CRIMEUCOPIA

We're All Animals Under The Skin

A Murderous Ink Press Anthology

****

Murderous-Ink Press

CRIMEUCOPIA

We're All Animals Under The Skin

First published by

Murderous Ink Press

Crowland

LINCOLNSHIRE

England

www.murderousinkpress.co.uk

Editorial Copyright © Murderous Ink Press 2021

Cover art (Mr Bananas) by BunsaDraws © 2018

Based on an original image composition (Gangsta Chimp)

by Matt Cioffi 2004

All rights are retained by

the respective authors & artists on publication

Paperback Edition ISBN: 9781909498235

eBook Edition ISBN: 9781909498228

Acknowledgements

To those writers and artists who helped make this anthology what it is, I can only say a heartfelt Thank You!

*Suspicion by Nick Boldock first appeared in *Off The Record* (2013)

** White Hell, Wisconsin by Weldon Burge is taken from *Broken: Stories of Damaged Psyches* (2013 Smart Rhino).

*** Three Hogg Tales and One Hairy Ending by Jeff Dosser previously appeared in *Yellow Mama* 4/19

****A Winter's Day has appeared on *Punk Noir Magazine* April 25, 2020

And to Den, as always.

Contents

You Can Call Me Crazy, It's My Middle Name....

(An Editorial of Sorts)

In this anthology the focus is on people and reactions. On a psychological level there may be some kind of common thread that runs though, but we doubt it. It's more about motivation, and the instinct to survive—in one form or another.

It's been the basis of many a NOIR fiction, from the creation of the anti-hero, or simply a tale where the 'Bad Guy' wins out for a change. But then who can say who's bad and who's good when there's always two sides to everything.

We put the idea to various people before putting it out on the website in order to see what would surface—and hopefully this time out we've been able to get as broad a spectrum as we could hope for without stepping into other, more specific genres, such as Horror, Macabre or Bizarro. Well, not too much....

So we have as our opening a piece from John Gerard Fagan, while Fabiyas MV uses a similar psychological theme, but with the added brevity that a poet can bring to fiction. Nick Boldock keeps with the animal theme, and Steve Carr takes a retro step back in time with a period LA PI tale of corruption.

Lamont Turner and Michael Bracken keep with the more traditional American Detective, but Al Hagan, Dan Meyers, Bobby Mathews and Edward Ahern take us down more darker roads.

Weldon Burge manages to put the psycho back into psychological, while Chris Phillips, and Robert Petyo tell tales of people and revenge—well, sort of.

Jeff Dosser give us a humorous slant on a similar theme, and Caroline Tuohey continues the dark humour in a tale that actually fits in rather well with the underlying theme.

To add even more to this international gathering, Emilian Wojnowski gives us a twist of 1960s NOIR from a different angle, and Eve Fisher brings a story to the table, which is recounted from a different perspective.

And to close out this anthology, June Lorraine Roberts presents a Flash Fiction tale, quite literally salted here and there with just a touch of dark humour.

Usually we don't consider Flash Fiction for these Paper First anthologies—mainly because the short word count can make it a bit of a lick'n'flick fest. However, June is very much an exception to our Roadhouse rules, mainly because we feel it is an exceptional piece when all's said and done.

So, with such a smorgasbord of Crime fiction, there should be something you immediately like. However, we're great believers in the Murderous Ink Press motto—that of:

"You never know what you like until you read it."

When What You Love is Broken

John Gerard Fagan

Eck ran greasy fingers across the glass and watched as it dripped with condensation. The garden was covered in frost. He stirred a mug of lukewarm tea and swallowed. An aftertaste of sour milk slugged back up his throat and onto the table. He let his sleeve soak in the mess and wiped his mouth with a plastic bag. His eyes wandered towards the patch of muck in front of the old willow tree. No headstone; Mum never allowed one on Pichi's grave.

"Eck?" Mum called, walking into the kitchen, fixing her hair. Her thick perfume made his eyes water. "I'm off to clean the church. Job centre today, is it?"

"In 14 minutes 23 seconds I'll get the bus."

"Well, don't be late. And remember to cash your giro right away. I'm going to the bingo tonight and I'll be needing it."

Eck nodded and stared back out the window. He closed his eyes with the sound of the front door slamming and high heels clicking against the concrete pavement. He had blanked out most things from his childhood, but Pichi's funeral was still clear.

The sun had disappeared behind the old willow tree, turning leaves the colour of blood. Outside smelled of bonfires. The grass was damp, so it didn't take long to dig a small grave. Wet dirt went deep under fingernails. He hugged the yellow shoebox containing his best friend's body. Mum's shadow passed across the curtains in her bedroom. He knelt into the mud, feeling it soak into his school trousers, and said a quick prayer to Mum's god. By the time he had finished, the rain was lashing. He crawled back inside the kitchen window and hurried back to bed. The loss hit as soon as he was safe under the covers.

Eck drew Pichi's cheery face on the window and felt a pain rise in his gut. He ran through all the fake jobs he had applied for and marched out for the bus.

*****

Eck pushed the front door and hurried inside. He grabbed a tea-towel and dabbed his head and face. Mum was sitting in the kitchen, blowing rings of smoke.

"Look at the state of you – your clothes are ruined. Why didn't you take an umbrella? Are you *that* stupid?"

"I didn't think it would rain. The weather channel said there was only a 30% chance of rain."

Mum sighed. "I don't know why I put up with you, I really don't. Did you find any jobs today?"

"Yes! Finally things are looking promising. There is a dish washing position going at Moodiesburn House Hotel. I handed in my CV on the way back."

Mum stubbed out the cigarette into a wet saucer. "Don't lie to me, son. Don't you fuc—"

"I'm not lying this time. The manager even said there was a great chance I'd get the job as he could tell immediately that

2

I had outstanding skills and determination. He was highly impres—"

"That fucking hotel has been closed for going on ten years. Just leave your giro money on the table and get out of my sight. And you lie to me again and I'll stub this cigarette out in your armpit like I was forced to when you were a spastic child."

Eck nodded and sprinted up the stairs. Couldn't fight the urge to numb the pain any longer.

*****

Eck opened one eye and grunted. A hangover was already circling his brain waiting to pounce. The curtain was blowing back and forth. He stumbled out of bed and closed the window. 02:13. He curled into a ball and shivered. A tug on the blanket.

"Hey, Captain Eck. You awake? Huh? Come on, buddy – don't be a grumpy grouch. It's me."

Eck rubbed his eyes and turned on the side lamp. "Pichi!"

"Shhh. Don't wake your mom. She'll be oh so very angry if she knows I'm back." Pichi jumped on the pillow and tap danced. "Did you miss me, buddy? Huh? Huh? Did you miss me?"

"Yeah," Eck whispered. "Every day."

Pichi hugged his finger and grinned. "Me too, pal. But not to worry, I'm back now."

"How did—"

"Gee, no need to know about that boring stuff. All that matters is I'm back, and ol Pichi won't ever leave again."

Eck nodded, wiping his wet eyes. "You look the same."

"Boy, have you changed – all grown up."

"Yeah."

Pichi leapt from the pillow to the floor. "What's this, huh?" he said, pointing to the empty bottle.

Eck shrugged. "It's my new special juice."

"Ah come on, buddy. I thought we only liked Barry's Red Cola?"

"I haven't drunk that in years."

"Well, only the finest red cola from now on. Deal?"

Eck smiled. "Deal."

"Right, go back to sleep, Captain, and I'll see you at breakfast. Say... do you still go to school?"

"Not for a long time."

"Wow, that's good. Let's meet at breakfast time anyway and we can go on an adventure. Would you like that?"

"Yeah. That would be amazing."

"Swell. Get some sleep, buddy. We've a big day ahead of us filled with joy and special times. I'll see myself out."

"Okay." Eck smiled. He laughed, covering his mouth as Pichi crawled out under the door.

*****

Eck jumped out of bed and smiled at the pink sky. He hurried down the stairs into the kitchen. Mum was drinking purple wine in her dressing gown. Ripped up bingo sheets lay by her feet and an unlit cigarette dangled from her bottom lip. Pichi was sitting on her shoulder and put a finger to his lips, signalling their secret.

"You're up early. Piss the bed again?" Pichi made a face in Mum's ear. Eck held in a snigger and shook his head. "You're not getting another new mattress if you have. You're nearly forty ye—"

"I haven't."

"Why God blessed me with a spastic child I'll never know. I've never had any luck. God is testing me to the limit with you."

Pichi jumped onto the table and sat in a spoon coated in wet sugar. Mum drained the wine and scratched her wrist.

"I'm going out today, Mum."

Pichi gave Mum the two-handed salute and Eck copied him. Mum closed her eyes and rubbed her temples.

"You haven't done that since you were a child." She pushed herself to her feet and spat on the table, saliva, dripping down her chin. "And you are not going anywhere. You'll clean this whole house up today. It's a disgrace the mess you've caused. If your father were here he would beat the living daylights out of you. My own child causing me so much hardship in my old age. I don't know why I bother."

"Let's get out of here, buddy and get some breakfast someplace else," Pichi whispered. "She's still the same old grumpy grouch, huh? Go grab your coat."

Eck nodded, and raced Pichi up the stairs.

"You here, me? Clean this mess up or you're getting your old kettle medicine."

*****

Eck secured a great seat by the window of his favourite

restaurant and went to the counter to order.

"What will it be, Captain Eck? Oysters? Venison?" Pichi said.

"Let's get big lobsters with caviar gravy and cranberry soup."

"Now you're talking."

A thin boy stared back from over the counter. Eck cleared his throat. "We shall have lobsters, served with caviar gravy and champagne truffles. Cranberry soup as an apéritif will be splendid, and champagne in glass flutes with be suffice to wash it all down, my good sir."

"W-w-we only serve f-f-fried chicken," the boy said, pointing to pictures behind his head with a shaky finger.

Pichi screwed up his nose. "Just get us six of those chicken buckets. This zib is obviously not on our level. Gee, his voice is making my head nip. Is he making your head nip?" Eck nodded. "Then I guess we have no choice. Can't be walking around with sore heads all day, can we?"

Eck smiled. "We shall have six of those buckets," he said to the boy, pulling out his wallet.

"No, no, buddy – it's my treat." Pichi said. "In fact, let's get takeaway. Go park your keister in the park – it's too nice a day to be inside. I'll pay these wise guys the ol way. Best way to stop our headaches."

"Thanks, Pichi."

"Don't mention it. Gee, it's good to be back."

*****

Pichi chased Eck around the swing park with his walking

stick and tripped him.

"Tag you're it!" Pichi said. A man pushing a fat child on the swing gave them a funny look. "Boy, ain't this place full of grumpy grouches?" Pichi said, arms on his hips.

"Yeah. Hey, is that a dog that behind you?"

Pichi spun around. "Where?"

"Tag, you're it!" Eck sprinted away.

"Ha-ha. Say, I'll meet you back home. I'm going to have a word with that Mr there over on the swing. I'll pay him the ol way, too. Pichi pulled out his sword from the walking stick and winked. "No-one disrespects us anymore."

Eck nodded.

*****

Eck's cheek nipped. Couldn't remember falling asleep. Pichi was standing by his face, still in his scuba diving gear. The neighbour's goldfish stank on the pillow, but it was a happy smell.

"Eck, wake up." Eck flicked the switch and rubbed his eyes. "I've some bad news, pal."

"What?" Eck said through a yawn.

"Gee, this is hard to say."

Eck sat up. "What are you talking about?"

"Well, I have to go."

"What? Why?"

"It's a long story. Gee I'm sorry, buddy," Pichi said, shaking his head.

"No, no, no, no, no, no! You can't. You said you wouldn't.

You promised. No!"

"Boy, have we had the best week ever, huh?"

Eck picked him up. "Is there anything I can do to stop you from going?"

Pichi faced his feet. "Ah shucks. Well, there's... there's one—" He shook his head.

"What?"

"It's nothing, pal. It's probably best I go away for good."

"No. I want you to stay with me."

"You do? Really? More than anything?"

"More than anything."

Pichi smiled. "Okay, buddy, well there's only one thing that can be done to save me."

"What do you mean?"

"Hmm. Well, if someone takes my place in the grave under the old willow tree I can stay forever. You could put your mom there. That would work, pal."

"You mean murder her?" Eck whispered.

"Wow, buddy, big words, huh?" Pichi smiled. "I just mean put her to rest the ol way."

Eck shook his head. "I ca—".

"I thought you wanted me to stay. Didn't you just say that?"

"I do. I really do."

"Did she even let me have a headstone?"

"No."

"Exactly. We were best friends and that ol gnashgab didn't even allow that."

"I don't know why she hated you so much."

Pichi unzipped the scuba suit. "Are we not having fun? We're cleaning this town up. Captain Eck and his great assistant Pichi are exactly what this town needs."

"Yeah we are, and it's great having you back."

"I feel the same, buddy. That's why I want to stay. I love you. Your mom doesn't."

"I love you, too."

"And she knew, Eck. She knew what your father did to you at bedtime and she did nothing about it."

"No she didn't. She wouldn't have—"

"Oh, she knew all right! Don't kid yourself. She knew everything." Eck nodded, tears running. Pichi smiled. "Hey, look we can make this right. I dug up your knife and it's under the bed. She's sleeping – do it quick and she won't feel a thing. We can have her buried before morning with the others. Cut her up real good just like we did your father."

Eck rubbed his eyes and took a deep breath. He slid the knife out with his foot. "Is this the only way I can save you?"

"Yeah, pal. I've thought over our options for many, many years and this is the only sure thing."

"And you'll definitely stay forever?"

"Yeah, buddy, I promise. I'll never leave you."

Eck fastened all the buttons on his dressing gown and pulled on slippers. He gripped the knife and headed for Mum's room with a smile so wide it hurt his face.

Pichi was back forever.

Superstition

Nick Boldock

Black cats are supposed to be lucky. Christ knows why. The damn things are everywhere – what's so lucky about that? I see them all the time – one in particular – and I've never been lucky in my entire life. Not once. Seeing a bloody cat never made any difference. Mind you, I could grow an acre's worth of four-leaved clovers and I'd still be the unluckiest bastard alive – that's just my lot in life.

Next door to me, there's a black cat, which insists on shitting in my front garden. Filthy animal. Why I should have to clear up the faeces of somebody else's cat is beyond me. There's some young tart lives next door. I don't really know her but perhaps I should go and introduce myself by presenting her with a faceful of her precious animal's shit, gathered from my admittedly rather downtrodden veg patch. Perhaps she'll be so repulsed that she'll help me hold the cat down while I gouge its fucking eyes out. Not exactly original I know, but it'd make me feel better.

She's unlikely to go for that though. Instead, predictably, she'll half-heartedly apologise and bleat on about how cats are wild animals and are compelled to follow their nature. Fair enough, but I'd much prefer it if it followed its nature in someone else's garden, thanks.

Right on cue, there it is on the windowsill, glaring at me. I give it the two-fingered salute but it doesn't move, although it does seem to frown at me in a feline sort of a way.

It's taken to doing that lately, sitting on the windowsill. I've stopped banging on the window and shooing it away because it only comes back five minutes later. I'd close the curtains but it's the middle of the day and the sun's shining and I'm buggered if I'm going to let that little furry fucker spoil the good weather.

It's lunchtime. Betting shop'll be open. Shoes on, out the door, money to lose. That's my Saturday really – perhaps a punctuating pint in the pub by the bookies, but aside from that it's just placing (and then losing) a few bets, really.

I step out the door and the bloody cat nearly knocks me arse over tit. It's decided to return home – propelling itself at high speed over the fence – just as I leave the house. Its fur brushes against me as it flies past. I aim a wayward kick at it.

I'm away down the bookies. I go in and study the form for a bit and then pick a couple of horses running in back-to-back races at Wolverhampton. One of them's at forties but I fancy it so I back it anyway. I never bloody win so it doesn't really matter. It's just an excuse to get out the house, really. I back both nags on a double, so if both of them win (yeah, right) then I'll be laughing. Bet placed, I fuck off to the pub for a pint. I'll come back in half an hour or so to see how long the horses ran for before falling over and being mercilessly shot.

The pub's quiet although I see a couple of familiar faces that I nod at, out of politeness. I nurse a pint of too-warm

Guinness for half an hour or so, watching the same news headlines tick over every two minutes on the tellies in the corner.

When the glass holds nothing more than some furry of-white foam, I trudge back to the betting shop to pick another couple of useless horses. I check my slip first – you never know; it could be my lucky day.

And it is. They've only gone and won – both of them. I'm shaking as I hand over the betting slip, unable to work out how much I've won. The cashier hands me just over two hundred quid. I'm grinning like Hugh Hefner at a convention for dumb blondes. My luck's in, for the first time ever.

I shove the cash deep in my jeans pocket and decide against any more bets. I'm thinking it's a good time to go down the shops and get some decent beer in for a change instead of the usual cheap shit. Maybe some proper scran too, something that costs more than a quid and tastes like actual food. I'm a tiny bit chuffed.

The door to the bookies swings shut behind me. I stand for a second, squinting into the sun and smiling. There's a weird noise beside me, down on the pavement. I look down and there, sitting and staring up at me, a loud meow still on its tongue, is next door's cat. I recognise it because it has a chunk missing from one ear, which I've always found amusing.

It meows at me again and I have to admit, it's quite cute when you look at it properly. It has a cheeky expression that reminds me of myself. And maybe – just maybe – it's lucky after all. I bend down and tickle its ears. The cat nuzzles up against my hand.

"I'm not going soft or anything", I tell it, "And this doesn't mean you can keep shitting in my garden, alright?"

*****

I have a fantastic week with my unexpected winnings. The following Saturday I'm getting ready to go out to the bookies when the cat appears on my windowsill again, just like last weekend. He doesn't look quite so evil anymore, and I can almost forgive his relentless urge to defecate on my carrots. I notice I'm thinking of him as a "he" and not an "it". I step outside and this time instead of hurdling the fence he skips over and rubs up against my legs.

In the bookies, I back two horses, my usual double bet. I go for a pint, come back, and I've won again. I can't believe it. Not as much as the last week but still a three-figure sum. The lass behind the counter jokes with me – she knows I never win, and she's saying congratulations on my newfound good luck. I'm not listening. For some reason I can't stop thinking about the cat. I don't even know his name. I'm being stupid. It's just a coincidence, nothing more. Just luck.

I go outside and the cat's there on the pavement, just like last week. This is getting fucking weird.

*****

The same thing happens the following week. And the week after…and so on. Each time I go and bet, and win, and the cat is outside waiting for me, as if to pat me on the back for my good fortune. He's my new best friend.

After a couple of months, the manager of the bookies threatens to ban me, but he can't find any evidence that I'm cheating so I'm allowed to carry on. But all the same, I'm getting worried. I can't keep this up forever, or they'll ban me regardless. So I make a decision.

I'm in the house, gathering up all my money. My winnings – almost ten grand's worth by now – are secreted in the loft. All this cash is laid out in front of me on the table. I'll stick it on one long-odds horse, clean up, and walk away a rich man. I can't lose.

The cat's already on the windowsill waiting for me. I look over and give him the thumbs up. As I leave the house he's bounding around my feet waiting for the tickle I always give him between his ears. Bless the little mite.

*****

They don't want to take the bet. I knew they wouldn't, but I insist it's the last time I'm betting. Eventually, they take almost ten thousand pounds on one horse that, in theory, can't win. As is customary, I don't watch the race – I go to the pub for a drink. I've graduated to large malt whiskies recently. I sit there savouring the taste of the Scotch, dreaming about what I'll do with the wads of money I'm going to win. I won't get cash of course. It'll be a delayed payment, probably one of those giant cheques. I am going to win nearly a million quid on an unfancied horse.

I drain the last drop of whisky and head back to the betting shop, almost floating above the pavement. I go in. I hand them the slip, waiting for the bells to ring and the confetti to fall around me as I'm proclaimed the biggest winner they've ever had.

It doesn't happen.

The horse fell at the second hurdle.

I've lost everything.

*****

The cat isn't outside waiting for me. My new friend has deserted me. I walk home in a suicidal mood, wondering how I'm going to pay the bills, when only a short while ago I'd been planning a holiday to the Caribbean. I'm panicking. I bet the rent money as well – everything.

I'm down my street and the lass from next door is outside in her front garden. She's crying. As I get closer I can see what she's crying about. On the floor in front of her is a prone black furry shape. The cat's laid there, looking pretty dead.

"You alright, love?" I ask, shaking.

"My cat," she says, "My cat… he's dead. He's dead!"

I go cold. "What happened? A car?"

"No, there's not a mark on him," she says through floods of tears, "Some bastard's poisoned him I think. Happens all the time nowadays. But not my Bobby!"

She scoops up the corpse and cuddles it to her face. It's horrible.

I go even colder.

I look over at my vegetable patch. She won't see it, but in amongst the carrots there's a small bowl buried to the level of the compost, and it's full of anti-freeze. I'd completely forgotten about it, but I put it there months ago, and the fucking cat never touched it.

Until now.

The little bastard had it in for me all along.

Just my luck.

White Hell, Wisconsin

Weldon Burge

"We're in for one helluva snowstorm!"

Jake Murphy recognized Bill Sweeney's gruff voice on the CB. He turned up the squelch to eliminate some growl of the blizzard, then lifted the CB's mike from its clasp on his dash.

"Bill? This here's Jake. What's the situation out there, c'mon?"

"Glad you could make it to the party, Jake. Where are you?"

"Just turned on Route 14. My plow keeps dipping into the blacktop, so I'm taking it slow. I keep telling those guys down at Highway to junk these antiques, but they just plug their fingers in their ears."

"Tell me about it! I'm on 23, but don't ask me why. Snow's fallin' faster'n I can plow it!"

"All the schools are closed," Jake said. "Banks. Stores. Haven't even seen any postal jeeps. We're the only ones stupid enough to drive in this shit. Got about two feet of snow on the major highways, and it's only been snowing a few hours. It's drifting on the back roads, up to five feet deep in some areas. Damned Wisconsin. Well, I can use the overtime, but it's sure like pissing in the ocean, ain't it?"

"Oughtta be in bed with my woman." Bill laughed. "Listen, I'm stopping at the 14-23 intersection, next to old man Gifford's farm. I'll wait for you there. Got some Kentucky bourbon stashed under my seat, perfect for melting the ice in your veins."

"Sounds good."

Suddenly, a muffled explosion came over the CB, followed by the sound of shattering glass.

"Bill?"

The CB buzzed with static, then Bill's sandpaper voice came quick, tainted with fear. "Lord, where'd they come from? Oh God–"

"Who? What's going on? C'mon?"

"Four!" Bill yelled. The sound of a nest of angry hornets filled the CB crackle in the background. "No, five. Five! Oh, sweet Jesus, they're on me!"

There was another explosion, then the CB died. Silence.

"Bill?"

Nothing.

Jake slammed the truck into gear. As his speed increased, the snow spilled away from the plow's blade, creating a curtain of white that hilled on the shoulder of the road. The blade occasionally screeched into the blacktop, ripping great hunks of asphalt. Even at top speed, it would take 15 minutes to reach Bill.

Jake hoped he wasn't too late.

*****

Snowflakes the size of quarters pummeled the windshield, a

heavy snow that made the wipers virtually useless. Jake managed to stay on the road by using the telephone poles as points of reference. Everything else was blanketed with lashing white.

Even in his fur-lined work gloves, his fingers were numb. He tried the heater switch again, knowing it was futile. The heater hadn't worked for the past two winters.

"Anybody with their ears on?" he said into the CB mike. Only static answered. He tossed the mike at the dash.

*****

Squatting like a mastodon in the middle of Route 23, Bill's truck was covered with snow and motionless. Dead.

Jake stopped his own vehicle just behind Bill's. On the left of the road was a dense forest, on the right Gifford's empty cornfield. He wondered how such a serene, Currier and Ives scene could seem so ominous.

Jake hopped out of the cab of his truck, left the engine running. He pulled the hood of his parka up around his head, but the bitter wind still penetrated to his ears. He yanked a snow shovel from the back of his truck, then slowly approached the other plow. Jake wanted to call out for Bill but thought better of it.

The shattered windows looked like jagged alligator teeth. Hundreds of small holes perforated the door on the driver's side.

Jake opened the door. Bill wasn't in the cab. The driver's seat had been shredded; springs protruded through the excelsior. All the gauges in the dash were smashed. What was left of Bill's CB was scattered on the floor with other debris.

The pint of bourbon was untouched under the seat. Jake slipped it into his back pocket.

He turned toward the forest. Bill would have run in that direction if he'd had a chance. Halfway between the plow and the perimeter of the trees was a mound of snow. Portions of the mound were red.

Jake stumbled through the deep snow, holding the shovel in both hands in front of him. He dropped to his knees and brushed the snow away from the mound. The shotgun blast had been at close range. Bill had been nearly blown in half.

Whoever did this was still here, in the woods, watching. He knew. He could sense the laughing eyes.

No, something moved behind him, not in the forest. He spun around on one knee, grabbing up his shovel. Stupid to sit out in the open, he suddenly realized. Stupid. He searched for movement in the swirling white.

Someone was in the cab of his truck! The engine stopped, then the driver's side door opened. His CB tumbled into the snow, followed by a kid in a white ski suit. Goggles disguised his face, but Jake guessed the kid was about 16.

The boy raised his foot over the CB radio. He smiled at Jake. Then the boy stomped the radio, grinding it into the snow.

"HEY!" Jake screamed.

The kid lifted a white-gloved hand, middle finger extended.

The snow whipped at Jake's face. He stood motionless, indecisive for a silent, angry moment. His fingers tightened on the shovel. He stepped toward the boy.

Then he heard the buzzing he'd heard earlier on the radio,

a drone slowly invading the wind. He turned just in time to see two snowmobiles burst from the forest behind him. The teenagers driving them were also dressed in white. One kid carried a small Panzer crossbow.

Jake jumped out of the path of one vehicle, but he wasn't fast enough. The other snowmobile struck him on the left thigh, sending him sprawling in the snow.

He rolled on his side to look back at his truck. One snowmobile picked up the boy who had mangled the CB, then crossed the road and sped across Gifford's field.

The other snowmobile, the kid with the crossbow, turned back toward him.

Jake pushed himself to his feet, despite the throbbing pain in his leg. He knew he couldn't outrun the approaching vehicle.

The kid stopped just 15 feet in front of him. Without saying a word, he raised the crossbow, aiming at Jake's face.

Jake stared down the shaft of the arrow into the boy's gleaming eye. He brandished the shovel like a shield, standing awkwardly with all his weight on his right leg.

The kid lifted his crossbow a mere inch and pulled the trigger. The arrow soared barely six inches above Jake's head.

The boy laughed. "See ya later, old man," he said. "We got a date, you and me."

The snowmobile then sped past Jake, disappearing into the snow-frosted forest from which it came.

Jake's heart jackhammered in his chest as he stumbled to his truck. The punks were all dressed in white. Even their snowmobiles were white. They could move like ghosts in the swirling snow that stretched forever in each direction.

Jake heard the snowmobiles moving in the forest. Had Bill meant five snowmobiles? Five kids? He didn't know who or what was out there.

He climbed into the truck, grimacing at the searing pain in his leg. He reached for the ignition. The keys were gone. He pounded the steering wheel with his fists, cursing. Maybe he could hot-wire it. Even then, what were his chances of getting help? The nearest town was twelve miles away.

As he probed for wires under the dash, the truck suddenly lurched to the left. He leaned out of the cab. An arrow had flattened the front left tire. Jake heard the faint *thhppt* of the arrow that then punctured the left rear tire.

Instinct told him to fall from the cab. He heard the shotgun blast as he fell. The buckshot shattered the windows, spraying glass fragments across his back. He looked up. He couldn't see anyone in the surrounding woods, but he knew they were there.

An arrow speared into the snow two feet in front of his face.

Jake skittered like a crab on his hands and knees to the front of the truck, positioning himself behind the blade of the plow. The blizzard had intensified. He could barely make out the details of the forest through the sheets of snow.

"WHY ARE YOU DOING THIS?" he screamed at the trees.

Then the laughter started. First a perverted chuckle, then there was a chorus of laughter seemingly from everywhere in the forest.

"WHY?" he screamed again.

The laughter abruptly stopped. Jake heard only the wind and the dreadful thumping of his own heart.

He sensed, but could not see, movement amongst the trees. They were toying with him. He also knew they had every intention of killing him.

If they had abandoned their snowmobiles, he'd never know where they were in the whiteout conditions. They could easily surround him, finish him off. Too much beer and too little exercise made him easy prey.

If he could get to Gifford's house, get to a phone, he could get some help. That would mean crossing an empty, fifty-acre field. No way. They'd be on him in a minute. His only chance was in the forest. If nothing else, he could hide until they tired of the hunt—if he didn't freeze to death first. There were other farms in the area. He could eventually get help. Eventually.

Of course, if he could get one of the snowmobiles …

Jake crawled to the opposite side of the truck. He opened the passenger side of the cab and grabbed the twenty-four-inch wrench and a flare from the toolbox under the seat. He stuffed the flare into the inside liner of his jacket. Then he popped open the glove compartment, tossed out the pack of Marlboros, and snatched up his cigarette lighter. Noticing nothing else that would make a respectable weapon, he wished he still had the shovel.

He tested the weight of the wrench in his hands.

"I'll teach those little bastards."

Jake moved again to the front of the truck. Pulling the pint of bourbon from his back pocket, he twisted off the cap and tossed it aside. He took one gulp from the bottle, ignoring the

23

fire splashing down his throat. He then pulled his handkerchief from his shirt pocket, twirled the fabric into a cord, and stuffed it into the bottle, leaving a tag hanging from the mouth.

"I'M STAYING RIGHT HERE, YOU LITTLE PRICKS," he yelled at the tree. "YOU PUNKS WANT ME? COME GET ME!"

At first, he thought they hadn't heard him. He started to repeat the challenge when he heard the snowmobiles revving. He smiled, his lips ticking. His trembling right hand pulled the butane lighter from his jacket pocket.

Two snowmobiles burst from forest. The boy on the first snowmobile held a single-barrel shotgun. The kid with the crossbow followed on the other vehicle.

Jake pulled the flare from his jacket and ignited it.

The kid with the crossbow stopped, but the boy with the shotgun continued his approach.

Jake touched the lit flare to his makeshift Molotov cocktail. When the snowmobile was close enough, he hurled the bottle.

The bottle exploded upon impacting the front of the snowmobile. A ball of orange-blue flame licked across the front of the vehicle, startling the boy. He jumped clear, his shotgun tumbling into the snow a few yards away. The passengerless snowmobile ripped into Bill's truck, screaming its metal anguish as it died.

Jake moved from the front of his plow, the burning flare in his left hand and the wrench in his right. The kid sprang toward his shotgun, but not before Jake was on him. He swung the wrench like a baseball bat, smashing the boy in the ribs,

24

lifting him off the ground with the blow.

"Get outta the way, Larry!" the other kid screamed. "I can't get a decent shot!"

"Shut up," Larry said through clenched teeth.

Jake noticed a glint of steel in the boy's right hand, just in time to avoid the swoop of the blade as it slashed his jacket close to the wrist.

"C'mon, Pops," Larry hissed. He made circles in the air with his switchblade. "I'm gonna slice your heart out."

"Move!" the other kid screamed again. Jake could see the crossbow past Larry's shoulder.

"Shut up, Kurt," Larry said without turning. "He's mine!"

The boy lashed out with the knife. Jake parried the lunge with the wrench. He started to back away, then saw Kurt's crossbow again and decided against it. Instead, he thrust the blazing flare at Larry's face.

The boy ducked beneath Jake's arm, easily evading the flare. He moved in close, plunging his blade into Jake's side.

Jake felt the sting of the steel sliding between his ribs, ignored it and lunged again. This time he successfully sank the burning tip of the flare into Larry's left eye socket. As the boy screamed, Jake swung the wrench like a nine-iron. The metal jaws bit into Larry's head just beneath the left ear, instantly snapping the neck and splintering the base of his skull.

Jake then heard the now-familiar whistle of an arrow. He bellowed when it ripped into his right arm just above the elbow, forcing him to drop the bloodied wrench. If he had turned a fraction of an inch, the arrow would have penetrated his chest. He coughed, bringing up bright-red, oxygenated blood from his lungs. The stab wound had been deeper than he'd realized. He fought to maintain his balance, but it was a losing battle. His legs became fluid under him. He felt his body shifting, but the sensations were all wrong. He heard nothing. The angry, gray-white sky swirled before his eyes. He seemed to float to the ground like a leaf, as if he were no longer a part of his body. He fought the blackness creeping into his field of vision.

Kurt stood next to his idling snowmobile, reloading his crossbow. He walked toward Larry, holding his crossbow loosely across his chest. He nudged Larry's head with his boot. Then his malevolent eyes turned to Jake.

Jake groggily raised himself on his elbows. He tried to push himself to his feet, but his wounded arm folded under him. He slipped again into the snow.

His hand fell on Larry's shotgun.

Kurt stepped toward him, raising his crossbow.

Jake, propping himself on an elbow, hefted the shotgun. "I… wouldn't," he said.

Kurt smiled. "I could put this arrow right between your eyes, you old fart."

"Not before I pull this trigger."

Kurt seemed to think on that for a moment. "It ain't loaded," he said. "Larry never carried it loaded while he was riding. Kept the shells in his vest pockets."

"Bullshit," Jake said. He leveled the shotgun at the boy's chest.

"I'm tellin' you, it ain't loaded." Kurt lowered the crossbow to his side.

Jake's finger teased the trigger. "Why haven't you killed me then?"

Kurt stepped closer. "You ain't goin' nowhere, not leaking the way you are. Looks like you're gonna die any minute. I think I'll just wait for the others."

"Others?"

"We're a club. Go out dirt-biking in the summer, snowmobiling in the winter. This year we thought we'd try something different." Kurt laughed. He took another step toward Jake. "When the others get here, you're dead meat."

Jake lowered the shotgun, more out of exhaustion than resignation. He concentrated on keeping his eyes open, despite the overwhelming urge to just sleep and be over with it all.

"That's right, old man," Kurt said. "Might as well put the gun down. Ain't gonna do you no good now."

Jake heard the snowmobiles approaching from the distance, from Gifford's field behind him.

Kurt suddenly lifted his crossbow. Jake twisted his body, but the arrow still caught him in the shoulder. On reflex, he pulled the trigger of the shotgun. The gun bucked against his chest, sending immediate, agonizing pain throughout his torso.

A load of buckshot eviscerated Kurt, blowing backward off his feet.

"Liar," Jake whispered.

He finally lapsed into welcome unconsciousness.

*****

A sharp kick to the temple woke Jake. He forced his eyes open. Three teenagers—two boys and a girl wearing the same white outfits as the two he had killed—stood over him. One boy cradled a double-barrel shotgun in his arms.

"What do we do with him, Kevin?" the girl said.

Jake looked into Kevin's eyes. With great effort, he managed to ask, "Why?"

"Well, it's like this," the boy said. "There's gonna be a lot of snow. Supposed to snow for the next few days, and who knows how much snow can pile up. Know what that means? Means the snowplows have to clear the roads. But how can we enjoy the snow if we have to go to school all day, every day?" Kevin opened the breech of the gun. "We figured, if the plows don't run, neither do the school buses. Buses don't run, we don't go to school. Simple, huh?"

The boy pulled two shells from his jacket and shoved them into his shotgun.

Kevin sighed. "That's as good an excuse as any, I suppose. Even if the school buses run, maybe we'll waste a few bus drivers. Would you drive a bus, knowing a coupla fellow drivers are stretched out at the morgue?"

He shut the breech, then lowered the gun. He pushed the end of the double barrels under Jake's chin, forcing his head up.

"Nah, I wouldn't either," Kevin said. "I think we'll be out of school for a long time."

A smile played across Jake's tired face. "I got two of you bastards."

Kevin sighed again. "Yes, but only two. Larry and Kurt

28

weren't the brightest. We can get five more kids to replace each of them, no sweat. The fun's just starting."

"You're all … crazy," Jake said.

"No, not crazy," Kevin said. "Just bored."

For an insane second, Jake wanted to laugh.

The last thing he heard was the click of the shotgun's hammer.

Then Jake splashed across the snow.

The three teenagers stood around Jake's body. Kevin's smoking shotgun rested against his shoulder, pointing to the clouds.

While the other two looked down on the twitching, headless body, Kevin looked to the moving sky. The swirling snow seemed to funnel toward his face.

He smiled.

"It's gonna snow for a long, long time."

St George's Day Massacre
Chris Phillips

It had all the trappings of a traditional East End gangland funeral. A Victorian carriage drawn by four plumed black horses. Behind it a line of stretched limos. Dominant among the wreaths decorating the hearse was one of white chrysanthemums which read 'Len, love you always, Val.'

Dozens of other floral tributes lay outside Manny's Pie and Mash Shop, an 'authentic' Cockney landmark next door to the funeral parlour. It was April 23rd 2010, and a neighbouring shop displayed the St George's Day flag.

Dominating the news that day was not a gangster's dead body about to be reduced to ashes, but the impending General Election, vying for front page space with the disruptive aftermath of an ash cloud over Europe following a volcanic eruption in Iceland.

Crowds jammed the pavements as the cortege made its way to the parish church, an ugly Gothic style building blackened by the chimney soot of previous decades. Most were curious bystanders, too young to have known Lenny Goodman personally, but aware of his reputation through recent newspaper headlines. Some of the old-timers cried out 'God bless, Lenny'.

Reporters and camera crews jostled for position, their attention focused on a knot of celebrities from TV and cinema, as the coffin was withdrawn from the hearse. Among the bearers was Lenny's son, Kevin, his eyes glistening with tears.

The vicar, who had known Lenny for 30 years and privately loathed the man, had initially been reluctant to carry out the service. It was one of life's ironies that a gangster should have the surname of Goodman and the Rev Charles Digby would have to be at his most dispassionate to say the words: *Lord, may you bless him and keep him; may your face shine upon him and be gracious to him; may you lift up your countenance upon him and give him peace.*

Besides, he was under no obligation to officiate. Lenny had lived near Chigwell, Essex, for the past 15 years. It was for sentimental reasons that the family wanted the service in his old home patch.

Three days before the funeral, there had been a knock on the vicarage door. Kevin Goodman, accompanied by two other men with the build and appearance of night club bouncers.

'A quick word, Rev,' said Kevin. 'I hear that you don't want to do Dad's service. Just to let you know that the family will be *most* disappointed if you don't.' Kevin shook his head to emphasise the word 'most'.

Charles Digby was about to reply, but Kevin silenced him by placing a finger on his lip. 'Here me out. What Dad did in business we'll leave out. You know he also did some good things. Raised thousands of pounds for charity. There's been a good many people round here who, if they were still alive, would have reason to thank him when times was hard. Times is still hard. You run a food bank at the church hall, right?'

Digby nodded.

'Right, well here's a contribution,' said Kevin, handing over an envelope. 'Now I have every confidence in you to give Dad a good send off.'

The thin, menacing smile on Kevin's face was imprinted on the vicar's mind as he closed the door and opened the envelope. Inside was £2,000 in used £20 notes.

Since arriving in the parish as a young curate Digby could count on the fingers of one hand the church being packed. This was one of them and as part of his food bank contribution, Kevin had arranged for the service to be relayed to the crowd outside.

In the committal, Digby left out the words 'and give him peace.' No one noticed. He was asked to the wake, but declined, saying he had two other funerals later that day, which was true.

'This manor's gone right down the craphole,' said one of Lenny's former associates. Frank Riley, known as T-Bone because of his fondness for steak.

'More fucking mosques than pubs,' added Harry Betts.

Both men were at the bar of the White Swan, favourite haunt of their Firm in the 1960s. The ceiling of embossed paper was stained dark brown from nicotine. Paper currencies from around the world were pinned between two gilt mirrors. Two bulbs from a chandelier were not working. 'Been like that since we was here last. Bone idle fucker,' said T-Bone referring to the landlord.

Drinks were on the house – or to be accurate on Kevin and his mother—for everyone in the pub who had been invited to the wake. The two bouncers who had accompanied Kevin on his earlier visit to the Vicar's stood at the door to ensure there were no gate crashers.

Harry Betts ordered two more pints with whisky chasers for himself and T-Bone before taking out a packet of pills from his jacket and popping one in his mouth. His face, the complexion of sliced salami, indicated heart problems.

T-Bone wrapped a veined hand round his pint glass, a thick gold ring on his forefinger bearing the initial F. Urban legend had it that he'd nearly beaten a gangland rival to death, repeatedly jabbing him on the nose and mouth with the ring, until his victim became unconscious through ingesting blood.

A woman wearing a black jacket and skirt and white blouse joined them at the bar.

'Hello darlin', how are you?' inquired Harry. She kissed him on the cheek, leaving an imprint of red lipstick. Patsy Reagan was a one-time star of TV dramas and former lover of Harry's. Now she fought to keep herself in the public eye with appearances on chat shows and panel games.

T-Bone left the pair to join three other men standing by the juke-box which was playing Lenny's favourite song, Frank Sinatra's *My Way*.

'Not a bad turn-out,' said one. His name was Don Halliday, but was often referred to as 'Blakey.' That was down to the reputation he'd gained back in the 1970s and 80s for his high quality printing and forgery work when it came to moody papers. Almost everything, ranging from MoT certificates for disreputable car dealers to international passports. His print shop was behind a steel door, accessed through a burger bar, his legitimate business 'front'.

With him was Joe Manning, who held the unenviable record of serving more time in prison than any other gang member, and Kenny 'The Crab' Lambert, so called because of his fearsome track record for collecting overdue debts with a pair of pincers. The joke in those days was that you could always spot one of Kenny's 'clients' because they were always missing one or two fingernails.

'Ronnie's not here,' said Joe looking round the packed bar.

'Nah, flight from Malaga got cancelled, so Val told me,' said Blakey, looking in the direction of Lenny's widow. She was in a group of five other mourners, wearing a wide brimmed black hat with the veil raised, eating a plate of buffet sandwiches.

'Pity, I was looking forward to a drink with him. How long's it been?'

Blakey screwed up his face trying to remember. 'Must be getting on for 10 years. Diabetic now. Someone said he had to have a leg off a couple of years ago.'

There was a pause in the conversation. It was as though mention of Ronnie's ill-health and this reunion was a sombre reminder that the hey-day of the Goodman Gang, as it had been known, was long past.

Lenny had always been the governor, a title tacitly acknowledged by the rest of the gang since their schooldays when Goodman had led a series of raids to steal copper piping from building sites in London's post-war building boom.

School had been a challenge to attend as little as possible. Spells in borstal and then prison was where they learned lessons that were to equip them for a life of crime.

It was the usual pattern for ambitious villains: petty theft followed by more profitable ventures into ownership of brothels and porn shops in Soho. And for really easy money there were the protection rackets, 'persuading' business owners to hand over money to ensure their premises didn't come to any harm. That meant establishing a vicious reputation, first to gain dominance over rival gangs and secondly to convince the targets of extortion that they really meant business.

One man who'd managed to defy the Firm had been Wilfred Gates, one-time landlord of *The Hoop and Grapes*, located in a side street off the Mile End Road. Gates, at the time a promising amateur boxer until an eye injury finished his career, told T-Bone Riley to 'fuck off' when Lenny despatched Riley to offer Gates protection.

Riley had gone back and advised Lenny not to pursue Gates, who was well respected in the community, but Lenny wouldn't have any of it. 'No fucking way. Before you know it, word will go round that I'm a soft touch, and next thing others will stop paying up as well.'

A week later fire destroyed the pub in the early hours. Gates, his wife and their son Barry were asleep upstairs when a petrol bomb was thrown through a bar window. Gates escaped with Barry in his arms and tried to re-enter the premises to rescue his wife, but the smoke and flames forced him back.

Gates had reported the earlier visit by T-Bone Riley to the police, but no one was ever prosecuted for the attack.

Nearly 50 years later, the old bill were also struggling to try and find any leads pointing to Lenny Goodman's murder.

He'd been found by his wife in the shrubbery of their three-acre garden with an axe embedded in his skull. That at least had ruled out suicide.

Detectives could find no obvious reason for the attack. For at least the past 10 years Goodman had led an apparently blameless life, even serving on his local Essex parish council.

'Maybe a case of revenge being a dish best served cold?' said DS Morris after he'd studied intelligence reports of Lenny's criminal past.

'Must have put the grudge in the freezer for it to have taken this long,' replied a colleague.

'Unless the perpetrator didn't have a choice,' observed another member of the inquiry team. The significance of this comment was not lost on the rest of the squad.

It had taken a further two months before the coroner finally released Lenny's body for the funeral. There had been no such delay for Wilfred Gates. His death at the age of 76 was from natural causes. He was found by his son Barry slumped in an arm chair at his council flat. At his side was an empty bottle of whisky.

By coincidence, his funeral was on the same day and at the same church as Lenny Goodman's. The only people at the service were Barry and Wilfred's carer.

Reverend Digby remembered Wilfred from his days as a landlord, and Barry had told him that his father had never recovered from his wife's death in the fire. He had quit the licensed trade and become a painter and decorator, before chronic alcoholism reduced him to a life on benefits.

Digby couldn't help but note the contrast between Wilfred's pathetic departure from Earth with that of Lenny's. *Nothing like a recent murder of someone with a notorious past to bring out the crowds*, he thought with a sardonic expression.

From the pulpit he looked at Barry, hands clasped, sitting in the front pew. The last time he had seen the young man he had been clean shaven with his hair cropped almost to the scalp. Now he had a full beard and hair curling round the collar of his shirt. He had been released from prison on parole three months ago, having served seven years of a 14-year sentence for armed robbery.

Two other men had taken part in the raid on a jeweller's in Knightsbridge, but the case against Kevin Goodman had been dropped due to a lack of evidence other than circumstantial. It had been an unofficial rumour that his father had paid £40,000 to the detective heading the inquiry in return for destroying evidence against his son. As part of the deal, Kevin had named his two accomplices.

As Wilfred Gates' coffin left the church destined for a Council grave, Kevin Goodman felt an arm clasp his shoulders. 'Bad business about your Dad,' said T-Bone Riley.

'Who's in the frame, Kev? Any idea?' inquired Blakey.

Kevin shrugged, gulping down another double whisky.

One of the bouncers came over to Kevin. 'Photographer outside giving me ear ache, wanting to take a group picture.'

'Which paper's he with?' asked Kevin.

'Says he's freelance.' The bouncer looked back towards the door.

'Can't do any harm, I suppose. Just one picture though, no more. You three, Harry and Kenny. For old times' sake.'

Blakey said, 'Tell him we want half a dozen prints, framed.'

The group nodded and headed to the bar to join Harry, who was still talking to Patsy Reagan.

The bouncer relayed the message to the photographer, who jostled his way towards the bar.

Patsy clung to Harry, wanting to be in the picture as well. 'Go on, let me be in it. It's been ages since I've had my face in the tabloids.'

Kevin scowled at her. 'Not a hope in Hell, now clear off.' She scowled and slunk off to join another of the one-time celebs.

The photographer gestured with both hands for the group to stand closer together. He also beckoned to Kevin to join them. Kevin was hesitant until T-Bone said: 'Yeah, come and join us. Your Dad would have wanted that.'

The landlord also tried to get in on the act, but one look from Harry Betts was enough to send him to the far side of the bar.

The photographer took two shots. He attempted a third but the flash had stopped working.

'Hurry up, we haven't got all day,' said T-Bone as the photographer bent down and one hand went inside his shoulder bag.

As he stood up, his camera now on the floor, the group looked in shocked disbelief at what he was holding. 'Fuck me...' said Harry Betts, who was on the extreme left. They were the last words he uttered as the first burst of 10 rounds from the FN P90 machine pistol ripped into the six of them. Within seconds, they were writhing on the floor. The gunman turned round and glared at the bouncers. 'You want some? Take a step closer!'

Then, when everyone had backed off, he turned and shot each of his victims once more, 'For good luck!'

Patsy was the first to begin screaming as the assailant headed towards the door, waving the gun from side to side.

Outside, he resumed firing, barrel pointing skywards, until the magazine was empty.

As he let the weapon clatter to the pavement, Barry Gates felt the adrenaline still coursing through his body and wondered, when the day came, how many would turn out for his funeral.

First Person Singular

Dan Meyers

The accommodation at the Old Lodge motel on the edge of Daxton isn't pretty. The only time that would apply is if you put the word 'crap' after it. Still, beggars can't be choosers. Not that I'm a beggar.

The single room is kitted out with a basic bed, chair, desk-cum-table. The wardrobe's one of those cheap flat-pack build-it-yourself – which is probably why the doors don't quite fit together. Tracks worn into the cheap blue carpet go from bed to wardrobe, via the small wash basin. Mirror over the top of it is actually bolted to the wall. Who the hell would want to steal a mirror?

I check the burner phone. Minimal functionality and no GPS. The display shows a quarter after midnight in soft green figures. It's probably still not safe to go out just yet. Too many potential dangers. I put it to one side and go back to watching the neon lights from the strip mall opposite as they flash and dance on the carpet. I pulled the curtains shut several hours ago, but the red and blue lights keep finding ways to insinuate themselves through the chinks and cracks. It's hypnotic despite the wayward spring in the chair continuously poking me in the back. When I first tried to get comfortable it'd been a real piss-you-off aggravation. Now it's something to focus on, keep me awake. Just in case….

I can feel myself mentally sliding again.

*****

Standing in front of me is my father – a Saturday Night drunk who extended it to the other six days of the week as well.

"You hear me, boy?" A big ex-steel plant man, knocked low, to the point where he could no longer get regular work. He'd staggered up from the worn out sofa in front of the TV. I was still standing in the doorway – home late, and I hadn't prepared his supper. When you're 16, with urges, you tend to lose track of time. It'd been happening more and more. He'd then start shouting, coming towards me while unbuckling his belt. "Going to have to strap some sense into you. Something I should've done after your mother ran off."

If I was lucky, before he got to me I'd turn and run out of the house, down the drive and hide under one of the neighbour's parked cars. It'd become a regular thing. As regular as a set piece played out at a college football match. Only the players didn't have scars when they'd not been agile enough. He'd then stand on the porch steps, looking all around for me. After a handful of minutes the near-empty bottle of bourbon would call him back into the house. I'd wait another five or ten, just to be sure he wasn't faking it, then come up from under, and make my way over to Mallory's Diner. Maxine, one of the waitresses, would take pity on me. She'd feed me fries, maybe a burger now and again – or, a piece of pie.

But after a while I'd gotten tired of running. The next time he'd tried it I didn't run. I waited until he was fumbling with his belt, then stepped forward and kneed him a couple of times in the balls – quick and forceful – so it finally registered in his dinosaur brain, and he'd gone down, belt still clutched in his right hand.

While he was wheezing and gasping I got his pants off, yanked down his boxers, and stuck his left hand in his crotch. It took several attempts and a few kicks to his stomach before I'd finally got the photograph right. The little camera might've been plastic and cheap, but it took photographs good enough.

I didn't go back home for several days. Maxine was always happy for me to sleep over, even though she knew I was under age. But when I did go back I still had to be careful.

He was sitting on the sofa, watching TV when I walked in. Didn't even turn round to see who it was.

"So you finally came back. Knew you would." He took a long pull on his beer can, then belched. After he wiped his mouth I started in on my piece.

"I want you to listen to me, and listen good. Things are going to be very different from now on."

He snorted, finished off the beer, and crumpled the can. I waited for him to say something, but he didn't. So I carried on.

"Don't you ever try and take your belt to me again. I took photos of you, and the next time you try anything. and I do mean anything, I'm going to tell everyone that you abused me. That you've been doing it for years."

He snorted again. "No one's ever going to believe you."

My turn to smile. "I don't care if they all believe me or not. That kind of thing will stick to you like shit on a blanket. Just takes one to start with, and they'll tell some people, who will tell other people, and just like a forest fire, it'll spread all over. Plus I've got the photographs. And the scars as well."

That'd shut him up. Even stopped him drinking for several days. But like a truly unrepentant alcoholic, it wasn't long before he'd crawled back into a state of spiteful remorse.

In the end no one went to his funeral. Not even me.

After that it'd been easy to exploit small town sympathy and gain knowledge of small town indiscretions.

*****

My foot twitches, bangs up against the sports bag, and I'm back watching the lights.

Martin Crowley, the bank manager, will claim $500,000 was taken, even though we both know the take was far less than that.

"It's all insurance, John. People do it every day, inflate their claim, so why should the bank be any different?"

"But won't you get audited?"

"Sure we will, and they'll fine all the money is missing."

I open the bag and look at the mass of money bricks and the loose notes stuffed in around them. First thing to go will be the wrappers, then check for any sequential numbers. They were supposed to be all used notes, but it always pays to be careful. All together it should be a touch over a quarter of a million. I thought it would've been heavier, but it's probably less than 10lb, spread out in a football bag.

I smile at it all. "Go Cubs!" Then feel a little embarrassed, talking to myself and feeling like I was a rookie line-backer again.

*****

The original plan had been Martin's. We'd been sitting in Chequers Bar & Grill on Main Street, around 8pm. I was slowly drinking a beer to pass the time when he walked in, sat down beside me at the bar, and ordered a large Regal and rocks. The drink arrived, and a quiet minute later he'd said:

"We've known each other for some time now, John. Would you say I was a bad man?"

I wasn't too sure as to where the conversation was going. "Not as far as I know, Martin. Why? You looking to confess something?"

"Not as such, but they do say that sometimes a thought is as good as a deed."

"And you've been thinking?"

"I've been thinking. About how to rob my own bank."

"And why should you want to do that? You don't strike me as someone on the breadline, or running short. Unless you've been spending more than you've been earning?"

"No, you're right, Ellie and I are better off than most in town. Kids don't want for anything. The mortgage is discounted through the bank and easy to keep up. Hell, even our relationship is still sweet after the kids left."

"So why the thoughts? And why are you telling me?"

"Well, if I were to put it down to anything, then it would be pure greed. Nothing more, nothing less. As for telling you? Well, I figure, what with your position, you're the best person I know who could help pull off a robbery."

I looked at him. A now-not-so-slim mid-40s ex-jock, dark blue suit, white shirt and dark tie. Little beads of sweat on his upper lip, caught in the evening stubble.

"How many have you had, Martin?"

"First one of the day – including the cabinet in my office. Still, it's taken some time to grow the stones to talk to you about it."

I'd tried to sound confused rather than curious. "So why should I come in with you on this venture of yours?"

"Same reason as me. I know what you get per month. Less bills and outgoings. But there are all those cash deposits you drop into your account on a regular basis. I suspect they're just donations to the John Cheslin Appreciation Fund, but I doubt it would take much to correlate someone's outgoings with your incomings, now would it."

I'd remained silent, the back of my neck suddenly hot and damp. "Are you trying to blackmail me, Martin?"

"Ah, John. Blackmail is such an ugly word. But I can't think of an alternative right this minute."

"And after?"

"When it's all over we'll be equal in what we know about each other. Knowledge is power, as you obviously know. Sharing it with each other is our safeguard. Think on it."

We'd gone back to drinking in silence, and I'd left shortly after. It wasn't until three weeks later that we'd met up at the bar in Chequers again.

Martin came in, sat down beside me, ordered me a bottle of imported Crystal Dark and himself a Regal and rocks.

As the barman moved on down to the far end of the bar, Martin asked: "Have you come to a decision regarding my proposition?"

I took a pull from the beer bottle, paused to belch discretely, then said, "I've had a little think on it all. First off we're going to need three extra bodies in on this. Two for the muscle and a wheelman. I need sketches of the inside floor plan, camera locations, details of the surrounding area, number of bank clerks, security guard's details."

"But you know all that, John. Hell, you even know old Frank. He's as local as you and I."

"And that's going to be the problem. I'm not looking to have someone decide that this was an inside job. We need to create the credibility that someone has studied and noted down details. Make the sketches on plain paper, no company watermarks. Maybe even photocopy the photocopies half a dozen times so they start looking fuzzy. That way they'll look good."

"Okay, so tell me the rest of it."

"Simple. I'll be on the inside, distracting Frank. The three walk in, all calm and no panic. Then they go bat-shit crazy, pulling out weapons and telling everyone to get down onto the floor."

"But the bank staff are going to be safe behind bullet proof glass."

"Which is why they'll be shouting to them to open up the side door otherwise they'll start shooting civilians."

"Okay, they've all been told to co-operate wherever possible. They open the door, then what?"

"Simple. Two of the three get the cashiers to clean out the tills and the reserve safe, then go back out the main entrance."

"And you?"

"I'll be keeping Frank from trying to use that fuck-ugly old Magnum of his while the robbery's taking place. Then I become their hostage, and we'll make good our escape."

Martin had put his empty glass on the bar and waved the bartender over for a refill. He took a sip from the refreshed glass, then half looked at me. "Sounds like you've got it all wrapped up. You got a team in mind?"

I'd smiled. "The less you know, Martin, the easier it'll be."

*****

I'd gone over the State line, then cross county until I found a place with no obvious connection. Then I'd started to use a non-descript hotel – the Belmont – over the following dozen or so weekends, until the manager and I were on chatting terms.

"I wonder if you could help me, Archie."

"I can try, what's the problem."

"I need to pick up a gun."

"Dobson's is pretty fair when it comes to cost. He's the only gun shop around, but he won't gouge you on the price."

"And that's the problem. I'm looking for something that's off the grid."

"And you figure I'd know where to get something like that?"

"People trust you, Archie. You have a thing for knowledge – and knowledge is a valuable commodity these days." I dug my wallet out and freed up two $20s.

Archie looked at them, fingers reflexively twitching a little in a grasping motion. "And if I did?"

"Then the forty's yours, no strings, provided the information is good."

"Okay," He thought for a moment, then, "There's a place out on the edge of McCarthy creek –"

"Which is an illegal biker bar." I hooked the two notes securely back into my fist. "I might not've been here long, but I do basic research, so I know that's a place I'd have a mind to avoid."

"The only other place I can think of is The Duce, over in Jess'ville. Richard Deveraux will sell you something. Or part trade if you've any Oxycontin?"

I gave him a half smile. "Why, look at you. Drumming up trade for Mr Deveraux. Maybe I should drop by McCarthy creek after all. Tell them you're his agent."

"I'm offering information, nothing more."

"Then let's hope there's no surprises when I meet him."

*****

As it turned out Deveraux was an old-fashioned dishonourable Southern gentleman from somewhere along the bottom half of the Mississippi. His security was called Clyde, who had biceps the size of melons and that twitchy, shiny look of a compulsive steroid abuser.

"To what do I owe the pleasure of your company, Mr Radford?"

The two of them were sitting in the back booth of the bar,

away from the overhead lighting and by a window, the top half open to keep the smoke and heat at bay. Clyde stood, silently patted me down, found nothing untoward, but remained standing, blocking anyone else from passing by us.

As I got myself settled I answered his almost rhetorical questions. "Well, sir, I understand that Archie Meritson may well have spoken to you regarding an item I'm interested in acquiring."

"That he has. Did he pass on the cost of such a thing?"

"He mentioned a figure, but I suspect it also included his brokerage fee." I handed him a sealed envelope. "I trust you'll see that he gets it."

Deveraux smiled, showing just a hint of teeth. "You let me worry about that sort of detail Mr Radford. Clyde?" The other man didn't move, but it was obvious he was waiting for the next statement. "If you would kindly give Mr Radford his birthday present."

Clyde went over to the opposite booth, picked up a holdall half hidden under the bench seat, and took out an oilcloth wrapped object. Placing it in front of me, Deveraux flicked the ends of the cloth open, exposing a small black steel .32 automatic and a pocket box of ammunition. There was some wear on the grips, but the barrel looked clear of any rust, and the ammunition seemed relatively new.

Deveraux leaned in and dropped his voice down low. "This came down from New York, and the numbers have been removed so they won't show up in any acid treatment. There's 8 in the clip and 12 still in the box."

I refolded the cloth, pulled a Benny's Big Burgers bag from

my pocket, and slipped everything into the takeaway bag.

Still leaning in, Deveraux added, "We would be willing to buy that back from you at a later date, and an obviously reduced price, on the understanding that you don't add any more history to it."

I smiled and got up to leave. "It sounds like a pretty good deal, though I can't guarantee anything, one way or the other."

"Think on it. I'd hate to see a nice piece like that become discarded in the heat of the moment."

Deveraux kept eye contact as Clyde moved to let me leave, though I didn't feel really safe until I was back behind the wheel of an old beater I'd picked up for the duration.

*****

I reach down to the ankle holster, take out the .32 automatic. It looks ineffectual, but I've seen .22 revolvers used in disputes where one side or the other had not walked away from the conflict.

*****

It had taken around another couple of months to start putting the crew together. Martin was in no hurry what with the robbery being motivated out of greed and not necessity.

There had been four of us. Murry Wilson, Floyd Barrett, Barrett's sister Carrie Ann and myself. Carrie Ann had been the driver. Mousey brown hair cut short – Pixie, she called it – brown eyes and a slight dimple in the middle of her chin. "Driver? I think you mean Wheel Person, Aaron. This might be a dead end spur off the 'I', but you still need to move with the politically correct times."

She had a way of laughing that felt natural and unforced,

as if she were one of those people who, no matter what, always saw the bright side of things. I'd like to say that she'd felt an attraction to me, but whether it was real or encouraged by her brother didn't matter to me. Friends are friends, but business is business.

She'd also doubled up as one of the masked bandits who stayed close to the bank's main doors. Last one in, first one out when everyone was moving for the exit.

I'd started grooming Murray Wilson first. I'd made him my 'favourite drinking buddy' from a sports bar three blocks away from the Belmont. He was short of money, long on resentment, and perfect for being worked into the role of a liberating bank robber. He recommended Floyd Barrett as his wing man, and Floyd's older sister, Carrie Ann. Floyd had a little record, all petty stuff, which he'd freely admitted to at our first meeting.

Wilson and Barrett had agreed to meet me in The Home Run sports bar, and they appeared beside me as I was part way through a Bud. They took bar stools to my left, ordered a couple of beers and bourbon chasers.

When the barman moved off, Wilson said, "Aaron, this here is Floyd Barrett. Floyd, Mr Radford here has a proposition for us."

Floyd looked at Wilson as if he were some kind of local idiot, then at me. "I hear you have money problems."

I nodded. "You could say that. The bank is about to foreclose on us as we haven't been able to keep up the mortgage payments. By the time they finish adding up the outstanding interest, plus administration fees, then selling it all, it'll leave us with barely enough to keep our heads above water in a rental."

Wilson nodded his head. "We hear you." Then he went back to sucking on his beer bottle. Floyd was more astute. "We?"

"Wife Susan and little Shelby. He'll be 4 come September. The redundancies hit us hard as we were both working for the same company. Dual income to zero almost overnight."

Floyd didn't comment, so I continued with the story. "You can only survive for so long, especially when there's nothing else to go to these days."

Wilson looked over to me. "You not a college boy?"

"Blue collar all my life."

"And you think a bank robbery would solve everything?" His head tilted a little to one side as he asked the question.

"Maybe not everything, but a whole heap of the problems would go away. We'd certainly move. West coast somewhere. I keep reading about old ghost towns out that way that're being reclaimed by people in similar situations."

Barrett said, "And you're prepared to risk it all?"

"I've got nothing left to risk except my family, and I'm keeping them out of all of this."

He nodded. "Wise move. How long you been planning?"

"About a year. I've already got floor plans, camera points, alternative routes in and out of town should we ever need them. I'm not just going at this head on. I need this to be a success."

Barrett took another pull from his beer, tossed his bourbon

down in one, then said, "And afterwards?"

"I know someone who'll buy my cut of the money, 75 cents to the dollar. I've been told he's reliable. If you want, I'll ask him if he's interested in taking your cash on as well."

Barrett paused. "Would I know him?"

"Probably not."

Barrett smiled. "Then we'll take our chances with our cut of the money."

I decided then it was time to get agitated. "Well, are you in, or am I just wasting my time?"

"You have the plans on you?" Wilson asked.

"I might be new to this but do I look stupid?"

"Point taken." Barrett took another sip of his beer, then, "Supposing it all comes off, what's the getaway?"

"We take the car down to Ellesmere, switch it there with a pre-parked vehicle, take that cross country to Felton, switch again, then one more at Blixby. From there we head on to the forest just outside of Daxton. I've checked out an area in the woods by one of the old open mining sites. From there the three of you go your way and I go mine. I'd suggest just the one car for the three of you so as not to attract any attention. We use the area to split the takings, and then go our separate ways from there."

Barrett ran the tip of his tongue over his lower lip. "Murry says you're going to be on the inside taking care of the floor security guard?"

"Yeah. I know Frank from way back. I'll be keeping him distracted when you three come in. Once the money's bagged you grab me as a hostage. That not only gets me away without any suspicion, but should make the local police cautious when it comes to pursuit. Changing cars in quick succession will throw them off vehicle and plate recognition. I make it back into Daxton on foot. I give the authorities descriptions of three random people I've seen while I've been down here, and after they're through and I'm back with my family, the following night we skip, using an RV I've already stashed away."

Wilson said, "See? I told you he had it all planned."

Barrett still didn't seem satisfied. "What's to stop us from just shooting you and making it a 3-way split?"

I took my smartphone out of my pocket. "Apart from the fact I've been stream recording the three of us to cloud storage? Susan has an envelope with the account and password details. It's the same as my living will, so she's not suspicious."

Barrett smiled. "Murry's right. You do seem to have it all planned. And you've no problem with Carrie Ann coming in on this?"

"If she's as good a driver as Murry says she is, then what's to worry about?"

Barrett finished off his beer. "She's ex-Army. Got herself a medal or two for seeing action. You might have seen her around. Drives a red '95 Dodge Avenger."

"As long as she can get 4 low profile vehicles, and remembers where she parked them, then fine."

"No problem. When are you looking to do this?"

*****

I put the gun back in the ankle rig and try to work out how I'd send it back to Deveraux. Putting it back in circulation would be better than just dumping it. He'd sell it on quick enough. I allowed myself a quick smile. That would really piss in the evidence pool. I'd thought about taking a small screwdriver and sliding it several times up and down the inside of the barrel to make some new score lines to help slow down any forensics ID. But they'd show up new if the gun was found too early, and I doubted Deveraux would waste time holding onto it.

I check again and the burner phone shows 23:51. Getting close to time.

******

On the day everything had gone according to plan. By 11:15 I'd been talking to Frank for a couple of minutes.

"How are the kids and grandkids these days, Frank?" Basic conversation friends tend to make in passing. I'd moved in front of him, blocking his view of the main glass doors, counting the sweaty seconds off until the three of them came running in, waving weapons and shouting through monkey masks like some outtake from a cheap remake of Planet of the Apes.

Frank immediately became hyper edgy, and started to unclip the holster on his belt.

"Better not, Frank. Nothing is worth becoming a dead hero over." He looked somehow crestfallen, until I mention his grandchildren again. All the while the other three were shouting for everyone to get down on the floor and toss out their wallets, bags and mobile phones. As planned, Barrett had gone directly up to the glass shielded counter, Wilson following several paces behind him, while Carrie Ann kicked the wallets and phones into a pile and scooped them into a lightweight canvas sack.

Still with my back to them, I got down on the floor, taking Frank down with me. Barrett, running true to script, shouted:

"Open the side door, and start putting all the money into this bag. No dye packs, no trackers – nothing that will get some of these innocent people out here killed."

The cashiers complied with the company's co-operation briefings because no bank wants the publicity that their actions got any of their customers killed. Barrett stayed the customer side of the door, watching them dump banded blocks of notes and lose money into the sports bag. Back on the main floor, Carrie Ann held up the canvas bag, indicating she's picked up everything worthwhile.

Wilson checked the stopwatch around his neck. "Thirty seconds…. Fifteen…. Five…. And we're done here!"

Barrett grabbed the money loaded bag, pulled the security door shut, then headed for the main doors. As he passed Wilson, he shouted, "Grab a hostage – the one over by the security guard."

Wilson came over and kicked the sole of my shoe. "Hey, you. On your feet. You're coming with us."

I'd paused for a count of five, which was the agreed cue before Wilson said, "Either you come with us, or I shoot you and your fat fucking friend here."

I stood up and let him pull me out through the main door and around the side of the building where Carrie Ann had parked the car. Barrett and Wilson went in the back and I took the front passenger seat as Carrie Ann drove the car out of the alleyway as fast as she dared, horn blasting so as to clear pedestrians from the entrance.

As we shot down Main Street, Wilson and Barrett had dumped the cell phones out the back windows before we'd gone more than a couple of blocks. Quicker and more efficient than trying to disable GPS, and stolen phones hold little value these days.

Then the monkey masks came off and were stuffed into the canvas sack. We'd planned to burn them in the forest so as to stop any DNA profiling. Leaving them out in the open would've degraded anything, but Wilson was paranoid about such things.

In reply Barrett had just said, "You watch too much CSI on cable." But he'd left it at that.

As we went past the city limit, I turned in my seat and held my arms out to Wilson.

"Okay, tie wrap my wrists."

He'd pulled one out of the bag, then hesitated. "I don't see the point of this part."

"Because it'll give me abrasion marks and bruises, otherwise my kidnapping will seem fake."

I'd made sure he'd pulled the plastic strap tight, then turned forward and started to push and work against them. After I'd started to bleed from the chaffing, I turned round to him again.

"Okay, now cut them off."

Both of them had looked at the cuts around my wrists. Barrett had shook his head. "Shit. You really do take this seriously, don't you?"

"You either buy in one hundred percent, or you get caught."

*****

In Ellesmere we changed to a Nissan, then in Foxton we changed and drove out of town in a non-descript beige Prius, all the while the money safely out of sight in the trunk. Blixby left us with a Chrysler, which was when I'd taken over the driving. It was partly because I knew where we were going, and Carrie Ann didn't, and partly to let all three of them start calming down and come off the adrenaline highs they were on.

By the time we made it up into the woods beyond Daxton, the sun was starting to touch the horizon, casting a glow over the water.

I'd picked the spot carefully. Off trail, and close to the ridge of an old abandoned open cast mine. Over the decades since the 80s and 90s the pits had filled with water. They were deep enough and the water filthy with God knows what so you couldn't see the bottom, even from up on the cliff edge.

Since circling around Daxton city limits I'd been passing a hip flask between the four of us, only I made sure I never actually drank anything from it. When the two in the back held onto it, Carrie Ann had been a little jealous.

"You better save some more of that for me, hear?" They passed it forward, and she'd taken a long pull on it. A minute or so later I took a sharp left onto a dirt road, hearing Carrie-Ann laughing at the way the two in the back were now sliding around, seemingly a touch drunk.

I passed her the flask again. "Here. We're nearly there so a couple more shouldn't hurt."

True to form, she slipped the neck between her lips and took a couple of swigs. She handed it back to me, saying, "That doesn't taste like common or garden bodega brand."

"Hardly. I figured something like this would call for some 25 year old quality. Let's face it, it's to celebrate our success."

In the back, Barrett and Wilson would've probably nodded their agreement, only the Rohypnol had steadily kicked in, doing what it did best. As I finally pulled into the clearing Carrie Ann seemed to realise something wasn't right, but by then it was too late to worry about such things.

After making sure all three of them were fully incapacitated, I'd gotten out of the car, took the money from the trunk, then went over to a large rucksack I'd hidden a week before. I transferred the money from the large black holdall into a nylon sports bag that had garish orange and neon blue panels and a local high school football team logo on it. Then I'd spent a couple of minutes going through the wallets, clearing out the ready money and anything else that might be useful later on. I still needed them and the canvas sack for the last part of the plan, but it seemed too much of a waste to just junk everything.

Putting on a disposable clear plastic rain poncho and rubber gloves, I went back to the car, gathering up some loose rocks on the way and putting them in the sack with the wallets. I'd dumped that by the driver's door, then went around and dropped the empty robbery bag and the rucksack into the passenger seat foot well alongside Carrie Ann's legs. Wilson and Barrett were still under the influence of the whiskey and date rape cocktail, but it was clear they were fighting it and slowly coming out of its control. I wound down the window, shut the passenger door, then opened the back door. Wilson started to loll to one side as I wound down the door's window, which gave me cause for concern that the drug was wearing off too quickly. Time to move things along.

I bent down, took the .32 from my ankle, then shot Murry in the temple. The poncho caught the blood splatter, and the gloves the GSR, which was why I'd packed both in the first place. I closed the door, went around the back of the car, and did the same to Barrett. His eyes might have twitched as I pointed the gun at his head, but that close up I was guaranteed a kill even if he'd succeeded in moving.

That just left Carrie Ann.

It had been tricky and more problematic moving her from the passenger seat, but after some flipping and flopping around I'd managed to get her securely behind the steering wheel before opening the driver's door window. Once everything seemed to be in position I pulled the automatic from the ankle holster again. I had no idea just how much she'd comprehended when I'd shot Wilson and her brother, but I suspected she'd already figured out what the outcome was going to be, regardless.

Somehow the belief of her knowing it was inevitable made things rest easier on my conscience. She seemed like the kind of woman who might've believed in Fate.

Another temple shot, then I arranged her feet on the accelerator and brake.

With the dirty work all done, I took off the poncho and gloves, and tossed them in the back with the two bodies. After that, firing the ignition was easy, but keeping some pressure on the brake pedal while I shifted the car into gear was tricky. With one hand on her knee keeping the brake pressure up, I gave the engine around 30 seconds to get warm again, then picked up the canvas sack and dropped it on the accelerator. Moments later I knocked Carrie Ann's foot off the brake and pushed myself backwards out of the car. The engine roared, burning gas as it shot forward, and in less than five seconds it'd become airborne as it sped off the cliff edge. For a moment it seemed suspended even though its momentum kept it moving forward, like one of those cartoon characters who doesn't realise they're treading air until it's way too late.

And like all those characters, it swan dived down, breaking the surface of the lake with a loud splash.

The engine had died immediately. Then the water found the open door and windows, pushing the air out and letting the car sink rapidly to the bottom of the pit. As I looked over the edge, all that was left was the occasional fart of air breaking the surface, and a thin oily residue that was already dissipating as I cleaned up the site.

*****

The strip mall was almost completely closed by 1am, but I gave it a little time to clear. The last thing I needed was for someone to remember me leaving the motel and make my way to the bus station. My feet were a little sore from walking cross country from the camp site back into Daxton, but the short journey was the least of my discomforts when compared to the money in the bag.

At the terminus I put the sports bag into a long stay rental locker, paid cash for a 60 day period, then I asked at the ticket counter if they could break a dollar so I could make a phone call.

"No problem, buddy. The phone's over there. Doesn't get much use, but then I figure that's all down to everyone having cell phones these days. Me? I can live with or without them, it don't bother me either way."

I nodded my thanks as I picked up the four quarters and moved off to the wall mounted pay phone. Lifting the receiver I dialled a well-remembered number.

Ray Caulfield answered on the second ring. "Sheriff's office, Deputy Caulfield speaking."

I could hear the tension in his voice.

"Hi Ray, it's John."

"John! I mean, Sherriff Cheslin, where are you?"

"I'm over the line, in a town called Daxton. They dropped me in the woods before they took off. Can you send a team out to the Old Lodge motel? I'm just going to rest up there until you guys come and collect me. Don't forget to let the local boys know what's going on. I know I wouldn't like it if strangers turned up unannounced, no matter how well their intentions might be. Plus it's their jurisdiction, not ours, so they'll probably want to pick it up from here."

"What? Yeah! Sure! You sit tight John! The rescue party'll be with you as soon as I can get it on the road! Just remember that."

"Good to know, Ray. After the day I've had it'll be nice to see a friendly face or two."

Three Hogg Tales and One Hairy Ending

Jeff Dosser

Kyle Hogg never dreamed the Sunny Acres Trailer Park would be a sight he'd long to see, but after the night he'd had, even the relative peace of his decrepit Winnebago was cause for celebration.

With a cursory check of the empty Tulsa streets, Kyle scurried from the shadows, his wet shoes squishing softly as he made his way to LOT 2B and home sweet home. Stepping inside, Kyle heaved a sigh of relief and flicked on the lights.

"About time, Fat Boy. I was wondering when you'd show up."

Kyle's heart skipped a beat as he spun to find his employer, Lawrence Talbot, aka, Hairy Larry, plopped down on his couch, pointing a blue steel automatic at him. Dressed in a pair of khaki shorts, and an open necked pink polo, the RV's light shimmered on the ebony forest of hair carpeting Larry's muscled arms, and exposed chest. In fact, the only part of the man which wasn't covered in thick fur was his clean-shaven face and the round smoothness of his bald head.

Larry ran his tongue around his bottom lip. "I missed you at our rendezvous, Kyle." He pushed up from the couch and with a wave of his pistol, motioned Kyle inside. "Go ahead and have a seat."

"Hey, Larry." A lame smile played across Kyle's lips. "I was gonna call, but I lost my phone in the river."

"Excuses, excuses," Larry smirked. "Because I was startin' to get the impression you were trying to avoid me."

As Kyle squeezed through the narrow gangway, Larry hurried him along with a pistol-jab to the ribs. Kyle squealed in terror and dropped onto the couch.

"Don't hurt me. It wasn't my fault." Kyle looked up, a whine in his voice. "There … there was nothin' I could do."

"What do you mean, it wasn't your fault?" Larry's eyes narrowed. "Where's my ice?"

"It was the police," Kyle said. "They had some kinda checkpoint set up on Riverside. They was stoppin' everyone, Larry."

He struggled to breathe through the tightness ringing his chest. Fumbling through the piles of fast-food wrappers and beer cans littering the counter, he spotted his inhaler, grabbed it and huffed down a couple of shots. Breathing under control, he continued: "When I pulled into the line of cars at the stop, I didn't know what to do."

"You left the Meth in the car?" Larry asked, brows rising.

"No, no, I'd never do that." Kyle waved his hands as if wiping away the allegation. "I knew how important that package was to you and Fat Sheila. But the cops. They saw me take off, Larry. They came after me."

He shook his head, tears welling in his eyes. "I'm no athlete." Kyle waved a hand over the swell of his gut and his pencil thin legs. "Just look at me."

Larry leveled a finger. "Then how the hell did you get away?"

"I jumped in the river before they could catch me. They had spotlights, an' the helicopter came. But the current was swift. I was past em' before they set up. I wanted to call, but I lost everything in the water."

"And the Meth?"

Kyle shrank away like a dog expecting a blow. "Gone."

Larry took an angry step, hand raised.

Kyle shrank beneath Larry's upraised arm. "Please, no!"

Larry paused, staring down on the trembling Kyle.

"God damn!" He slammed a fist into the faux wood cabinet leaving a jagged indention. "Sheila's going to be *pissed* when she finds out." He eyed Kyle suspiciously. "If you weren't so stupid, I'd think you were pulling a fast one. That's twenty-k worth of ice, Kyle. You think Fat Sheila's gonna just let that go?"

"No, I swear on my momma's grave. I didn't take nothin'."

Larry leaned back and jabbed the automatic towards Kyle. "How much money you got, Fat Boy?"

Kyle shrugged. "I dunno. A couple hundred bucks."

"A couple hundred?" Larry shook his head and laughed. "Shit! A couple hundred's not gonna appease Sheila."

Kyle did his best to roll into a ball as Larry stepped over and jammed the gun's muzzle into the back of his head. "You better find some cash pretty fuckin' fast or you'll be *floatin'* in that river." He stepped back wiping a hand across his head. "Shit!" Then looking about the camper, Larry's brows rose. "How much this piece of shit worth?"

Kyle's eyes darted about his home. Despite the faded carpet, sunken mattress, and quirky plumbing, the RV was his. The only thing of value he owned. "I don't know. Three ... maybe four grand."

"You got the title?"

Kyle looked to the glove box and nodded. "Yeah, the paperwork's in the cab."

Larry crawled into the passenger seat, the sound of crinkling paper and muttered curses drifting back to Kyle. When Larry returned, he swept a hand across the table, dumping the trash to the floor, then he slapped a pen and the title in front of Kyle.

"Sign it over, Fat Boy. I'll have my sister notarize it in the morning."

"But it's all I've ..." Kyle began before Larry's slap set his ears ringing.

"I said sign it, or I pop you right now." He rapped the gun on the table to prove his point.

When Kyle signed, Larry pocketed the document and held out his hand. "Keys."

"They're in the cabinet. Last one on the left."

As Larry rifled through the drawer, he asked over his shoulder. "You got family? A mom or dad? A bunch of little piglet brothers and sisters running around somewhere?"

As a key's rattle announced Larry's success, the big man turned, his dark eyes flashing. "Well? I asked you a Goddamn question."

"Y…y…yes. I mean no." Kyle said. "Mom and Daddy are dead, but I got brothers."

Larry weighed the statement, then shaking a finger, "Stay right there." He strode out the door and a moment later, Kyle felt the low throaty growl of an untuned engine and the complaining squall of failing brakes. The trailer door slammed open as Larry stepped back in.

"Okay, Kyle, here's what you're gonna do."

As Larry leaned in, Kyle shrank back trying to escape into the cushions. Larry's gleaming face pressed closer until they were nose to nose. Slowly, Larry lifted the pistol and pressed it to Kyle's temple. Larry's breath stank of Slim Jim's and grape Swishers.

"What you're going to do, is get in the car outside and go find your brothers. You're going to explain that if you don't come up with twenty-thousand dollars in the next twenty-four hours, you're a dead man. You understand me?"

Kyle whimpered a feeble, "Yes."

"Good. Once you've got the money, you're going to meet me on the 11th Street bridge tomorrow at midnight. "

The pistol barrel dug into Kyle's head.

"But you're taking my RV," Kyle protested. "Don't that count for somethin'?"

"Call it a restocking fee," Larry chuckled. "You don't have a problem with that do you?"

Kyle shook his head.

"And do you know what Sheila's going to say if you don't show up tomorrow night?"

Tears burned down Kyle's cheeks. "She'd have me killed?"

"No. she won't have you killed."

Kyle's eyes fluttered open, and he gasped out a, "Really?"

"Really," Larry said. "First, she's going to have me hurt you real bad…."

Kyle shuddered, a high pitched moan escaping his lips.

"Then, she'll have you killed."

Wet heat spread across Kyles lap.

Larry stepped back, his eyes drifting to the growing dark spot on Kyle's already damp shorts.

"Now get out, before I change my mind."

*****

The buzz of cicadas and box-fan hum saturated the humid July air as Michael Hogg sat on his couch, the game controller firmly in his hand. Clicking his game to 'pause,' he watched for the umpteenth time as his brother, Kyle, thudded across the hardwoods and peered through the shuttered blinds.

"He ain't comin'," Mike said, returning to his game. "You said yourself, there's no record in the trailer of where you're from." He looked up and met Kyle's stare. "An' we parked that heap you came in behind the barn." Mike set down the controller, then rocking his prodigious girth from its indention on the couch, rose ponderously to his feet.

"There's no way anyone could find ya, even if they did have an address. The mailbox's been gone since the tornado last spring, an' no one 'round here's gonna give up a neighbor."

The screen door protested with a high-pitched whine as Mike waddled onto the porch and considered the cow-dotted fields surrounding the Hogg family farm. The sun sat like an ember on the darkening Oklahoma horizon, the shadow cast by the two-story farmhouse stretched to cover a parking lot of rusted hulks squatted in the weed-strewn yard.

Leaning onto the gas grill at the edge of the porch, Mike lifted a hand against the sunset and squinted at a dust trail boiling up the road.

"What kinda car this fella drive?" he asked.

Kyle bustled out, the screen door slapping shut as he joined Mike on the porch.

"He's got a candy-apple-red F150 with chrome rims." Kyle squinted into the light. "Oh, God. It's him." He stumbled back shoving the grill against the window and ripping open the screen. "It's him ain't it?"

It was a red pickup, that much was certain, but there were plenty of red pickups. The vehicle slowed as it approached the drive, the pursuing cloud of dust enveloping it as it ground to a halt beneath the gnarly old elm.

Mike turned and stomped inside. By God, this was Hogg property, had been for generations. As he rummaged through the hall closet, the smell of mothballs and old cardboard filled the air. At the back, he found Daddy's Remington 870 and a box of shells. Stepping onto the porch, Mike thumbed in three rounds of 00 Buck.

The crunch of tires on gravel announced the arrival of the intruder and as Hairy Larry stepped from his pickup, Mike worked the 870's action – Cha-Chunk -and jacked in a shell.

"Go on and get back in your truck," he called from the porch. "We don't want no trouble."

Larry wore a tank top and an OU Sooners ball cap. The fur on his shoulders shone like a dark aura silhouetted in dusk's fading glow.

"Look," Larry called. "I know Kyle's here. All I need is twenty-thousand, and I'll be on my way."

Mike laughed. "Seriously, I ain't got no twenty-thousand dollars."

The screen door gave a squeak as Kyle poked out his head.

"Hey, Kyle," Larry called. "I missed you on 11th last night." He pulled off his cap and ran a palm across his gleaming head. "But, tell ya what." He turned, eying the open fields and grazing cattle before returning his gaze to the front porch. "You got a nice place here, Kyle. I'm sure if you sign it over, Sheila will let bygones be bygones."

Heat rose in Mike's face. His grip tightened on the 870's stock. After Daddy and Momma's death, their older brother, Deon had worked to keep the family whole. Once he'd left, the responsibility of maintaining the homestead and protecting Kyle had fallen to him. He'd be damned if some drug-dealin' trash would threaten his brother and kick 'em off their land.

"How about you take this with ya instead?" Mike hefted the shotgun and fired.

The blast sent Larry diving for cover as an explosion of dirt erupted beside the truck's front wheel. With a hiss of escaping air, the Ford sank onto its rim.

"How's he supposed ta leave now?" Kyle grumbled from

the doorway. "You shot out his tire."

Mike turned to answer when Larry rose above the hood, a semi-automatic gripped in his hand. Bullets zinged and thudded sending Mike and Kyle diving inside. With the sharp ting of metal and low, deep thuds, more rounds careened through the walls sending clouds of plaster dust and splinters of wood into the air.

Rising from the floor, Mike raised his head and peered through the window in time to see Larry drop his pistol's spent mag and load another.

"What's that smell?" Kyle asked.

Mike sniffed in the sharp bite of propane. One of the bullets must have punctured the grill's tank. If he fired back now, the muzzle flash would ignite it and blow up the porch.

"Come on," Mike called, dragging Kyle to his feet. "We gotta get."

As they raced towards the kitchen and out the back door, Larry opened up once again. The fan in the window took a hit. One of its plastic blades shattered, throwing the entire mechanism off balance. As it tumbled from the window and struck the floor, the cord was yanked from the plug. In the shower of sparks which followed, Mike had time to shove Kyle through the doorway before the porch and living room were consumed in a swelling ball of flame.

*****

From the bed of his Chevy Silverado, Deon Hogg took a drag from his cigarette and puffed a gray cloud into the humid Oklahoma night. Although Mike, in his frantic call, hadn't explained everything, he'd told Deon enough. Kyle was in trouble…again. Only this time, he'd brought trouble home.

Although Deon wasn't Kyle's father, he felt the same guilt of his decisions. Hell, he'd been only eighteen when Momma and Daddy had died, petitioning the courts to keep the family together; three brothers eking out a living on insurance money and what little the cattle brought in each year. Yet somehow, it had been enough. He'd barely been more than a boy himself, doing his best to raise a ten-year-old Kyle and fifteen-year-old Mike. By the time, he'd volunteered for the Army and left Mike in charge, Kyle was an uncontrollable fifteen-year-old, experimenting in boys, weed, and wine.

He shook his head and flicked the cigarette into the night. Hell, if he'd stayed at home, there was no guarantee his baby brother wouldn't have ended up an addict anyway.

He watched the headlights turn into the empty neighborhood and splash across the billboard announcing:

Willow Creek Estates

2 & 3 Acre Lots Starting at $100k

Build Your Dream Here

Deon reminded himself that blood was blood and if you messed with one Hogg, you messed with 'em all.

"Deon," Kyle wailed as he tumbled from the car and raced into his brother's arms.

Kyle smelled of weed and sweat as Deon pushed him back and forced a smile. "Well, you really put your foot in it this time."

Kyle's face fell as Mike stepped up beside him.

"Yeah, we all know Kyle fucked up," Mike said. "What we

don't need is a lecture." He kneaded Kyle's shoulder then met Deon's stare. "What we need, Big Brother is help."

Deon nodded and tapped out another cigarette, lit it, then said, "You're right." He looked his siblings over, acknowledging inside that Mike was beginning to take control. It would be easy to slip into the father role and dish out blame, but that wouldn't help them escape the problem.

He took another drag, feeling the icy menthol chill, and jabbed a finger at the car.

"This your ride or the heap the drug dealer gave ya' after he stole the RV?"

Kyle spared a glance at the dented Taurus and nodded. "I don't have a car. This is the one Hairy Larry gave me to find ya'll. To get the money."

"Twenty grand," Deon's brows V'ed into a frown. "That what he wants?"

Kyle nodded and looked away.

Stepping over to the Taurus, Deon opened the door. "And you're sure there was no paperwork details inside that RV as to where you grew up?"

"None," Kyle said. "I have no idea how he found us."

When he'd first received their call, Deon assumed Hairy Larry had found his brothers by searching the web. You could find almost anything on the internet, cooking recipes for grilled snake, how to build a deadfall trap, the phases of the moon in 1901. He'd searched himself and found nothing on Kyle or the family farm outside of Bartlesville, Oklahoma; drug arrests, court dockets, and more crap about his brother's lifestyle than he ever wished to know. But nothing on the farm.

Deon climbed inside the Taurus. The Ford's trash covered carpet was crusted stiff from spilled pop, and God only knew what else. He searched beneath the seats pulling out layers of crushed food wrappers, used tissues, and faded receipts before climbing out with a fist-sized bundle in one hand.

"What's this look like?" Deon flipped a balled sock into Kyle's hands.

When Kyle dumped the contents, a rubber-banded cell phone and portable charger hit the trunk with a metallic thud.

Mike peered over Kyle's shoulder and shook his head. "GPS. He's known where you are the whole time."

"Do we destroy it?" Kyle asked.

Deon shook his head. "I don't think so."

As he studied the empty lots and the handful of half-built homes lining the neighborhoods empty streets, a plan began to form.

Deon grabbed a lantern from the toolbox in the back of his truck and motioned towards the house in front of them. Three stories high, brick and stone exterior, gabled roof, and a three-car-garage. It would one day be the centerpiece of the neighborhood.

"Grab that phone and follow me," he said as he led them up the sidewalk and through the front door. "I've got a plan."

*****

Lawrence, 'Hairy Larry' Talbot, studied the tracking app as he maneuvered onto the pristine concrete roads snaking through the open fields and lines of partially constructed homes. Chain lighting arced and chased itself through the cloudy horizon as a warm breeze sighed through his truck's open window, bringing with it the sharp tang of cut grass and the scent of approaching rain.

Flicking off his lights, he cruised the vacant streets until he spotted the Taurus parked in front of a three-story mansion at the top of a rise. The car was parked beside a new Silverado whose doors and truck bed sported bright images of a cap-wearing pig, a brick in one hand and a trowel in the other.

HOGG MASONRY AND BRICKWORKS
GO THE WHOLE HOGG

Was written beneath the dancing swine.

So, Kyle dragged both brothers into this little drama, Larry thought. He eased the F150 into a spot just short of the house.

Pulling out his pistol, he crept through the shadows to the front door. A yellow glow stained the front windows and seeped through a hole in the front door where a handle should be.

Leaning down, Larry peered through the opening and spotted the three portly brothers standing at the center of an expansive living room. He recognized Kyle and the brother who'd shot at him from the front porch of the now burned down farmhouse. The older, fatter of the three had to be the owner of the Silverado.

A battery powered lantern at the room's center cast tilted shadows from 20-foot scaffolding onto the plastered wall behind. Except for a pile of bricks, and lengths of 2x4s leaning against the scaffolding, the room was empty.

"Little pig, little pig, let me come in!" Larry announced as he kicked open the door.

The brothers turned, Kyle's face flush with terror. The farm boy glowered, and the head Hogg scowled. Beside the stack of bricks, a partially constructed hearth and chimney scaled the thirty-foot wall and disappeared into the ceiling. Larry wondered what kind of people could afford such luxuries. He wondered if someday he might be one of them.

"Hands up, my three little piggies," Larry chuckled. "Or should I say, Hoggs?"

Kyle and the farm boy's hand's shot up as they stepped back from the door. The oldest of the three held his ground before letting something fall clattering to the floor. Then he too raised his hands and stepped back beneath the scaffolding.

"Ah, I see you found my phone." Larry's voice echoed through the cavernous room. The entire space stank of dust, and fresh pine lumber, and the muddy wetness of new cement.

"You don't have to do this," the older brother said. "I've got all the money I could lay my hands on. $8,000 bucks." With one of his upraised hands, he pointed to the front door. "It's in the glove box of my truck. Take the truck too."

Very slowly, the older Hogg lowered a hand and dug into his front pocket. With a flick of his wrist, the keys clattered to the floor beside the phone.

Larry clucked his tongue and stepped closer. "A fine offer, but Sheila has a code to maintain. You start lettin' people rip you off and word gets around. Pretty soon you're either out of business or six-feet under." He shrugged. "It's not personal. Just business."

Never taking his eyes from the three Hoggs, Larry stepped over to the phone and knelt down to pick it up. "Any last words?"

In the instant Larry lowered his eyes and reached for the phone, he caught a flicker of movement. He glanced up to see the older brother kick away a board lying beside his foot.

With a ropey twang, a leaning 2x4 shot away from the scaffolding and slapped against the floor. Glancing up, Larry watched in horror as the entire steel structure tilted over. Slowly at first, then gaining speed, it smashed down upon him. Sheets of drywall and metal framing slammed to the ground in an ear-splitting roar, surrounding him in an explosion of pain and sudden oblivion.

*****

When Larry woke to his cramped darkness, the only illumination was a rectangle wedge of light close beside his head. The air was stifling and humid yet bright with the stink of his own cologne and the coppery tang of blood.

Rising to an elbow, he ignored the lightning bolt of pain lancing through his ribs realizing suddenly that his arms and legs were bound. Larry peered through the rectangular opening into the room, recognizing he was sealed inside the hearth.

With the gritty scrape of trowel on stone, Larry watched as the older Hogg spreads a line of mortar along a brick he held in his hand. He turned and meet Larry's eye.

"Ah, you're awake." A smile dimpled Deon's chubby cheek as he leaned closer.

"You asked if we had any last words?"

As the brick was slid home and Larry's fate sealed, he could just make out the bricklayer's muffled voice:

"Not by the hair of our chinny chin chins."

Collateral Damage
Eve Fisher

It was around ten o'clock on that particular hot June night, when I heard a scrabbling sound that wasn't from the Sci-Fi channel. It came up the alley, by my garage, and onto my back steps. Then somebody started banging on the back door.

I looked through the kitchen window and saw Barry Tripp, Grant's brother, fist raised. I whipped the door open and he jumped back.

"I've got a front door and a door bell –"

"Linda," he said, gulping air. "I need some help." He waved to the man sprawled on the ground beside him.

"Who is it?"

"Andy. Andy Bentz. He's a friend of mine. He's drunk."

"I can smell that. What's he doing here?"

"I brought him. Could you give us a ride to my place? I can take care of him till he sobers up."

To my left, the lights went on in Mrs. Domagala's place.

"I think I should call Grant."

"No!" Barry almost shouted as Andy groaned. "Please. He's on parole. Grant'd just have to bust him again. And he's already mad because Grant busted him before. They don't talk any more. Grant's upset already. And he didn't mean to do it."

"Grant or Andy?" Barry looked at me, puzzled. "Barry, it's my experience that alcoholics usually mean to get drunk."

"No. They do it, but they don't mean to. Really. I know. I never mean to when I do. Well, I mean, I do, but I don't mean to -"

"Okay, Barry. Come inside, while I find my purse."

"What about Andy?"

"He'll be fine where he is." Once inside I switched off the TV and asked, "Where did you find him, anyway?"

"I just got off my shift. I come out the back door, and there he was. Lying in the alley. I almost stepped on him."

"Was he there earlier?"

Barry shook his head.

I fished my car keys out of the bowl on the worktop by the window. "Do you think we can get him into my car?"

"I got him here."

We went back outside. Now the lights were on at Art Mohnen's, the postman who lives to my right. I'd have to call him later and tell him that Barry Tripp came by, upset, and I gave him a ride home. That would fly: Barry's known all over town for being needy but harmless.

I helped Barry maneuver Andy up. His shirt was splotchy wet with bourbon. *How often does a drunk spill booze down his back?* I turned on the yard light and saw his face: swelling fast, and a crust of dark red on his upper lip and chin.

"Who beat him up?" I asked Barry.

"Nobody. He's just drunk."

I ignored Barry and grabbed Andy's chin. His right eye glared at me through puffy, half-closed lids. "Andy, you need to go to the doctor."

"I told him that already," Barry said.

"No," Andy mumbled. "Home."

"That's what he told me," Barry added.

I turned to Barry and said, "We could take him to the hospital anyway."

"No!" Barry yelped. "They'll call his parole officer. They'll call the cops. Please, Linda. Just take him to my place. I can take care of him. I know what to do when someone gets beat up. You give them ice and aspirin. I've done it before. Please. *Please.*"

So I took them to Barry's.

*****

Whatever happened to Andy, no one seemed to know about it. When Grant Tripp came in with paperwork, I asked if anything exciting had happened over the weekend. Nope, quiet shift, and he was glad of it. At lunch, nothing. The old men who come in afternoons to the courthouse to complain about the morning news – nothing. Finally I called Nordstrom's Autos and asked to speak to Andy.

"He's not here," the receptionist said. "He called in sick. Can one of the other mechanics help you?"

"Oh, sure. It's just that I ran into him Saturday, and there's this weird sound in my engine –" there's always a weird sound coming out of my old Chevy – "and he said to bring it in

Monday. So, anyone else got some time to look at it?"

"Not today. We're backed up. Maybe Thursday? Can it last that long or do you need a rental car?"

"Oh, it'll last."

I'd call and cancel the appointment Wednesday.

A week later, I was taking my early morning walk out at Lake Howard along with about a dozen or so other people. Andy pulled up next to me in a car that was obviously not his, and in need of a tune up.

"Thanks for taking me home that night. I was in pretty bad shape."

"Yes, you were. What happened?"

"Just horsing around."

"That was a hell of a horsing. Your eye's still swollen." Andy shrugged, so I carried on. "You know, I'm still trying to figure out if they wanted to send you to prison or set you on fire and got interrupted."

He tilted his head and squinted at me. I moved closer to the open window. "Look, there was booze all over your shirt – one lit match, and I think you would have been a whole lot more hurt. They suddenly turn nice, or did Barry get in their way?"

"It was just a warning."

"Mm."

"Look, I found out something I shouldn't have, and they didn't realize I don't snitch. They know better now. That's all I'm going to tell you, Linda."

"Fine. I'm just glad you're okay. I hope you're going to stay okay."

"Oh, yeah. Especially since neither you nor Barry told anyone. Right?"

I sighed. "I don't snitch, either."

"I know. Thanks," he said, and drove off.

I kept walking. Small towns are full of unsolved mysteries. Why did Mary Nelson move from Laskin to Flandreau in the middle of the night? Gloria Munsell passed me – I saw her once, shaking and white as a sheet, throwing something into a dumpster just before her boyfriend came driving up. Carla Hovis – why was she window-shopping a new washer and dryer two months after she'd bought a brand new set? What made those crop circles out at Lyle Pederson's? Who beat up Andy Bentz and why? What was Puffer Davison doing riding his bike out here at seven a.m.?

Small towns are also all about connections. I used to be married to Gary Davison, whose entire family are always the usual suspects in Laskin. Gary's older sister, Kristin, used to date her cousin Puffer, who used to be a major drug dealer in town, and Barry – Grant's little brother – had been one of Puffer's mules who supplied Neil Inveig, who in turn supplied the more respectable druggies in town. I'm not sure how much Grant knows about Barry's involvement – I'm not sure how much *Barry* knows about Barry's involvement – but Grant knew enough that it's one of the reasons why he's suspected of having killed Neil, even though someone else confessed and is doing time for it. Puffer is currently clean, sober, working a 12-step program and a construction job, so all is well with the world. But back in the day, Andy had hung out with Puffer, too. And Andy was currently dating Puffer's wild-child baby sister, Rhiannon. And it was my all too personal experience that Davisons never get entirely clean. And it struck me, as I finished my walk, that drugs or sex were both damned good reasons to beat someone to a pulp.

*****

That Saturday night was the Laskin street dance. I stopped at one point and watched the Laskin elite, slumming in full force. It was like a car wreck: you know you shouldn't look, but you just can't help it. Jim Mackenzie was passing a bottle of scotch around a group that was already pretty well tanked. Jennie Mackenzie, dressed like a Klondike hooker, was dancing with a tall, wanna-be cowboy. As one after another went out to dance, Jack Hofer drifted over, picked up their plastic cup, and drained it. I was sorry to see that – Jack was a month out of his third spell in treatment – especially when I passed his wife Nancy (another Lake Herman walker) coming from the VFW fundraising booth with a couple of pops.

I bought a beer and two pork loin sandwiches at the same booth from Rob Stroh, Andy's boss. I bit deep into the first when Puffer Davison leaned into me and said, "I love a good two-fisted eater. How ya doing, Linda?"

"Just fine. What are you doing here? Isn't this a dangerous event for you?" I waved my beer in his face.

He waved his pop in mine. "Not any more. I don't drink, I don't smoke –"

"Good for you."

"Did you hear that Gary's up in North Dakota, working the oil fields?"

"Good place for him. Good wages."

"Want me to say hi?"

Eve Fisher

"Not particularly."

"Hey, what's the deal with you and Andy?"

"What are you talking about?" It wasn't like Puffer to ask questions.

"I saw you two out at the lake together."

"Oh. Yeah. I saw you, driving around. What were you doing up so early?"

"I'm a morning guy these days." I snorted. Behind me, I could feel Rob listening to us. "Clean living all the way. But Andy. He just broke up with my sister and I was wondering if it because of you."

"Not hardly." I started to walk away, and Puffer put a hand on my arm.

"I'm just asking. I mean, you're hot, I know that –"

I pulled away from him. "Are you checking up on me?"

"No. Well, Gary likes to hear –"

"You tell Gary to go to hell. And no, I am not dating Andy, have not dated Andy, will not date Andy. Not that it's Gary's business or yours or any other damn Davison. You got that?"

"You always were a firecracker."

"And I've blown up in your face before."

I'm really not sure what would have happened next, because Barry came running up and grabbed my arm. "Linda!" he cried, pulling me out into the street. "It's time for our dance!"

News to me. But I danced with Barry twice, then I worked my way out and around the corner, away from the street dance, and on home. On the way, I overtook Edie Wilson and

Marilyn Nordstrom.

"You two done for the evening, too?" I asked.

"I may be done for life," Edie said.

"Dan's been drinking again," Marilyn volunteered.

"I could kill him," Edie said. She described the unhappy relapse in great detail, repeating over and over, "I could kill him."

"Nobody's worth going to prison over."

We stopped at my house, and Edie turned to me. "You work at the courthouse. You ever hear of any special way to get away with murder?"

"By the time I hear about it, they got caught."

"CSI has ruined it for everybody," Edie complained.

"True," Marilyn agreed.

"How about a drive by?" I suggested brightly. "Say, after a meeting. You could wear gloves and a disguise." We all started laughing. "Just don't use my car!" I called out as they walked on up the street.

*****

I was joking. I swear to God I was joking. But you might understand my sense of responsibility when, two weeks later, someone pulled up in a dark car with tinted windows and sprayed bullets all over eight people who were standing, talking and smoking outside the old Paulson building after an AA meeting.

Why did I feel so guilty?

Because I'm Norwegian Lutheran, and guilt is in my DNA.

Because I secretly believe that ideas are the equivalent of

action: if you put it out there into the universe, and it's bad enough, the universe will pick it up and run with it.

Because I also shared it with a group later that week, and we all had a real big laugh.

Because, specifically, it looked like someone took my idea and thought, "here's the perfect solution," and did it. With horrific results: Brian Daugherty was shot in the leg; Andy Bentz was shot in the chest; Jack Hofer was shot dead.

Both Barry and Grant Tripp had actually been there, because Grant had gone to pick Barry up after the meeting. Grant came in the next morning for magistrate court and said, wearily, it was just like out of the movies, only worse. "Who's the judge today?"

"Judge Hauser from Sioux Falls," I answered. "He's talking with the state's attorney right now. Are you okay?"

"Sure."

"Is Barry all right?"

"Yeah. Thanks to Brian. He dove down, right on top of Barry. Probably saved his life. Got shot in the leg. He works for the co-op."

"I know who Brian is. Biker, Afghan vet, hangs out with Puffer Davison a lot. Where was Puffer?"

"Right behind me."

"What do you mean, right behind you?" I asked, as Detective Jonasson walked in with more paperwork.

"I mean he pulled up next to me on his bike. I got out of my car, Puffer got off his bike, the shooter came, and there we were, standing with our mouths open, like a couple of freaking idiots."

"I'm sorry, I didn't mean –"

Jonasson interrupted. "I see Grant's filled you in on last night's excitement."

"Yes. Any hopes it's a random shooting?" I asked.

"Hopes? If it is, I'm moving to Gann Valley to raise sheep."

"I'd prefer Yellowknife," Grant said.

"Who invited you?" Jonasson growled. And we were all back to normal as the judge came out.

*****

Later, Grant took me to lunch at the Laskin Café. He was so sweet, trying to make up for snapping at me, that finally the guilt drove me to tell him what I'd said. "I'm sorry I said it. I mean, I was just joking at the time."

"Just joking?"

"Uh-huh."

"That was a hell of a thing to joke about. Do you have any idea what last night was like? I saw three people shot. I watched Jack Hofer's head explode. Oh, that's one hell of a joke, all right."

"Grant –"

He stood up, his mouth grim. "You know, I need to get back to the station." And walked out.

*****

Nothing improved over the next two days. Nobody had seen the shooter. The car had been dark, with muddy license plates. Andy was still in ICU, still unconscious. Every possible theory was floated. The old men at the courthouse decided, after much debate, that it was a deranged serial killer, and they urged me to keep my doors locked and my guns loaded. At Mellette's, the consensus was some punk from Sioux Falls. At the Laskin Café, it was… well, they're a crazy bunch there, and the apocalypse comes up a lot in casual conversation. And the only meetings people admitted going to were prayer services.

Everybody's alibi was being checked, especially those of us connected with AA or Al-Anon. Grant came for mine late the afternoon of the second day.

"So, where were you the night of the shooting?"

"I was at a library board meeting. Seven to eight-thirty. Afterwards, a bunch of us went to the DQ for ice cream. We were there until nine-thirty. Nancy Hofer was there. I can give you the rest of their names if you'd like."

He nodded wearily. "Anybody leave early?"

"No. We were having a good time. Any sign of the car?"

"Nope. Any chance of a lead from any of your Davison connections?"

"Those days are long gone. I'm out of the clan, remember?"

"That's not what I hear."

That damned street dance. I thought of Rob Stroh, standing and listening behind me at that damn booth. He went hunting with Grant. And there were the Mackenzies, or… It could have been anyone, including Barry. Especially Barry, who seemed to be everywhere I went, keeping his distance with a thoroughness that was very suspicious. "Just because they talk to me doesn't mean they trust me. Or vice versa."

"You could ask. Pry. Flirt." I think my jaw dropped. "Look, if Puffer Davison is sniffing around you again, why not use it?"

"And why don't you just go to hell?"

*****

The visitation for Jack Hofer that night was even more depressing than you can imagine. Nancy Hofer was pale, thin, and devastated. Standing next to her was her dad, my neighbor Art, looking grim. Barry hovered near, and looked away every time I glanced at him. Grant was huddled with Fran Cochrane, a nurse at the hospital who lives down the alley from me. I'd tried to apologize later on at the courthouse, but he'd ignored me. Fran, however, had his full attention.

Fran was in AA, and she was busy almost violating anonymity on Grant's behalf. She'd told him what they'd talked about at the meeting. She'd offered to interview her fellow AA members. Randy Walworth, Laskin coroner and mortician, told me all about it over a quick cigarette out back, adding,

"Personally, I'm hoping that she confesses to the shooting in an over-zealous attempt to win Grant's attention. Anything that works. They had a one night stand a long time ago. I wouldn't bet that she remembers much about it, but now that she's sober…"

"She wants to try again?"

"Honey, she wants somebody. Anybody. Any. Body. And she is ruthless. I'm sure she's told him stories about your Davison days. And you and Puffer were seen together at the street dance. Who, by the way, she wouldn't mind hooking up with, either."

"She can have him. Both of them."

"If you say so. Anyway, a delegation of her fellows,

including yours truly, is going to remind her that anonymity is the foundation of all our traditions, and basically tell her to keep her big mouth shut about anything and anyone other than that night."

I went back inside, and there was Puffer, dressed in black, offering his condolences. Nancy flushed slightly – God only knows what he said to her – and turned to the next person in line. Fran gave me a bitchy glance and then went back to Grant. I thought about having a chat with her myself, but decided to leave it to Randy and go home to a half a bottle of wine.

I was sitting on my deck and on my second glass, when I saw Art coming up his back walk. I waved at him, and he walked over.

"So, how are you doing?" I asked.

"Me? I'm fine. It's Nancy who's a basket case. But she's young. She'll recover. Even if she doesn't believe it right now." And he drifted into telling me – again – about that terrible foggy day, twelve years ago, when his wife, Nancy's mother, died in a tragic auto accident. "Nancy was what got me through it. She's always been the best daughter a man can have…" He sighed. "She'll be okay. She might even be better off. Jack was a nice enough guy, God rest his soul, but he wasn't what I had in mind for her."

"You wanted someone with ambition and a better job and –"

"No, I wanted somebody with character. With strength. Someone she could depend on."

"Not an alcoholic." He nodded. "But she fell for Jack.

Personally, I think it's because he made her laugh. Guys don't understand how attractive that is to women."

"That might be true, but I'd think a woman could get real tired of laughing when it's at a clown that can't stay sober." There was a pause. "Anyway, at least now Nancy can quit going to meetings every week." As I looked politely puzzled, he continued, "Al-Anon meetings. Oh, she tried to keep it from me, but you can't keep secrets in this town."

I nodded. What he didn't know was that Nancy didn't go to Al-Anon, she went to the AA meetings that were held the same night. You can keep secrets in a small town if you're devious enough. Most of us learn.

I said, "True. But I hope she won't quit coming. She's still going to have a lot to deal with – maybe more now than ever."

"Jack's dead. Once she gets over that, she'll be fine." He got up. "So how is that mechanic? Andy. The one in intensive care?"

"Still unconscious."

"I hope he makes it. One death's enough. See you later."

*****

That weekend a black car with tinted windows was found out near Dark Hollow. There was no proof that it was The Car, but it had been stolen from Nordstrom's Auto, and it was abandoned, and that was enough for rumors.

And after dinner Sunday night, Puffer came banging on my back door.

"What do you want?" I asked through the locked screen door. Sometimes I listened to the old guys.

"I need to talk to you."

"Fine, talk."

"Come on, Linda. Let me in."

"No."

"I'm not going to attack you or anything."

"You're right about that. Back up." He did, I came outside and closed the door behind me. "So. What do you want?"

He rolled his eyes at me, but got on with it. "That day you were talking to Andy out at the park. What were you talking about?"

"Puffer –"

"Look, he's still unconscious. He might die. I need to know what the hell you were talking about!"

"He was thanking me for taking him home after he got beat up."

"Did he say anything about why he got beat up?"

"Nope. Wouldn't tell me a thing."

"Linda, this is no time to be keeping secrets."

"I'm not. That's all I know. But you keep asking me about it, so obviously you know something I don't."

"Okay. Rob Stroh beat him up."

"What? His boss?" I remembered Rob, standing behind us, listening…

"You heard me."

"How did you find that out?"

"His girlfriend Carrie told me."

"Why would she tell you?"

95

"Hey, she was upset. Bunch of crap's going down. She needed a friend."

I gritted my teeth. That was Puffer. If there's a woman with relationship trouble, he'll be at her door before she can snap her fingers. And he'll talk his way into more than her door, don't think he won't. But I had more things to think about than that old resentment.

Andy had said he'd found out something he shouldn't have: well, it wasn't Rob's infidelities. Rob's been screwing around for years, and everyone in town knows it, including his wife Jan, who never sets foot in public. So that left theft, or drugs – and with that, my blood pressure spiked as the memories flooded in: Gary's mom and pop; the stench from the house that blew up on 81; the blister packs spilling all over Puffer's van; Kristin screaming bloody murder; Dave Davison's expression as he stomped out of my house; Gary dumped like a sack of bruised potatoes on our back porch...

I could see Art lurking in my lilac bushes, and I was glad of it.

"What about Jack?" I asked.

"Collateral damage?"

"If it's what I think you're hinting at, you're lucky to be alive."

"Damn straight. And I want to stay that way. I was thinking you could ask some of your buddies down at the courthouse. Keep my name out of it, maybe. They'll listen to you, Linda."

"Why should I risk my neck doing your dirty work?"

"What risk?"

"Don't hand me that. I remember what happened to Patty,"

I snapped.

"Don't look at me. I didn't do anything to her. Jesus, Linda, I don't hurt women. You know that." I nodded. "So, will you?"

"I'll think about it."

"Linda –"

I lowered my voice, and kept it firm: "I said I'll think about it. So you need to leave. Now."

Amazingly, he went. Art came out from the lilac bushes.

"Everything okay?"

"Oh, yeah. No problem."

"I wasn't sure when I saw his bike pull up. And then you wouldn't let him in the house." He was too much of a gentleman to mention the night long ago, when I'd kicked Puffer to the curb, though that's why he'd shown up now with his gun in hand.

"I was just being cautious. You want a beer?"

"Sure." He holstered his gun, I opened my back door and we both went into my kitchen. "Can I ask what he wanted?"

"He wanted me to tell the police something that might have something to do with the shooting." I put a beer in front of both of us, and sat down across from Art. "Drug related, not that he ever officially told me anything, if you know what I mean. I have no idea if it's true or not." I rolled my head on my neck, trying to get the tension out. "God, I don't want to be in the middle of this."

"Then don't be. Share it with me." I must have given him a funny look, because he added, "Listen, it's my son-in-law that got killed. I want to know what's going on. What does that son

97

of a bitch know?"

"I don't know if he knows anything or not. He's got information about a fight between Andy – the mechanic still in ICU? And Andy's boss out at Nordstrom's."

"Oh."

"I just wish I could talk to Andy…"

"And it's drug related?" Art asked.

"He never said that. But I speak Davison all too well."

"Hmm. Maybe we should check into it before you talk to the police."

"What?"

"Come on, Linda. You know you want to find out what's going on. And I sure as hell do."

I actually thought about it for a second. But then I reminded myself that even though Art sort of looked like an old Rutger Hauer, he was no action hero. He was a rural delivery postman who watched too much TV, sitting at my kitchen table with a loaded gun, dying to go out and hunt down the drug lords of Laskin.

"I really appreciate it," I said. "But I need to think about this. I want to do the right thing, and not just go off half-cocked."

"You sure?" I nodded. "I'd be your back-up." I shook my head. "All right. Just… keep me posted?"

"You bet."

He left, I waited a few minutes, then went out to my car and headed down to the Man Hole, a pool hall that serves pop, beer, and whiskey, nothing else. As you can tell from the name, it serves pretty much an all-male crowd, but I'd shot pool there before, back when I was married to Gary. It was Rob's favorite hangout. And I wasn't the only woman at the Man Hole that evening – Carrie, Rob's little girlfriend, was with him, sucking on a longneck in between shots. She was the one I really wanted to talk to.

"Hey, Rob. Carrie."

"What do you want?" Rob asked, swiveling around on his right leg, which was heavily braced.

"To get out of the house. Have a social beer. Maybe shoot some pool. What happened to your leg?"

"Wrenched my knee getting out of the bay the other day." He sat down and rubbed his leg. "Hurts like hell."

"Sorry to hear that." I turned to Carrie. "So, how are you doing?"

"I'm fine. Why?"

"Just asking."

I went over to the bar, got a beer, and then came back and watched as Rob made a couple of shots. He was good enough so I knew he'd be excellent without the brace. Carrie never took her adoring eyes off of him. If she'd been upset about anything, she was over it.

"You know Puffer Davison?" I whispered.

"Who?"

"Biker. Hangs around a lot."

"Rob doesn't like bikers."

Rob missed a shot and came limping over. Carrie went out and lined up a shot as he sat on a stool beside me.

"Okay. Something's on your mind. What is it?"

"Mm. Well, you remember, back at the beginning of June, when Andy Bentz got beaten up?"

"I remember him coming to work all bunged up, yeah. Why?"

"Who did it?"

"What do you mean? How should I know?"

"Oh, come on Rob – he works for you. He was out for a week. He must have told you. Or you must have known already. I just want to know who did it."

"Why do you care?"

"Because. A lot's happened since then. Maybe it was tied into the shooting..." Rob stopped rubbing his leg, and went very still. "I mean, first he was beat up, then he was shot. What do you think?" Nothing.

He stood up and waved at Carrie, who put her cue away and came over to him. "I can't tell you squat. And you can tell Puffer –"

"I never said –"

"You didn't have to, Linda. You and those goddam Davisons... You got shed of them once. Why can't you stay the hell away from the rest?" He started limping away.

"I'm trying to!"

"And you –" to Art Mohnen, who was standing by the door, "You need to tell your daughter the same damn thing."

"I just want to know what happened to Andy!" I called after him. But he flipped me the bird and was gone. I stomped over to Art and hissed, "What the hell are you – you followed me!"

"What was he talking about?" he asked.

"Who knows. Why did you follow me? Oh, never mind." I pushed my way out the door and started walking to my car.

"Wait a minute." Art came after me, grabbing my arm. "What was all that about?"

I pulled free and snarled, "What that was about is that Puffer Davison is playing a game, and I got conned into playing it with him. And I am now going home and staying there."

"I mean, about my daughter?"

"I have no idea." I opened the car door and flung myself in. "There's Davisons everywhere. The only way to avoid them is to move to Canada."

I gunned the motor and zipped past Barry, sitting on his moped. I had too many followers, and not enough friends. Back home, I locked the doors and went upstairs to bed. But I couldn't sleep. Carrie hadn't turned to Puffer. And just talking about it had spooked Rob. Something was going on, something that no one wanted to talk about. I got up and texted Grant:

In June Andy Bentz got beat up – ask Puffer – I talked to Rob Stroh – he's freaked – drugs? – shooting? Send.

Then I looked up Yellowknife on Wikipedia and went back to bed.

*****

By mid-week the word spread that Rob Stroh had left town. Rumor said he told Nordstrom's he was going to Rochester for therapy, but that he'd really fled because the police were looking for him on suspicions of drug trafficking, which was the real reason for the drive-by shooting at the AA meeting.

"So is any of that true?" I asked Grant.

"Maybe." But he was trying not to smile as he went out on patrol.

*****

Friday, and no word about Rob. The appalling incompetence of the police – who should've had Rob or someone arrested a week ago – was being discussed in depth at the Laskin Café when Rhiannon Davison showed up and sat down across from me.

"Hi, Linda," she said, as if we'd exchanged more than ten words in the last ten years.

"Hi, Rhiannon." Behind her, I saw Barry come in and sit down at the counter. "What's up?"

"Nothing much. I'm going down to see Andy this afternoon."

"I thought you two had broken up."

"So what? He's been shot. He needs all the support he can get. He woke up yesterday, you know. He was in a lot of pain…"

"That's great. That he woke up, not that he's in pain. Does he remember anything about the shooting?"

"I don't know. I'm no cop, I didn't ask."

"By the way, do you know who beat him up back in June?"

"No. You ask a lot of questions, don't you?"

"Just curious," I replied, smiling.

"Uncle Dave says you always were a pain in the ass." A shiver ran up my spine. "I told him you were pretty cool. I remember you teaching me to knit."

That was back in the days when I baby-sat her. "Mm-hmm. You made the lumpiest scarf in history, I believe."

"I've gotten a lot better. I knit scarves for my boyfriends," she said proudly.

"That's great."

"Yeah. They like it. You seen anything of my brother?"

"Puffer? Not since Sunday night. Why?"

"Well, he's kind of disappeared. I mean, I don't know where he is. And yesterday was my birthday. He never misses my birthday. But I didn't get a card or a present or even a phone call, saying sorry I can't make it or nothing. It's not like him."

I believed that. The one true thing in Puffer's life was his devotion to Rhiannon. She was twenty years younger, more like his daughter than his sister.

"I asked everyone at my party, and none of them knew where he was. I called his girlfriend, but she didn't know."

I was curious. "Who's his girlfriend?"

Rhiannon looked at the wall. "Kind of a secret. Program stuff. Messy. You know you weren't the only one Puffer was seeing."

"Puffer wasn't seeing me at all. He was talking to me about what happened to Andy."

"Uncle Dave said he might have left for Sturgis early." Another shiver. "We're all going there this afternoon. But I don't think so. Puffer didn't say anything about it, and he would have told me."

"I'm sorry, Rhiannon, but I have no idea where he is." I took a deep breath. "But he might be in trouble. He told me something your Uncle Dave might not have appreciated him talking about." Rhiannon shifted slightly. "So when Uncle Dave said that about Sturgis –"

"No," she protested. "Uncle Dave… he wouldn't do that. Not to Puffer –"

"Rhiannon –"

"And besides, Uncle Dave didn't give a rat's ass about what happened to Andy."

"So it was discussed?"

Rhiannon bit her lip, so I said, "Don't worry. I don't know, and I don't want to know. Say hi to Andy. Who knows, maybe you two will get back together."

"Not hardly. Brian's driving me. You know. Brian Daugherty." She grinned. "He's ex-special forces, you know. Hot."

"His leg all healed up?"

"Everything's healed up." Then she got serious again. "If you do hear anything…"

"I'll let you know. Give me your cell phone number."

"Here. Thanks, Linda. See you."

I finished my dessert, paid, and went over to the counter. "Hi, Barry."

"Oh, hi, Linda."

"Everything okay?"

"Sure? Why not?"

"Because you haven't ordered anything."

104

"I've got coffee."

"It's lunch time."

"I'm not hungry."

"Is there something you want to talk to me about?"

"No. I'm having coffee."

"Okay."

Later that afternoon, Grant came in with paperwork, and I told him that Puffer had disappeared. He shrugged. "Probably went off with someone from Squeegee's. Why? You two have a date?"

"And how is Fran doing?"

Grant grimaced. "Okay. Truce. Besides, I haven't talked to her in days."

"Maybe she met someone."

"Maybe she and Puffer ran off together."

"It's a thought. I like it."

"You do?" Grant looked surprised.

"One Davison is enough, thank you. Look, the point is, Puffer gave me enough information to spook Rob. Don't you think there's a chance that Rob might have had an altercation with him before he left? Or that someone else did?"

"Mm. When we get him, I'll make sure to ask."

"Did you talk to Puffer at all?" I asked.

"No."

"Did anybody?" Grant shook his head, so I tried again. "Did you ever think that something might happen to him?"

"He's a big boy, Linda," Grant said. "Why do you care?"

"He's a witness you might need alive. Why the hell don't you?"

"All right. I'll have a look round."

And he stalked out. This was getting to be a habit.

*****

I went home after work, and sat on my deck to think.

Where do you look for a vanished Puffer? What was the deal about the secret girlfriend? Did it have something to do with what Rob had said to Art? Messy program stuff – Nancy? Nah, I couldn't believe that. But what if it was? Was that what Andy had found out? Had Puffer beaten Andy up, and then offered up Rob Stroh as the sacrificial lamb? And had Puffer actually been the shooter, killing his rival? Yes, Grant had said Puffer was right behind him, but how could he be sure? In the heat of the action, Grant could have gotten the timing all wrong, even if he did think he was perfect.

Or was Puffer's secret girlfriend someone else entirely – and God knows that would make a lot more sense – and the whole thing really was all about drugs? In which case, why had Puffer got involved? Why did he turn Rob over? Was Dave Davison lying? Did the sun rise in the east? And what would he do with Puffer? Or was Puffer doing this for Dave, an old score settled or an old debt called, in which case, was Rob the one who'd really disappeared, and Puffer who had hit the road? Maybe he had left early for Sturgis, after all…

"Hey, Linda!"

"Barry. What are you doing here?"

"You know, when you asked me earlier, if I wanted to talk to you?" I nodded. "Well, I do." He sat down. "It's about

106

Grant."

"I don't care about Grant –"

"Don't say that!" Barry pleaded. "He likes you, he really does. It's just that Fran, she was after him. And I know he was only using her to get information. But he wouldn't tell you. And I told him he should tell you so. I told him he wasn't treating you right."

"You can say that again."

"The thing is, I know Grant. I know he likes you. And I like you. A lot. And I want –"

"Barry, did Grant send you?"

"No! I'm just worried about you."

"Why?"

"Grant says you're in over your head with Davison stuff. And I know what that means."

"I'm fine, Barry. You worry about anybody, worry about Puffer Davison. He's disappeared."

"No he hasn't. I saw him just the other day at the post office. He was talking to Siv Davison. You know. Dave's son. Siv's scary. He scares me. And then he talked to Art, your neighbor? And Fred from Nordstrom's. And a couple of other guys. And then he talked to me."

"What did he say to you?"

"Not much. I asked him for a ride to Squeegee's and he said no. Said he had to meet someone at the old goose farm. I think he was just trying to get out of giving me a ride."

The cold chill ran through me again. When Gary had run afoul of Dave Davison all those years ago, it took him almost

Collateral Damage

a month to heal. For a week, he couldn't walk; for two weeks he couldn't sit up or straighten up without grunting. I thought the bruises would never go away. He never told me exactly what happened, and I really didn't want to know. The one thing he did tell me was that he'd been taken out to the old goose farm, where no one would interrupt them and no one would hear him scream.

"Maybe. Maybe not." I looked at Barry. "Listen, don't worry. It's all going to be all right. Grant and I talked today. Things are much better. So you go on home." Barry started to say something, but I shook my head. "No. You need to go home, Barry."

Barry left, and I sat there thinking for about two minutes, and then went inside to change clothes. I also texted Grant:

I'm going to goose farm – Puffer may be there – back up? Send.

It was worth a try.

When I came back outside, I saw Art having a beer on his deck and waved at him. He got up and came over.

"What's up, Linda?"

"Good news. Andy Bentz is awake."

"Thank God."

"Yeah. I thought I'd go down and see him later. See if he'll finally tell me who beat him up. Though I don't know that it matters. Oh, and Art, a couple of days ago, were you talking to Puffer Davison at the post office?"

Art looked surprised. "Uh… yeah. He was asking how Nancy was doing. Why?"

"His sister says he's disappeared. He mention anything to you about the old goose farm?"

"No. But, you know, it's kind of odd you bring that up. Day before yesterday, I had a special delivery for Ole Ahler, up Old Meridian Road. Right past there. And I could have sworn I saw Puffer out there, at the goose farm, with a guy that looked like Rob Stroh. Now, to be fair, I wasn't that close. But it sure looked like them."

"Could you see what they were doing?"

"I don't know, Linda. I had to keep moving. I've got a route, you know."

"Yes. Maybe you should tell the police."

"I did. When I heard that Stroh left town, I told Grant Tripp about it, but he didn't seem interested." He looked at me. "You're worried, aren't you?"

I nodded. "The thing is, I'm not sure which one of them I should be worried about." Art raised his eyebrows. "It's all got to do with drugs." I took a deep breath. "How'd you like to come with me, check out the goose farm? Be my back up?"

Art's face shone: his TV fantasies were about to come true. "It'd be my pleasure, Linda."

"Let's go."

*****

Up until about twenty years ago, the old goose farm was a standard summer job for every young man in Laskin, where they could earn pretty good wages for hard work and long hours in filthy conditions. But then it closed and the old one-story metal sheds have been sitting empty ever since. I parked in what shade I could find – it had been in the 90s all day –

and as we got out, Art said, "We'd best look around for tire tracks."

Well, there were plenty. But of course, the goose farm's been used by a lot of people for a lot of stuff over the years. I opened the door to one of the sheds and was about knocked out by the heat and the stench. Even Art gagged behind me and stepped back.

"You're not going in there, are you?" he asked.

"Yep." I pulled out a tissue from my back pocket and held it to my nose. I thought: *If I get psittacosis from this, I'll kill Puffer myself*, and walked inside.

Inside it was filthy with feathers and dirt and fossilized dung. Brown cobwebs streamed from the wooden framing that held up the roof and made up various stalls and gates. It was dark, too, and getting darker. I walked slowly down the center of the long shed. Nothing.

I turned around and nearly ran into Art. "Not here," I said, and went outside where I took deep lungfuls of fresh air. Or rather, I tried. The air was stiflingly humid, and purple clouds were boiling up in the west. A storm was coming.

"Maybe we should split up," I said. "You take the north shed and I'll take this one."

"Sure."

I went inside mine. More heat, stench, feathers, dung, brown cobwebs. Also more trash. Maybe Puffer had been joking with Barry. It would be like him. Why on earth was I doing this? I picked my way down to the far wall, and started back. There was a larger pile of trash in one stall to my left, and I went over to it. I prodded it with my foot – I certainly wasn't going to touch it with my hands – and felt my heart thud as my foot hit something solid.

I reached forward and started pulling away trash: there was a leg. I choked from the stench. I rooted some more, and Puffer's head emerged, filthy, dried blood around his mouth. I was stunned to see that he was still breathing. Barely. I reached for my cell phone, to dial 911. I looked up and saw Art coming down the center of the shed.

"Art! He's alive!"

"I was afraid he might not be dead yet," Art said, raising the gun from his thigh and pointing it at Puffer's head. "I didn't kill one drunk son of a bitch to have my daughter hook up with another." He fired, the noise thundering in the shed as Puffer's head exploded in front of me. Then he turned it on me. "Gonna have to be a murder suicide. Poor Linda, getting mixed up in it all. The question is, where do I shoot you to make it look right?"

"They'll never believe that, the way he was beaten," I babbled. "And I texted Grant before I came."

"Grant doesn't give a damn about you," Art said. "Nobody does."

I thought about how true that was as Art aimed and said, "I'm sorry."

As I struggled to breathe just once more.

As the rain poured deafeningly on the tin roof.

As a voice and another gun shot reverberated through the shed.

As Art spun around, red spraying from him.

As I realized that I wasn't the one who'd been shot. Which is when I finally looked and saw Grant running down the length of the shed towards me, two other cops and a deputy sheriff behind him.

*****

My initial statement was babbling but informative about Art and the drive-by. How he must have heard my bright idea the night of the street dance. How fed up he was with Jack. How fed up Nancy was, but Art didn't know that. Art didn't know the half of it, that Nancy was seeing Puffer, until Rob blew that.

And then I shut up as the ambulance arrived. I stood outside, gulping in the air and drinking in the feeling of the pouring rain while the EMTs worked on Art, Grant hovering over them. At one point Randy Walworth passed me to go look at Puffer and I bummed a cigarette from him.

"You okay?" Officer Johnson asked. I nodded. "You want a coat or an umbrella?"

I shook my head. The EMTs loaded Art into the ambulance, and Grant came over to us.

"Don't you want to get inside?" I shook my head. I was sopping wet and it felt great.

"Andy's conscious," I said.

"That's good. Who beat him up? Art?"

"No. Puffer. Probably to shut him up about him and Nancy. If Barry hadn't brought him to my door, I'd never have tried to find out why. Puffer…"

I shook my head, went over to my car, and got in. I sat there, smoking, and watched the tall slough grass bend deeper under the rain. I felt immensely calm, until they brought

112

Puffer's body out on a stretcher. He was a bastard who went after broken birds, he was a lousy son of a bitch, but he hadn't deserved this... And again I saw Gary, beaten almost to death, all those years ago...

"You okay?" Grant asked as the hearse left. I nodded. "You sure?"

"It's going to break Rhiannon's heart," I said, blinking hard.

"How about yours?"

"Mine got broken a long time ago. By Gary." In another minute it would all spill out. "I've got to go home."

"Linda –"

"Please."

He nodded, and I drove away. Later, I'd give a formal statement. Later, we'd talk, maybe mend our friendship. Later, I'd have to go to a funeral. Later, I'd be fine. But right now, I stopped on the other side of the lake, and cried harder than the rain.

Ditch Digging
Emilian Wojnowski

For Kowal and Suchy, whom I'd accept as my cellmates

The sun knew no mercy that day, so you may think it was doing us a favor while the prisoners were digging.

"Straightenin' my back here, Boss!"

"Yeah, straighten it!"

The dust was terrible there, thus I kept my head down most of the time. Just by looking at the depth and width of a ditch I could tell who'd dug it.

"Scratchin' my back here, Boss!"

"Yeah, scratch it!"

A lot happened at the prison—and what happened there, there it stayed. Well, it was a high security prison for a reason, thus I didn't take anything home, to my family or friends. As a guard, I simply kept order there. That was all. I was doing my job and repeating to myself that I was a human among humans… to maintain humanity, which didn't come so to everyone there with such ease.

But one memory got stuck in me for the rest of my life. It's settled in me because it affected me directly. It didn't happen as an aside.

"Adjustin' my hat here, Boss!"

"Adjust it!"

I was working at Polteen Correctional Institution, in North Florida, and it was the hot summer of 1969 when we went "on a trip," on one of many over the years. "On a trip"—it's hard not to agree—sounds better than "a punishment that will exhaust you so bad that you won't even think about running away" or "digging drainage ditches of little importance in the scorching sun, which will melt away all your desire to live, if you still have any."

"Wipin' the sweat of my brows here, Boss!"

"Yeah, wipe it," I said when it was my turn.

We took twelve inmates. Sometimes we chose them, sometimes we drew lots as to who we should take, allowing God to decide who to punish, who to reward. I stuck with two guards, with Jacob and Dominick—and it was mostly Jacob who wanted to draw lots. He thought most of the prisoners would go to hell anyway, so as long as they were on this Earth, we should allow God to decide; to make a decision that would do good to whoever needed it; and would end somebody who had to be disciplined.

"Takin' a deeper breath here, Boss!"

"Yeah, take it!"

Who worked next to whom… we decided. Jacob would say that neither the law nor God knew the prisoners as well as we did, so that decision was in our hands. The order and the effect of their work depended on the setting. There really was no need to legcuff or chain gang them.

"Pourin' sand here. Outta my shoe. Boss!" said Harpoon. He was the oldest prisoner I'd ever met.

"Yeah, pour it out!" I said.

Harpoon was pale as sugar, his face looked like it'd been cut in wood, and his eyes were half-closed, no matter whether he slept or worked.

One of the guards had explained to me why Harpoon was in the prison.

Well, when he was about twenty, he caught his wife in a room with his best friend. Harpoon grabbed a revolver and blew their heads off, then he put the barrel to his temple. Fortunately, or unfortunately, he didn't shoot off enough of his brain to die.

Some guards thought he didn't even know what he was there for. He barely spoke, swayed, and smiled a lot. If a mosquito was teasing him at night, he'd catch it just to let it go through a window. That's what Harpoon was like.

"Harpoon," I said, "new glasses, huh?"

"Yes. Boss."

"Put them away so they don't get damaged."

"No. Boss. They'll be fine."

I knew something was up. I hadn't seen him wearing glasses in a long time. Glasses were the dream of most of the old prisoners. Reading is the most beautiful game that humanity invented, as one poet said.

"They'll get dusty," I said.

"Yes. Boss."

"Don't you really wanna put them away?"

"No. Boss."

So that he didn't feel worse, I'd told him to work at the very end of the ditch, next to Young Bobo. His age made it difficult for him to keep up the pace, so next to Young Bobo, who'd been stabbed in the ribs with an ink pen sixteen times two months earlier, Harpoon didn't stand out at all.

And next to Young Bobo was some proud fish, whose name I don't remember. He was sentenced to two hundred years for a heap of accumulated offences, none of which amounted to him being hanged. After a month in the cell, he ripped off his penis with his bare hands and explained on his way to the hospital that it'd make him a better person now.

But back to Young Bobo: he came back to us after two months, having spent seventeen days on some ventilator. And, I admit, he had some power to dig. Strong son of a whore. He no longer felt like teasing other inmates, though. Anyway, he'd gone crazy after coming back. He cut his palms and started slapping his fellow inmates. They had allegedly been trying to steal something from him, but he, in revenge, just wanted to infect them with some make believe Hepatitis C.

His hands hadn't fully healed because of being on the work gangs, and now a thin line of blood from his makeshift bandages was smeared down his spade. But he kept digging, his teeth clenched and his eyes filled with tears. His part of the ditch was one of the widest and deepest ones anyway. I guess he'd decided to finish faster in order to have a moment of rest.

"Harpoon, come on. Let's take a walk. Let me show you something."

"Fine. Boss!"

"Take the shovel."

"Yeah. Boss!"

When we went away from the others, I told him to start digging again. It was fine for him.

"Harpoon, be honest. You know what happened to Young Bobo?"

"Was stabbed. In the ribs. Sixteen times. A pen with a. Silver nib."

"I know that, Harpoon, I know. But who's responsible for that? And why did they do this to him?"

"I dunno. Boss."

"Harpoon, look me in the eyes."

"Stoppin' diggin'. And lookin' ye. In the eyes. Boss." He raised his head and leaned against the shovel.

I was standing on a slight hill. The sun was behind me, so Harpoon probably saw only the outline of a black figure, plunged in the orange dust. Because the soil in that area had been dry for quite a while—for months, maybe—it resembled more of sand, or dust, or dirt, and its color was rather dark orange with brown overtones.

"Can't. Sun's hurtin' me eyes. Boss."

"Who did this to him and why?" I repeated.

Harpoon stuck the shovel in the soil and put his hands on his hips.

"Can I. Ask ye. Boss. A few questions?"

It tempted me to shout out that I was the one asking questions, but I just made sure Jacob and Dominic couldn't hear us, and then I nodded.

119

Ditch Digging

"Ye read. Boss. Books?

"Yes."

"For ye children?"

There were many sex offenders, but I was sure Harpoon wasn't one of them, so I said:

"Yeah, for my daughter."

"What's. Her. Favorite book?"

"A book about a dog. Can't remember the title."

"She cried?"

"What?"

"At the end?"

"Yes, we cried together."

"Beautiful moment."

"Sure."

"What if. That moment. It never. Happened?"

"I'd be very sorry, because it was a beautiful moment."

"What if I. Boss. Said that. I can't." He squeezed his eyes shut. "I can't. Experience a moment. Like this? By meself."

"Why?

"Boss. Lean over here."

"Don't want you to get shot, Harpoon. Tell me what you need to tell me. No one can hear us here."

"I been. Waitin' long. To have. Glasses. So that I. Could be moved. The last. Couple of times. A couple dozen maybe."

"And?"

"Young Bobo. Don't want him. To trample them again. He

120

knew. That I. Been waitin' for. My glasses. Long time."

"Aha."

"He ripped. Every last." Harpoon shed a tear. Drifting down the cheek, it became pinkish from the dust. "Every last chapter. Of every novel. In gloves. To have proof that…"

I left Harpoon there and took a little walk along the ditch.

"Hey, Harpoon!" I said after a while.

"Stoppin' diggin'. Boss." He'd already dug quite a hole, but it was nothing compared to his previous one, let alone the ones of the younger and stronger inmates. "Yeah. Boss?"

I looked at Young Bobo. In spite of his cracked hands and the drying bloody marks on his shovel, he didn't stand out in terms of digging.

The law or rules can be changed, twisted, patched. Worse is with scumbaggery. Scumbaggery can't be regulated. Scumbaggery is born in people. And it's incurable. And infinite. And could only be fought with yet more scumbaggery only. Vicious cycle, I know, but it still went on.

"Bobo," I said, "swap places with Harpoon."

And that was when that particular memory started digging a ditch in me. The one it's been living in until now. Dear God, forgive me, but the vicious cycle went on, and I don't want the ditch to be any deeper.

Yiyo

Fabiyas M V

A whining rises above the pit-a- pat of rain.

"Don't you hear that sound, Dad?"

"Put the pillow over your ear, and sleep well, my darling."

The animal-whining and the wind-howling continue. Rain bathes the night.

Darkness melts away in the dawn light. The hair-raising sounds of the previous night still echo in Kanishma's mind. She opens her bedroom window, looks at the fresh face of the day. There is a puddle in the yard waiting to be dried in sunlight. The wet sand has been carpeted with fallen leaves, green and yellow. A bunch of brown coconuts lie scattered. Frogs croak, mistaking the summer rain for monsoon rain.

Soon her eyes catch a puppy, sooty in hue, under the eaves of her house.

"Poor thing!" falls from her lips.

"Dad, please come. See a puppy down the window!"

The puppy is in a tight spot, his eyes communicate. It's distinct that he needs food and shelter.

Yadhu goes to the puppy, with his daughter Kanishma following closely behind. He is a mason with limestone-like physique and fruity psyche. He takes the puppy in his hand, pats him on the crest.

"How did this puppy come here, Dad?"

"Perhaps, his mother brought him here, finding a shelter under the eaves. It'd been raining all night."

"Then, where's his mother?'

"The dam may be wandering for food somewhere."

Yadhu rounds his lips like the snout of a pig, producing a squeak to catch the attention of the puppy.

Kanishma touches her new friend with wonder. She calls him 'Yiyo'. She doesn't know the meaning of this name. Though *Yiyo* is not in her vernacular tongue, she likes it for its auditory charm.

The traces of trauma slowly vanish from Yiyo's eyes. Soon he becomes a member in Kanishma's family. Human-canine bonding is thousands of years old.

Kanishma's dolls are discarded in the nook of her bedroom. For a child, a real live playmate is more important. She enters his heart, feeding him with boiled rice, sardine heads, chicken pieces… He is a voracious eater.

Yiyo gets love and care of Kanishma's parents as well. They permit him inside the house. When Kanishma reads Stevenson's Treasure Island, Yiyo sits on the tiled floor, brooding.

Kanishma beautifies Yiyo, combing his fur. She applies Cuticura talcum powder to his skin, and then polishes his nails. With a merry mien, he lets her antics on his body.

"Yiyo is growing fast. Certainly, I don't dislike him. But I can't let him sleep inside our house, especially at night", Kanishma's mother opens her mind.

"You're right. We want his service outside at night." Yadhu finds a night watchman in Yiyo.

One murky midnight in October, not only Kanishma's family, but their neighbors also wake up, hearing Yiyo's loud bark. His eyes shine in the dark. He is no longer a puppy.

The people don't come out, fearing an ambush. Instead, they shoot sharp lights from their torches. The light-arrows create an abstract art on the black canvass of night.

Now Yiyo stops his barking. He pants heavily, staring into the dark.

Next morning, Kanishma's mother is sweeping the yard. She finds paw prints, not a dog's, in the sand.

Yadhu stands with arms akimbo, gaping at the paw prints.

Now his neighbors stand around the paw prints. They reach a conclusion that a tiger came there last night. So Yiyo barked continuously.

The Forest Department officials visit Yadhu's yard in the afternoon. They confirm the tiger's presence in the area, examining the paw prints.

How did the tiger come there? This is a distinct question with an indistinct answer.

There is a tea shop on the roadside within the walking distance of Kanishma's home. Weary drivers from the distant states stop their trucks near the tea shop to take lime tea and snacks, and refresh themselves. They reach here at night, driving along forest roads. So there is a possibility for a tiger to leap into one of these opens trucks, hide among the goods, and alight here as the vehicle comes to a halt.

The shadows of fright fall over the whole village. Even then, what comforts Kanishma is the valorous presence of Yiyo. She believes that Yiyo frightened the tiger yesterday. Yiyo becomes her true hero.

Next day, the tiger is trapped by the Forest Department. People come in large numbers to see the tiger prancing in the iron-barred cage. Kanishma calls on the ferocious guest of their village, along with Yiyo. Now that Yiyo loses his temper before the tiger, she takes him back home quickly.

January 10, 2020.

Yadhu and his wife enter their portico in the gloaming. They have bought a Red Velvet Cake from a bakery in the town. The front door of the house is open. Yiyo is fast asleep beside a flowerpot. A tiny piece of dark chocolate lies close to his right foreleg.

Yadhu puts the cake on the dining table.

"Kanishma... Where're you, darling?" Yadhu raises his voice. But no response.

12th Wedding Anniversary

Mr. & Mrs. Yadhu

is visible in black letters on the cake.

They search for their daughter.

"Where's Kanishma?" Yadhu asks Yiyo.

Finding Yiyo's death-like sleep, Yadhu suspects a tragic happening. *Who brought the dark chocolate here? Is it a sedative chocolate? What happened to my daughter?*

Soon the police arrive. Their dog sniffs, and then runs to

the copse on the riverbank, not far away from Kanishma's house. The police and locals follow the dog with torches. They search through the night chill in the copse, but in vain.

Sun logs a new day. Waking up from his long sleep, Yiyo hurries to Kanishma's bedroom, where her mother sits propped against the pillows. She broods about her daughter. Yiyo steps out of human-canine silence.

Kanishma's photo with the caption *MISSING* goes viral on social networks. Her winsome face, with a red ornamental dot in the center of the forehead, wets the eyes of the world. People pray for her safe return.

Yiyo goes to the copse, sniffing. There are leeches lurking for blood in the copse. He stands among the trees, throwing his eyes into the river. He spends the whole night here.

9 A.M. Yiyo darts like a bullet train, carrying a mind full of pangs. His destination is Kanishma's home. Hearing his loud bark, Yadhu comes out of the house. Yiyo barks unusually, turning back frequently.

Yiyo is fretful. Again, he walks to the riverbank, barking, turning back... Yadhu follows him. His nephew is willing to accompany him into the copse. Yiyo stops beside a fallen tree – its trunk on the land, and its branches in the river. He jumps onto the trunk and barks, looking towards the branches. An empty hemp sack hangs on the root-wad of the tree.

Yadhu crumples up in grief. His nephew holds him tight, consoles him. Kanishma's bloated body lies upside down among branches of the fallen tree. The corpse has begun to rot – the right ear is eaten by fish.

The police file a first information report (FIR). They

suspect sexual assault on the girl before the murder. The culprit might have given the sedative chocolate to both Kanishma and Yiyo. Maybe, she was suffocated within his lecherous hands. He might have flung the dead body into the river, bringing it in the sack.

Really Kanishma's body was found by Yiyo's keen senses. The police and people admire Yiyo's brilliance. He comes into the limelight.

The smell of cremation lingers in the air. An everlasting emptiness spreads in Yadhu's house.

Now the full moon wipes off darkness. Yadhu hears Yiyo's howling from the copse. His voice is not down in the mouth. Sixth sense is a beautiful reality beyond the murky mysteries in the universe.

Concrete Bimbo

Lamont A. Turner

Robert Doverman stared up at the life-sized statue of a nude woman that had mysteriously appeared at the edge of the pond in Eden Park, blocking off access to the foot bridge. It didn't matter. None of the leering boys milling about, drunk on beers pilfered from unwatched coolers, planned to cross the bridge. They'd stood guard all night, paying giddy reverence to their frozen goddess, and had no intention of abandoning their post.

The woman, her ample gray breasts making pointed shadows that extended beyond the path into the grass, stood atop a pedestal about four feet in height. Carved into the pedestal was the legend: "Concrete Bimbo."

"Are you sure it's her?" asked the towering slab of a police detective, watching the scattered raindrops plink against the statue's face, making the gray woman cry.

"It's a damn good likeness from the neck up," Doverman responded. "I can't speak for the rest of it."

"Seems like a lot of trouble just to get our attention," the policeman said. "Most kidnappers just send a note."

"Maybe they ran out of newspaper headlines to make the letters," Doverman said. "When'd it show up?"

"Sometime after midnight as best as we can tell. A jogger

came past a little after eleven and Venus here hadn't landed in her shell yet. Her fan club was already here when we showed up, but none of them knew how or when she'd landed."

Doverman pushed back the brim of his fedora with a thumb and let his gaze burn into the detective. Realizing he'd given himself away, the big man's already ruddy face seemed to burst into flame, the clouds riding his chilled breath adding to the effect.

"Venus? You're still seeing that girl at the art museum." Doverman said, wagging his index finger. "Better wipe that artistic pretension off your collar before your wife notices it, Glenn." Glenn flashed a pained grin as he shriveled, finally allowing Doverman to catch a glimpse of the sun rising behind him.

A man on a ladder dropped a tarp over the statue to a chorus of boos from the congregation as it scattered to make way for the approaching crane. Several of the boys wandered into the path of the flatbed truck pulling up behind Doverman and Glenn, prompting an exchange of obscene gestures and horn blasts that bounced painfully off Doverman's skull, reminding him he hadn't completed the journey from the bar to his bed before receiving Glenn's summons. Doverman and Glenn stepped off the road to allow the truck to back up.

"Handle her with care," Glenn shouted. "That's going in my backyard next to the barbecue pit." The driver chuckled from behind his half open window, but Doverman knew Glenn wouldn't hesitate to set up the petrified goddess right outside his bedroom window if given the chance. If ever Glenn turned up dead, it would be a sure bet his wife had made him that way, though it was doubtful any jury would convict her.

As the pre-dawn drizzle grew heavier, threatening a morning downpour, Doverman left Glenn to manage Venus' relocation, and trekked back to his yellow 1978 Nova, trying not to slip on the wet leaves littering the pathway. On the way, he considered calling his client, the father of the young lady immortalized in stone, but thought better of it. He didn't like unleashing wild speculation on the people paying him. They might get ideas from it that were at odds with his own, and get their feelings hurt when he didn't devote enough time to their pet theory. He'd just have to hope his client didn't recognize his daughter in monotone if he saw her on the news, at least not until Doverman made some sense of it.

Holly Bakerson had been missing for just a day shy of two weeks. In that time there had been no ransom note or calls, and no clues that made sense to anybody. She'd spent her last Friday before becoming invisible throwing down shots of Tequila in an Over-The-Rhine after hours dive with a man no two people could manage to describe in the same way. As for where she ended up on Saturday, most bets were on the river, but a few dissenters had suggested she would turn up in a dumpster, or perhaps in several of them. Her father disagreed. His feeling his daughter was alive was so intense he was willing to pitch every dollar he'd ever made at the problem if that's what it took. Doverman had been there with his catcher's mitt, but he didn't put a lot of hope in the old man's feelings. He thought Bakerson's money would have been better spent on a fishing rod, and told him as much. The old man couldn't be swayed, though. Guys in his situation never could.

"She's all I have since her mother died," Bakerson had said, pleading with Doverman to take the case, though his money had already sealed the deal. "She's a good girl, Mr. Doverman. She studies hard, and has never caused me the slightest problem other than having to deal with the sometimes unscrupulous men drawn to her by her looks. She couldn't help that though. She couldn't help being beautiful. She always broke up with them when she found out what they were."

Doverman wasn't so sure about Bakerson's daughter's stainless character, but he was right about one thing, she was beautiful. The pictures her father had provided were a bonus to the piles of money the old man dumped in his lap. Tall, with large soulful eyes and dark shoulder length hair highlighted with just a trace of auburn, Doverman could see how she'd have to work hard to stay ahead of the wolves panting at her heels. To the old man, she would always be the chubby cheeked girl smiling at him from the frame on the edge of his desk, though. Doverman made a note to keep that in mind when sharing any details he might turn up. There was no point in disillusioning the old guy if he could help it. Like Doverman, he was former active duty, only he'd come home without the color scraped off the lenses. For him the expectation of brighter days still seemed reasonable, and people actually suited the frames you put around them.

*****

Unlike his office, Doverman's apartment was clean and fairly organized, the pair of bare feet sticking out from under the blanket on the couch being the only thing out of place. Those feet belonged in the bedroom. Doverman was about to run his finger down the sole of the foot on the left when he noticed the bottle of Merlot on the floor, wrapped in a slender hand. He bent down and slid the bottle out from under the fingers, leaving the hand dangling from the side of the couch. Empty. It looked like those feet would be staying in the living room. Doverman downed a few shots of bourbon, took a cold shower, pulled down the blinds over his bedroom window, and went to bed.

The naked woman snoring on the pillow next to him when he woke up that evening had tousled blonde hair and dark shadows under her eyes. He brushed her bangs away from her forehead and gave it a peck, causing the snoring to sputter to a stop.

"Rough night?" he asked as a pair of red-rimmed eyes fluttered open then disappeared under a tan forearm. Maggie Taft moaned before rolling over to mutter curses into the pillow. Doverman left her there to finish the fight she'd started the night before, and went into the kitchen to put on a pot of coffee. He'd already finished his second cup by the time Maggie, wrapped in his bathrobe, stumbled out to sit across from him.

"They found the Jaccobs boy," she said, watching Doverman fill the mug he'd placed on the table in front of her.

"Dead?" Doverman asked.

"Very. Somebody used his body parts to make a collage. It was supposed to be a portrait of him." She paused, hugging herself. "Whoever did it used his eyes. They painted the outline of his face in his blood and glued that kid's eyes in the center."

"Did this masterpiece have a title?" Doverman asked.

"As a matter of fact, it did," Maggie said, staring at Doverman like he'd just pulled a rabbit out of his nose.

"'Prodigal Son' was scrawled on the wall behind it. It was set up in a warehouse owned by the boy's father. How did you know?"

"I've seen some of the artist's other work," Doverman said, finding his cell phone on the counter by the coffee maker. He punched in Glenn's number.

"I think you might want to take a better look at that statue," Doverman said in response to Glenn's groggy hello.

"We did," Glenn said.

"And?"

"I've decided I don't want to take it home," Glenn said. "By the way, we've solved your missing persons case."

"The girl was in the statue?"

"Yep. We've already informed her father."

"I guess you know about the Jaccobs kid," Doverman said.

"Yeah," Glenn responded. "That's what made us take a closer look at our girl from the park. How'd you find out about it? It hasn't made the papers yet."

"I'm psychic," Doverman said. "A few more predictions and I'll be able to quit my day job and buy that island paradise I've always dreamed of."

"Or you've been screwing the reporter assigned to the case," Glenn said. "I thought you were going to stay away from Maggie."

"We both knew that wasn't going to work," Doverman said, letting his gaze linger on the woman peering at him with hungry eyes over her coffee mug. She'd let the robe fall open, making him wish he could hit the fast forward button on

Glenn.

"Have her stop by at the station and see me," Glenn said. "I'd like to know how she ended up at the warehouse when we found the body."

"Sure," said Doverman, hanging up the phone without waiting to hear if Glenn had anything else. He walked over to Maggie. She looked up at him with a grin, pulling the robe off her shoulders so he could get a better look.

"How'd you come to be at the art gallery the same time the cops showed up?" he asked.

"The foreman who discovered it called me. The boy had been snatched from in front of the warehouse, and I'd given the foreman my card when I interviewed him about it. I think he had a crush on me. Any more questions?"

"None at all," Doverman said, taking her hand and leading her to the bedroom.

Doverman's involvement should have ended with the discovery of the corpse he'd been paid to find, but he felt he still owed the old man. There was no way this would have turned out differently, the girl was probably dead, smothered under a concrete mask, when her father had sent Doverman on his quest, but Doverman had done nothing. He hadn't even been the one who found her. There was a lot of fresh money sitting in Doverman's bank account. Doverman felt he should do something for the man who'd put it there. Besides, Maggie was in it now. Her best shot of not ending up plastered on a canvas while she chased the story was if Doverman took away the killer's brushes.

It was around dawn when Maggie finally decided they'd

both had enough and fell asleep in his arms. He'd lost a whole day, but he considered it necessary for Maggie's sanity, as well as his concentration. Maggie always did get too wrapped up in the stories she pursued. He slipped out from under her and got dressed, carrying his shoes until he was out of the bedroom. Going through the notes Maggie left on her laptop, he got the name and location of the warehouse the Jaccobs kid had ended up decorating, and the name of the foreman who'd found him. Right now, Glenn would be neck deep in records, looking for any trace of shared history between the victims. Doverman planned to come at it from a different angle, concentrating on the killer. It's not unusual for witnesses to give wildly divergent descriptions, but there should have been at least some common element. At least fifty people had seen Holly Bakerson's escort on the night she disappeared. The only thing their testimony had in common was that Holly's companion was a man, and three of them hadn't been sure about that. Either Holly had been shuffled between fifty different people, or something strange was going on.

*****

The warehouse foreman, a dissipated little man named Flint, had so many cracks in his embankment he would have shattered if Doverman blew on him. The contrast between his chalky complexion and the dark smears under his eyes was as pronounced as that of a vampire at a junior high Halloween party. The red tic tac toe board etched in his cheek between the patches of stubble said he'd tried to stay away from the bottle before coming to work. His breath said he'd given up at some point after he got there. The last nip had been a while ago though, long enough to make razors dangerous again. His watery eyes shifted in every direction but forward, and the clipboard in his hand beat double time on his thigh, threatening to wear a hole in his pants.

"I understand you were the last to see Ronnie Jaccobs alive," Doverman said.

"And the first to see him dead," Flint said, hanging his head and shaking it like he was trying to throw off the memory. "It was the worst thing I've ever seen, and I served a stint in Afghanistan."

Doverman took a mental inventory of the horrors he'd been subjected to while toting a rifle for Uncle Sam, and concluded Flint was probably right. The killer had outdone Al-Qaeda in the attainment of shear ghoulish depravity, if not in the quantity of misery attained.

"I'm more interested in the last time you saw him with his eyes still in his head," Doverman said. "You told the police he was talking to a man."

"Yeah," Flint said. "It was the damnedest thing. It'd started raining, and I thought I might have left my car windows down. Turns out I hadn't but on the way back from checking, I saw Ronnie standing out in the rain, talking to a man in a hat and a long dark coat. The hat was kinda like yours, only black and with a wider brim. The guy in the hat was standing still as a statue, but Ronnie was pretty animated. Ronnie was a good looking kid, could have probably been a movie star, but the way he was twisting up his face—he looked like somebody had saddled him with a lifetime of misery in one quick jab. I almost went over to check on him."

"What stopped you?"

"I believe I mentioned it was raining. My dad died of pneumonia from going out in weather like that, and he was younger, and a hell of a lot stronger, than I am."

"Get a look at the stranger's face?" Doverman asked, shaking off the memory of his own father, gunned down in an alley when Doverman was still dreaming about being tall enough to reach the cookie jar on the kitchen counter.

"Naw," Flint responded. He kept his head down. All I saw was the top of his hat." He paused; his gaze focused on his shoes. "There was something weird about him though."

"How so?"

"That's just it," Flint said. "I'm not sure. There was something abnormal about him, something creepy, but I can't explain where the impression came from. It was just a feeling. The guy was tall, and stood kinda hunched over. I keep wanting to say he was deformed somehow, but I can't say why."

"That's not going to be of much help," Doverman said. "Sure you can't remember anything more specific?"

"Only that I had that same feeling when I found what was left of that poor kid. I had no doubt it was that freak who did that to him."

Doverman could see Flint had had enough. It was time to wrap it up, but he still had one more question.

"Did Ronnie work here?"

"Ronnie didn't work anywhere," Flint said, glancing over his shoulder. "He was probably here hoping his father would be around to throw some money at him. The kid liked to party, and was usually in some kind of trouble. It wasn't anything he wouldn't have grown out of if he'd had the chance, though." He paused to shake his head some more.

"Mr. Jaccobs didn't know how to, or didn't want to, deal with him," he continued, his voice now a whisper. "Ronnie would show up looking for some money to get out of a fix, and Jaccobs would fill his pockets and send him on his way."

"Thanks for your time," Doverman said, patting the man on the shoulder rather than forcing him to expose his quivering hand. Flint nodded, and drifted off toward a hallway lined with lockers, oblivious to the questions being shouted at him from a man on a forklift below the catwalk.

Suspecting this was going to be one of "those" cases, Doverman sat in the Nova outside the warehouse, scrolling through his phone and watching Flint sneak out to his car to bolster his nerves with a sip from the bottle in his glovebox. Finding Morrison in his list of contacts, he pressed the nose of the cartoon wizard on the screen next to it and then pressed the green call button that popped up to replace it.

"What have you stumbled into now, Doverman?" asked Morrison, jumping past the usual hello. He sounded more distracted than usual.

"You tell me, Professor," Doverman said. "What kind of spook looks different to everybody who sees it and likes to make art out of—repurposed materials."

"Andy Warhol, but he's dead," Morrison quipped.

"I was thinking this might be one of those things only you seem to know about," Doverman said, "maybe some demon with too many vowels in his name, from some country nobody's heard of."

"Nothing like that comes to mind," Morrison said. "It's more likely a human with a talent for witchcraft. You say they make art?"

"Yeah. Out of people."

"It's possible they're performing sacrifices," Morrison said. "They could be attempting to unleash some malignant entity."

"It doesn't seem like it to me," Doverman said. It seems more personal and a lot less structured."

"Then I'm afraid I won't be much use to you," Morrison said. "Witches performing rituals follow certain patterns. Their actions can be predicted. A person using witchcraft for revenge or personal gain are just like any other criminal and have to be caught using the same tools you'd use to catch a man who kills with a gun or a knife."

Doverman hung up just as Flint was flinging an empty fifth from the window of his car as he backed up out of the lot, apparently resigning his position. Doverman considered following him, wondering if he might be able to get more out of the man now that he'd probably washed away a wall or two of inhibitions, but decided his time would be better spent quashing his own inhibitions with Mickey, his favorite forensic scientist. Doverman was on the outs with Alonzo, the M.E., but Mickey was his way around that. Any stiff that was attached to an open case would get passed to Mickey after being processed.

*****

It was Mickey's day off, but Doverman knew Micky wouldn't mind him dropping in on him if he brought company. Mickey was always happy to see Johnnie Walker.

Lamont A. Turner

"This is for later," Doverman said, stuffing a fifth of Walker into the pocket of Mickey's robe as he pushed past him.

"What's the other bottle for?" Mickey asked, watching Doverman stomp through his apartment toward the kitchen.

"This one's for now," Doverman said, digging through the cabinet over the stove. "Looks like you're already dressed for a pajama party. I should have brought my blankie." Mickey glanced down at his pajama pants and shrugged.

"Like you don't sleep-in on your day off," Mickey said, setting down the fifth next to an ashtray shaped like a skull.

"I sleep-in every day," Doverman said, handing Mickey a plastic tumbler with less than an inch worth of air left in it. "That's what happens when all your friends are vampires."

"You trying to get them all drunk?" Mickey asked, peering into the tumbler. "You know, I have shot glasses."

"My next stop is a joint where politeness is frowned upon. I wanted to go in with the right attitude," Doverman said, raising his cup in a toast. "What can you tell me about the department's latest art acquisitions?"

"I should have known you'd be mixed up in that somehow," Mickey said, dropping into a chair under a framed four sheet from the original version of The Wolfman. It went with the cartoon werewolves on his pajamas. "What do you want to know?"

"Anything stand out?" Doverman asked.

"Naw," Mickey said with an exaggerated wave of his hand, "just your run of the mill double homicide. All the killers turn their victims into statues these days. First prize at the art fair is a chainsaw and leather apron."

141

"You know what I mean," Doverman said, shifting a pile of old movie magazines from the chair to the kitchen table so he could sit. "Did you find anything that seemed like it was from the wrong script?"

"The girl in the statue got me thinking a little," Mickey said. "The male victim was a mess. Anybody could have done that if they had a sufficient amount of crazy. The statue was different. It was—good. I mean, whoever made it had real talent, and to complete it in such a short period of time…"

"I was thinking the same thing," Doverman said. It seems like a guy who could pull that off would have been noticed by now. You guys checking the galleries for someone with a similar style?"

"Not my department," Mickey said. "You'd have to check with Glenn. It does seem likely the perp had more of a relationship with the girl, though, even if it was only in his head. He went to a lot of trouble, and he left her in a place where he could show her off."

"That's something else," Doverman said. "Why leave the boy in a warehouse? Unless he was making some sort of artistic statement, it looks like he was sending a message to somebody in particular. The kid's father maybe?"

"I enjoy watching you plot it all out," Mickey said, "especially when you get me drunk first, but I'm a lab guy. My opinion on the motivation of the latest demented maniac isn't worth more than the next guy's."

"Sometimes it helps just to bounce it off of somebody," Doverman said, setting his empty cup on the table and rising from his chair. "Besides, I've been drinking alone too often lately. People might start to worry."

Mickey got up and followed Doverman to the door, hopping over the pizza box next to the video game controller and the pile of empty beer cans.

"There is one thing you might not have heard about yet," Mickey said, as Doverman stepped out into the hall. "The statue girl was about two months pregnant."

"You couldn't have told me that at the start?" Doverman said.

"I just thought of it," Mickey said, rubbing his belly. "The pizza box made me remember I'd promised myself to go on a diet because I had to let my belt out, and…"

"Yeah, I get it," Doverman said. "I should have waited until after our conversation to break out the booze."

*****

Doverman's buzz had worn off by the time he reached Fred's Goodtime, the dive bar that had been the last known stop Holly Bakerson had made before sailing off to Sarpedon for tea with Medusa. Fred's Goodtime used to be known as Fred's Goodtime Girls and Games before the bottom of the sign out front took a hit from the shotgun of a man ejected for emptying his bladder on a woman passed out on the floor next to the jukebox. It was probably for the best since the games consisted of a warped pool table, pockmarked with cigarette burns, and the "girls" were mostly around fifty and in about as good a shape as the sign above the door. Holly Bakerson would have stood out like a nun at a cock fight. Getting people to remember her was never the problem.

The brown man behind the bar had a pink lightning bolt extending from the left side of his forehead down to the middle of his cheek. The knife that carved it had also taken out his left eye, leaving an ugly indentation barely disguised by the dense lenses of his glasses. He was short but thick, his tattooed forearms protruding from his rolled up shirt sleeves having a greater circumference than Doverman's thighs.

"I hate to break this up," Doverman said, taking a stool next to the bar's only customer, a middle-aged woman whose mascara made black tears on her sallow cheeks as she regarded Doverman, rolling her eyes to demonstrate her contempt. Looking at the rotten teeth between the cracked lips, Doverman decided she was probably not so much middle-aged as she was used up. For all he knew she was only twenty. He wondered whether the man behind the bar was her dealer, her pimp, or both.

"You back again?" the bartender asked, the veins in his thick neck swelling as he straightened his spine and puffed out his chest. He still had to bend his head back to look Doverman in the eye, and, despite all the muscles, Doverman would have chuckled if he could have been certain the hand under the bar wasn't resting on a gun.

"I missed you," Doverman said. "You say things that interest me."

"Like what?" growled the bartender, baring gold fangs worth more than the building he was standing in.

"Like the description you gave of the man who was in here with Holly Bakerson the night she disappeared," Doverman said. "By the way, we found her. She won't be stopping by for another drink anytime soon."

"We'll be alright," the bartender said. "There's plenty of drunks in Cincinnati." He was looking at the woman, but she didn't take offense; he was the man who kept her glass full.

"You said the guy wore a broad brimmed black hat, was tall, though I'd guess you'd say that about everybody, and had stringy white hair. Sound about right?"

"He was a lot taller than you, smart ass," the bartender said, his hand still out of sight. "But yeah, that's right. The guy was weird looking, dressed all in black with a long coat that looked more like a cape."

"The guy I saw her with was a Mexican," The woman said, "and I mean a Mexican, sombrero, poncho, the whole bit."

"Sure you hadn't been watching too many old cartoons that day?" Doverman asked, tossing a fin on the bar and pointing at the woman's glass. It wasn't a necessary business expense, the woman was already loosened up, but it would get the bartender away from whatever it was he was fondling under the counter.

"I know what I saw," the woman said. "I wasn't that drunk. The funny thing was he spoke perfect English. The girl kept calling him Robbie."

"Could it have been Ronnie?" Doverman asked, starting to think his investment in her might pay off.

"Yeah, maybe," the woman said. "I was paying more attention to the hunk giving me the eye at the end of the bar."

"Sure," Doverman said, tossing another five spot on the bar. It was time to go. She was starting to depress him.

Doverman checked his watch on the way out. Glenn would be on his way home if he hadn't gotten a call from any of the women he'd left his number with that day. The women on the force knew enough to keep their distance, but there were plenty of waitresses impressed enough by his badge to ignore the ring on his finger. Glenn ate out a lot. Doverman called him to confirm he was going to be at the house, then pointed the Nova in the appropriate direction.

On the way, he tried to work out what the killer's magic might run on. How was he able to make a roomful of people see different things when they looked at him, and what did he really look like? It seemed like he employed the imagination of each viewer, letting them paint him with whatever was already in their head. The woman at the bar didn't have much to work with, so she'd conjured up a caricature. Others probably saw people they'd previously encountered, or put together a person based on the type they expected to see. It depended on the locale and who the killer was with at the time. Of all the descriptions, only two had lined up, Flint's and the one given by the one-eyed man tending bar. Flint had come upon the killer when he wasn't expected, stumbling on him while he was distracted by his prey. As for the bartender, Doverman wondered if his impaired vision hadn't somehow revealed a limitation to the murder's magic. Maybe you needed two eyes for the spell to take.

*****

Glenn lived in the small but well kept house of an honest cop. Nestled between two nearly identical houses, all with two mid-priced cars in the driveway, there was nothing there you couldn't have bought on a police detective's salary. Doverman rang the bell, and was greeted by a pretty but dour faced woman, peering through the gap between the curtains.

"Glenn's out back," said the woman, fading away as soon as she'd opened the door. Doverman knew better than to try to make pleasantries. Glenn's wife had a strict limit on the amount of conversation she was willing to expend effort on, and she'd usually hit it by the time she'd finished brushing her teeth in the morning. He found Glenn on the patio, staring off at the holes in his privacy fence.

"Is that where you'd planned to put the statue?" Doverman asked, nodding at the lawn beyond the string of tiki lights on the edge of the patio.

"Speaking of that," Glenn said, digging out a beer from the cooler next to his chair and holding it out to Doverman as though it were the keys to the city, "turns out the D.A. is going to want it classified as a triple homicide."

"Yeah. I heard Bakerson was expecting," Doverman said, taking the beer and settling into the wicker chair next to Glenn.

"Of course you did," Glenn said. "One of these days I'm going to make you give up that crystal ball you keep in your pocket."

"You couldn't afford it," Doverman said. "It runs on scotch and expensive cigars. Any idea who the father was?"

"Not a clue," Glenn said, shaking his head. "As you probably know, she wasn't seeing anybody. All her friends were in the dark about it, and she hadn't been to see a doctor as far as we were able to determine. It's possible she didn't even know she was pregnant."

"After two months, I'd think she must have had her suspicions," Doverman said. "Any luck tying the two victims together?"

"Other than both having rich parents and attending the

same exclusive school, we couldn't come up with anything. As of now, we're going under the assumption the victims were selected at random."

"Doubtful." Doverman said, flicking his beer cap at the squirl peering at him from behind one of Glenn's garden gnomes. "Stopped by the school yet?"

"What's the point?" Glenn responded. "The girl graduated three years ago. The Jaccobs kid was still a junior."

"I think I might go poke around there anyway," Doverman said. "I might pick up some clue as to what sort of temperament the Jaccobs kid had and who he might have been running with."

"Don't let me stop you," Glenn said. "You still working for the girl's father?"

"I am, though he doesn't know it." Doverman said. "He paid me a lot of money. I figure I still owe him some labor."

"Good luck telling him about it," Glenn said. "The guy's in Beacon. They say he's almost catatonic. He doesn't even know his daughter was pregnant."

Doverman sat around for another hour, drinking Glenn's beer, and trying not to think about the old man, before heading back to his apartment to find Maggie hunched over her laptop next to a fresh bottle of Merlot.

"Come up with anything?" he asked, walking over to rub her shoulders.

"Not a damn thing," Maggie said, bending back to scratch her head on Doverman's shirt buttons. "You?"

"Nothing you could print," he said. "Turns out the killer was using witchcraft."

Maggie pulled away and spun the chair around, hoping to find a grin attached to his statement. Seeing the corners of his mouth slide down to pinch his chin, she slumped back and let out a sigh.

"How is it since meeting you, every other story I work on involves devils or space monsters?"

"It was always like that," Doverman said. "You just didn't see it because you'd convinced yourself those kind of things couldn't happen. It's like when people are surprised when the plane goes down, or that bad cough turns out to be cancer. People filter out the ugly possibilities when planning their day. If not, most of them would never get out of bed."

"Not you though," Maggie said, suddenly overwhelmed with pity for the tired-faced man standing over her. "You rush at it head on. Why spend any more time in hell than you have to?"

"That's where I'm going to end up," Doverman said, finally giving her that grin. "I might as well get used to the place."

Maggie didn't return his smile. Everything was fine as long as they both insisted on traipsing through the sewers, but someday she might want to shower the stink off. Someday she might finally get a story big enough to earn her the justification to let it all go and live a normal life. She wasn't sure if Rob was capable of doing normal. For him, the monsters would always be there.

"Feel like going to school tomorrow?" Doverman asked, grabbing Maggie by the hands and pulling her out of the chair. "You might get a few paragraphs out of it."

"Way ahead of you," she said, wrapping her arms around

his waist and squeezing while he buried his face in her hair. "I've already interviewed Ronnie Jaccobs' principal."

"That was before you knew Holly Bakerson was an alumni," Doverman said. Maggie pushed away and looked up at him, getting a kiss on the forehead for the effort. "We could get lunch at Corky's afterward."

"It's a date," Maggie said, "but don't think I don't realize you only want me along because you think my press credentials will get you farther than your P.I. license."

"Press credentials?" Doverman said, raising an eyebrow. "I was counting on your bright smile and winning disposition to get me in."

*****

Doverman wasn't kidding. Maggie's smile could open doors he'd normally have to empty his wallet or bruise his fists to get through. Sitting before the principal's desk like a couple of kids who'd been caught skipping math class to sneak a smoke behind the gym, Doverman let Maggie do most of the talking.

Principal Wheatley was a squat, round, fussy man with more hair on his chin than on the crown of his head. He wore his glasses on the end of his nose so he had to tilt his head back to look people in the eye, even with everyone seated, creating an impression of arrogance somewhat undermined by the soft, breathy delivery of his words. Doverman doubted if he had ever gotten close enough to a woman to smell her perfume. Maggie had him working for them after five minutes, checking to see which teachers had instructed both victims, and offering to provide introductions to all of them.

"I have to be honest," Wheatley told them, "I really don't

remember the Bakerson girl. However, I was quite familiar with Ronnie. He was a handsome boy, physically a man, but he was always getting into trouble. Nothing serious, mostly childish pranks. I always felt people reacted to him far too seriously because of his appearance. They thought he should have been acting like an adult, when he was still really just a boy."

The list of teachers still employed at the school who had taught Bakerson as well as Jaccobs consisted of a math teacher, currently out on maternity leave, an English teacher, an art teacher, and the gym coach.

"We have a high turnover among our staff," Wheatley said as he escorted them through the halls toward the teacher's lounge. "I'm afraid many of our instructors trade on our prestigious reputation, using us as a stepping stone to the more lucrative university positions. Mrs. Robbins, however has been an exception. We've been fortunate enough to have benefitted from her knowledge and high standards for nearly twenty years. Coach Youst has been here nearly as long."

"What about the art teacher?" Doverman asked, noticing he wasn't getting the same build up as the other two. Wheatley pushed his glasses up the bridge of his nose until they were nearly crushing his eyes, and quickened his pace.

"Professor Leiber has been with us for five years." he said, almost curtly.

"A professor? That's quite a pedigree for a high school teacher," Maggie said.

"There was some dispute regarding the professor's tenure at the university," Wheatly said with a hint of irritation.

"Could we talk to him first?" Doverman asked, intrigued by Wheatly's hesitancy.

"I suppose you could," Wheatly said, but you won't find him in the teacher's lounge. He's most likely in his classroom.

Art class was held in a room at the end of the hall, separated from the other classrooms by the restrooms and a fifteen foot stretch of empty wall on both sides. Wheatley stuck his head in the door just long enough to announce the pair and give an indication of their intentions, before scurrying off. Doverman noted he didn't once make eye contact with the man seated behind the desk.

Leiber, a taciturn, almost prim man, with a shaggy white mane, prominent nose, and deep set hollow eyes to match his hollow cheeks, ignored Maggie's outstretched hand, barely glancing up as she introduced herself as a reporter for the Cincinnati Enquirer. Doverman didn't waste any effort trying to be polite. He left the interrogation to Maggie while he made his way around the room, working his way toward the easel set up in the back corner, pretending to examine the paintings taped to the walls as he went.

"I understand Ronnie Jaccobs was a student of yours," Maggie said.

"He was," responded the white-haired man, his attention still focused on the papers on the desk.

"How would you describe him?"

"High spirited," Leiber responded, making it sound ugly. "I can't say he was much interested in art, or that I was much interested in him. It struck Maggie as an odd thing for a teacher to admit.

"I understand you also taught Holly Bakerson," Maggie said. "Was she 'high spirited' too?"

Leiber finally raised his head to glare at Maggie, conjuring the image of a hawk about to peck her eyes out.

"I don't recall having any student by that name," he said, daring Maggie to dispute him.

"It would have been several years ago," Maggie said, accepting the challenge. "She was an attractive girl, about my height, with brown hair."

"I don't pay attention to the physical attributes of—Leave that alone!" Maggie turned to see Doverman dropping the edge of the sheet over the painting on the easel.

"I'm sorry," Maggie said. "I can't take him anywhere."

Leiber was standing now, towering over Maggie.

"Sorry, pal," Doverman said with a shrug. "I didn't mean to defile your masterpiece."

"I don't think there's anything I can help you people with," Leiber said, shrinking back down into his seat.

"Thanks anyway," Doverman said, tilting his head toward the door to let Maggie know it was time to go.

"What just happened in there?" Maggie asked as soon as they were in the hall.

"We just found our killer," Doverman said, handing her his phone. She stared at the blurry picture of a painting of a young woman on the screen for a second before identifying it as a portrait of Holly Bakerson.

"I got my phone up under the sheet and snapped a few pics while he was busy trying to ignore you."

"Why would he keep it in his classroom?" she asked, passing the phone back to Doverman.

"Because he's obsessed with her," Doverman said. "He probably disguises it with the same hocus pocus he uses to hide his real face. Speaking of which…" He swiped at his phone, bringing up another picture.

"That's impossible," Maggie said, staring at the image of the cadaver seated at the desk in the photo. "I was standing right next to him. He didn't look like that. He was younger, handsomer."

"I told you it was one of 'those' cases," Doverman said. "Despite his hard to get act, he couldn't help but spruce himself up a bit for the pretty lady leaning over his desk. Since he was only concentrating on you, he didn't need to rely on your imagination to fill in the blanks. He painted the picture he wanted you to see."

"What do we do?"

"I haven't figured that out yet," Doverman said, "but at least we don't have to waste anytime questioning Mrs. Robbins."

*****

After a lunch spent watching Maggie try to make sense of the images on his phone while he tried to decide if he'd made a mistake of pointing out the killer to her before he'd defanged him, Doverman headed to the Beacon Psychiatric Hospital. Doverman had served in Afghanistan with several members of the staff, and he didn't hesitate to remind them of all the times he'd pulled their asses out of the fire. It was his admission ticket to see Bakerson. Positioned in a wheelchair before a window with a decent view of a brick wall, Bakerson seemed frail enough to be threatened by the weight of the blanket draped over his legs. The lack of stubble on his chin told Doverman he was being well cared for, but he couldn't imagine how they managed to feed him.

"I want you to know I've found the monster who killed your little girl," Doverman said, crouching down to whisper in the old man's ear. "I know it won't bring her back, but I promise he's going to pay for it. I'm going to see to it that taking her from you was the worst mistake the bastard ever made."

Bakerson's finger may have twitched a little in response, or it may have been Doverman's imagination, or maybe a muscle spasm. Either way, Doverman was determined that if Bakerson woke up, he wouldn't have to share the world with the man who murdered his daughter. There wouldn't be any arrests. No prosecutor would be able to get a conviction with a jury unwilling to accept evidence relying on the belief in witchcraft. Leiber would have to die. It would mean Maggie would never get an ending to her story, and Glenn would spend the rest of his life regretting that case he'd never managed to solve, but there wouldn't be anymore parents slobbering in hospital beds, unable to process how they'd ended up with artistic travesties instead of grandchildren.

*****

Doverman did his best thinking at his office in the company of the bottle he kept in the drawer of his pasteboard desk, so that's where he went, spending the next several hours staring at the cracked plaster and filling his ashtray with butts. He'd almost come up with a plan, half way into the fifth of bourbon, when his phone started buzzing, letting him know he had a text from Maggie.

"Followed Leiber to abandoned church on corner of Wood and Crandal in Price Hill," it read. "Need you here now!"

Doverman knew better than to call her back. If she'd left her ringer on it could mean disaster if Leiber was within earshot. He filed his bottle back in the drawer, found his battered fedora on the floor next to the hat rack, and headed for the Nova.

Damn her! Doverman thought as he backed out of the parking lot, braking just in time to avoid being hit by an approaching motorcycle. Ignoring the biker's curses, he pulled out and gunned it, blowing through the red lights on his way to the interstate. He pounded his fist on the steering wheel, smoke billowing from the cigarette he was mauling. She just couldn't wait! She had to go after Leiber on her own!

Maggie's car was parked on the street across from the church. She wasn't in it. Doverman stood in the shadow of the church steeple, scanning the edifice for unfriendly eyes. The windows were boarded, but there were plenty of gaps. If he'd been dealing with a sniper, rather than a witch, he would have already been dead. With no way to be sure he wasn't being watched, Doverman marched past the broken bottles and sheets of crumpled newsprint, the discarded blankets of abandoned parishioners, to the door. Seeing it setting askew in the frame, the faint glow of candles seeping through the cracks, he waited until he was under the cover of the overhanging arch to shift his revolver from his waistband to the pocket of his overcoat, and pushed his way in.

Standing at the end of the columns of toppled pews,

Maggie reached out to him, backlit by the candles burning on the alter behind her.

"Maggie?" Doverman said, trying to detect signs of movement in the surrounding shadows, his hand on the revolver in his pocket. Maggie hushed him with a finger to her lips while her other hand waved at the stale air, urging him forward. Doverman waited until he was close enough to see her eyes before ruining his coat, putting a bullet in her leg.

"How?" shrieked the tall man huddled on the ground at the foot of the alter, blood oozing between the fingers clutching his leg.

"It didn't take much to beat your parlor trick," Doverman said, leaning over Leiber with an exaggerated wink. "As wizards go, you're about as accomplished as a cartoon on the back of a cereal box. You should have stuck with the water colors."

Suddenly, Leiber was standing. Doverman guessed he would have been almost seven feet if he wasn't slouched over. His white hair had grown both longer and thinner, hanging from his pale scalp like patches of wet cobwebs. There was something unsettling about his asymmetrical features and the way his thin lips curled back away from his uneven teeth, combining with the sunken cheeks to create a death's head. If not for the beak-like nose, it would have been a face at home on a bottle of poison. Doverman closed his left eye again, and Leiber was back on the floor, trying to squeeze the blood back into his leg.

"Nice try," Doverman said, "but I told you your party tricks aren't going to work on me. All I have to do is close one eye, and you're beat."

"What the hell does your eye have to do with anything?" Leiber shouted. Doverman stared at him for a second in disbelief, then threw back his head to let out the laughter welling up in his belly.

"Was the instruction manual for your evil spell kit in Japanese?" Doverman said, clutching his side. "That's some funny shit! You thought you had everybody by the balls when all it took to see past you was a wink!"

Leiber mumbled something in Latin and started to gesture with his right hand, but Doverman grabbed a handful of elongated fingers and bent them all the way back to Leiber's wrist.

"No more bullshit," Doverman growled, stepping over Leiber to stomp on his left forearm. "Where is she?"

"She was fooled a lot more easily than you were," Leiber said. "Nobody ever notices the things they've been taught not to see. Nobody but you. What the hell are you?"

"I guess my parents forgot to teach me to ignore the clowns when the circus came to town. Trust me, I'd rather not see you. Now, once more, what did you do with Maggie?" Doverman shifted his weight to the foot on Leiber's arm, grinding it into the concrete floor.

"She's going to be my masterpiece," Leiber hissed between clenched teeth. "I'll take more time with her than I did with the whore and her boyfriend. I was actually mentoring that slut, guiding her through her college curriculum. What a waste."

"You mean the two kids you butchered?" Doverman said to the tune of cracking bones. "Turning them into art projects was your way of signing your work. You're proud of what you did, aren't you?"

"That punk was actually bragging about what he'd done!" Leiber shouted, pounding his free hand on the steps of the alter. "He came into my classroom, bragging about his latest conquest. He said he'd gotten a college girl drunk and 'took her to town.'" The pained expression Leiber wore was real, but Doverman had nothing to do with it. Leiber was somewhere else now, immune to the weight bearing down on him. "Imagine my horror when Holly wrote to tell me she was dropping out of college because she was pregnant!" he screamed. "He ruined her!"

"You murdered her, you son of a bitch!" Doverman said. "Did you really think she'd ever be with you?"

"I didn't want her to be with me! She wasn't supposed to be with anybody, certainly not with a spoiled cretin like Jaccobs! Can you believe his father actually tried to bribe me to pass him? It was a pleasure to lead him off to the slaughter. The fool thought he was taking Holly to get an abortion," Leiber chuckled.

"And what did Holly think?" Doverman shouted. "Did you dress up like Jaccobs and tell her you were going to do right by her? Did you tell her you were going to get married and buy a cozy little house in the suburbs?"

"Something like that," Leiber said with a grin.

"I've had enough of this soap opera," Doverman said, taking his foot off Leiber's arm long enough to bury his heel in his ribs. "What did you do with Maggie?"

"If you'd just gotten here half an hour earlier, you would

have seen her rushing up to save you," Leiber said, the blood seeping from the corners of his mouth, turning his smirk into a jagged gash like the mouth of a jack o' lantern. "She thought you were the one in danger. You should have seen how surprised she was when 'you' punched her in the face."

Doverman took his foot off Leiber's arm and crouched down, patting him on the chest. "You saw the Bakerson girl as the avatar of purity? Tell me, what do you see me as? If you were painting a picture of me what would you title it?"

Leiber stared up into Doverman's dark empty eyes, studying them for a moment before whispering, "Monster."

"Works for me," Doverman said, taking the gun from his pocket as he rose.

Leiber didn't have time to offer an objection. His body danced with each blast from Doverman's gun. It continued to twitch for a few seconds after the music stopped, made a rattling sound as his last breath vacated his punctured lungs, then was still, a bloody offering before the alter of an absent God. Doverman wasted a second to send Leiber off with a face full of spit and then headed out to Maggie's car. He fumbled around with the keys on the ring until he found the right one, and used it to open the trunk.

Doverman let out a sigh. Maggie was there, staring up at him with eyes that were wet and a little swollen, but very much alive. He hoisted her out and cut the rope binding her wrists, leaving her to peel off the tape from her mouth.

"Was it my turn to save you?" Doverman asked to the accompaniment of distant sirens. "I thought I was the one doing the saving last time."

"How did you know where I was?" She said, turning to wrap herself around him.

"Leiber told me," Doverman said. "He said if I'd shown up a half hour sooner I'd have seen you. There wasn't many other places he could have hid you in that short span of time."

"Is he…"

"Yep," Doverman said, giving her a squeeze. "Dead. We had a nice chat before he checked out, though. It ought to get you a Pulitzer." Maggie could feel his gun through his jacket. It was still warm.

*****

All that was left was the usual sweeping up. Maggie wrote her story, playing up the killer's obsession with an innocent young woman, while leaving out the magic spells, and, at Doverman's request, the unwanted pregnancy. In the final story, Jaccobs died because he'd disrupted class. There was plenty of evidence to support it, and it was less likely to add more pain to the heap already sitting on Bakerson's chest. Holly would get to stay a statue, forever enshrined as a paragon of virtue in her father's mind.

Glenn wrote his report, giving Leiber a gun to hold when Doverman shot him. Doverman could have planted one to make it more authentic, but why bother? Glenn knew the drill. Anyone who'd worked with Doverman knew the dirt they swept under the rug for him was poison. It was better to let Doverman live with it than to get it on your hands.

Holly's father passed away two weeks later. Doverman was told he'd snapped out of his trance just before the end, and that he'd died with a smile on his face, knowing his daughter had been avenged. Doverman didn't believe it for a second, but he appreciated the lie.

The Home Front
Edward Ahern

The dimly lit figure raised its arm, holding an iron shaft, and Collin shot him twice. The blasts from the snub-nosed .38 deafened him.

He took three steps toward the man, who lay unconscious, eyes closed, air bubbling out of a hole in his chest. Collin yanked the crowbar free.

Panic froze his reflexes, his body fritzing in emotional static. Then he dropped the gun on the sofa, and went through motions like a zombie. He eventually grabbed his phone and dialed 911, talking while holding a sofa cushion to the man's chest.

"Hello! It's Collin Meacham, 202 Euclid Drive. No, listen, somebody just broke in and I shot him. I think he's dying. Send an ambulance!"

Collin followed the dispatcher's orders, staying on the phone and in his underwear until a police car, a fire truck and an ambulance arrived at the house within two minutes of each other. The cops had their guns drawn. Collin pushed his hands up and stood still, nodding his head toward the sofa where the gun and crowbar rested.

The room filled with uniforms. The cops waved Collin into a corner and cuffed him, while the EMT's knelt over the body and the firemen stood around. Collin wanted to scream but kept his voice muted.

An EMT pulled a medical mask off the intruder's face and Collin jolted. "Hey! I think I know him."

The older cop recited his Miranda rights to Collin, then asked. "What happened?"

Collin told about hearing the front door being broken open, coming downstairs in shorts and tee shirt, and seeing a man wearing a covid mask and waving an iron bar. "I told him to get out, but he took a step toward me and raised the bar. I was shit scared and shot him."

"That the gun?" The cop pointed to the .38 on the sofa.

"Yeah."

"Registered to you?"

"Yeah."

One of the EMTs looked up. "He's gone, no breathing, no pulse."

The cops glanced around the living room, furnished by Ikea and Pier 1. "Okay, Mr. Meacham, here's what's going to happen. We're going to take you into custody while we sort this out. If this guy is a perp we'll find out, and there's a fair chance you'll be able to claim the castle rule."

"Pardon?"

"Connecticut has a castle rule. If you were defending your safety and home then there may not be any serious charges. But we're a long way from figuring that out."

*****

The interrogation room had a metal table bolted to the concrete floor, four metal chairs, neon lighting and a smudged two-way mirror. Two of the chairs were occupied.

"The guy was Ignacio Torres. You admit to shooting him?"

Collin Meacham nodded slowly. "I already told you I did, Sgt. Harkins. It was self defense."

Harkins sat back in his chair. "And you knew Torres?"

"Not really, but I'd seen Iggy around."

"How?"

"We go—went—to some of the same AA meetings."

Harkins rested his arms on the metal table and leaned in to Collin. "So you were both drunks?"

Collin winced. "I'm a recovering alcoholic, Sgt. Ignacio was a recovering addict. Lots of cross-addicted folks go to both NA and AA meetings."

"And the two of you had a fight at a meeting?"

"No sir, we barely ever talked to each other."

Harkins leaned forward again. His breath smelled of burger and tooth decay. "The dispatch cops said your place had basic furniture. You divorced?"

"A year ago. She got the kids."

"I got divorced too. It happens. The revolver's your gun?"

Collin shifted his buttocks back and forth on the metal seat. His face was blotched with red patches. "I don't feel well."

Harkins' lips turned down. "I'm sorry about that. Please Mr. Meacham, just stay with me. If you're thirsty I can get you a soda or water."

Collin shook his head from side to side.

"You local?"

"St. Francis high school, then straight into work after that."

"No kidding. My sister Mary Beth went there, about your age. You know her?"

Collin smiled. "Yeah, we dated a couple times."

"Your case for self defense looks okay, but we need to iron out the details. I believe the .38 with the hollow points is yours?"

Collin rested his hands palm down on the table, his fingertips nervously twitching. "You probably already know it's registered to me. I was defending myself in my house."

"We understand your situation, Mr. Meacham, most of us support home defense. Let's just go back over what happened last night."

Collin's sigh was expressive. "For the umpteenth time, I was up a little late, and heard the door shatter from downstairs. I grabbed my gun, took off the trigger lock and went to check things out. Only the night lights were on, but I could just see a masked guy in a hoodie holding something in his hand. I yelled at him to drop it, but he raised his arm and stepped toward me. I thought he was going to hit me, and I reflex shot him twice quick, one after another.

"He dropped to the floor. I called 911 and tried holding a towel against his chest to slow the bleeding. You guys got there in maybe five minutes, but he was already dead. I showed you where I'd put down the gun and you guys arrested me and have held me till this afternoon. Do I need a lawyer?"

"A good one will ask for twenty-five hundred up front, and you might not need one. Let's just go through the facts and see if we can't get you home again. What do you do for a living?"

"I install security systems for Binks."

"About the gun. Those hollow points could blow a man's arm just about off. Funny slugs for home defense."

"I'm not a good shot, sergeant, I need to stop someone if I hit him anywhere. When he made a move on me, I just panicked and jerked off two shots. When can I go home?"

A smile seeped across Harkins' face. "You're going to have to spend what's left of the day here, Mr. Meacham, but you might get released tomorrow. On the face of it, you have a decent self defense plea under the castle rule."

A uniformed officer took Collin to a cell. He couldn't sleep, and spent that next night sitting on a metal bunk bed. The toilet had no seat, he had no belt or shoe laces. A breakfast of reconstituted eggs and cold, greasy toast was provided at 8:30 the next morning. He sat alone for several hours more, then was cuffed and escorted back into the interrogation room. Harkins was waiting.

"Can I go home now? I really need a shower."

Harkins lips snuck out in that same ambiguous smile.

"For now. But I need you to come back in for follow up in two or three days. Enjoy the shower."

*****

Harkins called back the third day after the shooting.

"You may need to spend that twenty-five hundred now."

"Hah?"

167

"For a lawyer."

"Why, it was self defense."

"So it appears. With or without a lawyer, I need to see you at two this afternoon."

Collin returned to the station without the lawyer, and was escorted back into the interrogation room. Harkins started in by re-reading Collin's Miranda rights. He had a file folder in front of him that he kept closed.

"Funny thing, Collin. Mary Beth heard about you on the news. She said you were a slimy little sucker, and I trust her judgement, so I started doing some cross checking. A few hours before you offed Mr. Torres there was a break in at a local business. Door was jimmied with what we think was a crowbar just like Torres carried into your house."

"What does that have to do with me?"

"Your manager was kind enough to provide us with your appointment schedule for the last year. Guess what? A month or so after you made sales calls several places were broken into and cash and equipment stolen."

"So what? That happens all the time."

"It does. Our dear, dead friend Ignacio liked to facilitate his break ins using a crowbar. We'd caught him before. It was part of his M.O. But he liked empty offices with cash and computers, not homes with armed owners. That was another major part of his M.O. So why do you suppose he broke into your place?"

"Maybe he thought I had money."

"Maybe. We're starting to get reports back from pawn shops and it looks like Ignacio was indeed the break in artiste.

He must have been psychic, seemed to know exactly where the petty cash lock boxes were kept. Something you would also have known from your security sales calls."

"I don't like what you're implying, Harkins. I just quit talking."

Harkins' smile was beatific. "No need, Collin. Your credit checks show that you went from delinquent to good boy about a year ago. Found a new source of revenue, did you?

"I figure you two best buddies had a disagreement. We may never know whether you told Ignacio to break in so you could claim insurance, or if you invited him in and bust open your own door after you shot him. Doesn't matter. I'm betting you and Ignacio used the same diner or parking lot every time to discuss splitting profits or the next job. Cell phone records will tell us where."

Collin sat in silent, catatonic rigidity, his mouth twitching.

"But Collin, aside from being a creep with my sister, the clincher for me was your gun."

Collin blurted out, "my gun?"

Harkins' smile slithered out again. "I favor a wheel gun myself, and I took yours out of storage and dry fired it. Absolutely brutal trigger pull, must be twelve, fourteen pounds. No way you cracked off two shots on impulse, you'd have to clench your trigger finger like a death grip. After you get a lawyer you may need that drink."

.

Legacies

Robert Petyo

On his fiftieth birthday, Billy decided it was time to punish Sam Richardson for ruining his life.

Tuesday morning, he loaded his derringer and secured it inside the plastic frame in the bottom of his briefcase. He tossed a few papers and files into the case and locked it, then drove downtown, parked his sister's SUV on the second level of the parkade on Courtright Street, and took the elevator to the fourth floor which held the offices of Golding Investment Advisors.

"Can I help you?" The young woman behind the desk seemed too tired to smile.

"I'd like to speak to Sam Richardson." He fought to keep his voice firm, but the woman distracted him with her beauty. Her smooth shoulder length hair and the sprinkling of freckles on pasty white cheeks reminded him of Anita, his grade school crush, the girl who laughed when Sam Richardson called him *Baby Girl*. That was the last time he ever spoke to Anita.

The secretary surveyed him like she was at the mall shopping for a new outfit, and her deep green eyes broadcast that she didn't like what she saw. "Do you have an appointment?"

"No."

"I can't disturb Mr. Richardson." Her back stiffened. "He's in conference right now. What is the reason for your visit?"

Billy reflexively moved his arm, sliding the small briefcase behind his thigh. "I- I'm an old f- friend of his." She waited for him to say more, but he remained silent as he struggled to control the nerves that always made him stutter. *Shut your stutter face* Sam used to taunt him.

"Your name?" she asked.

"Billy Pankowski."

She scribbled something on a pad. "How do you know Mr. Richardson?"

"We went to grade school together."

Her brow tightened as she inspected him again. "What is this about?"

"Please." He almost dropped the case when he heard the whine in his voice. "I'd like to speak to Sam."

With an impatient sigh, she pointed toward the chairs lined up against the wall. "Have a seat." She glanced at her watch. "Mr. Richardson should be available in about fifteen minutes."

"Thank you." Billy carried his briefcase like a service tray, keeping both hands underneath it. He sat at the end of the row of stiff backed chairs and kept the case on his lap. There were two other people seated there, both paging through magazines, and both ignoring him. A small video screen near the ceiling broadcast a talk show with no volume.

He watched the secretary turn slightly away and pick up the phone.

Robert Peyto

Richardson wasn't in a conference, he thought. That was a standard excuse. But he couldn't blame Anita for doing her job. Richardson was the one he came to punish, not his underlings, who were probably terrified of him just as much as Billy had been.

Twenty minutes later, after the two other clients had been escorted inside by other advisors and Billy sat alone, the secretary stood. "Mr. Panski?"

"Pankowski," he said as he stared at her but remained seated.

Huffing, she beckoned him. "Mr. Richardson will see you now."

He clamped one hand on the handle of the briefcase and stood. He messed with his collar like a nervous salesman and walked toward the door that she pointed to.

"You'll be fine," she said as she gave him a thumbs up. "First right turn. His secretary will meet you."

Another secretary?

He swallowed noisily as he realized that sweat was tugging at his armpits. He shuffled through the door and faced a long bare hallway swamped with fluorescent lighting. After two steps another hall broke off to the right and Billy turned to it.

A big man with crazy blondish hair and wearing a gray suit and tie stuck a hand out toward him. "Mr. Pankowski?"

Billy stared at his hand but made no motion toward it. "I'm here to see Sam Richardson."

The hand hung between them for several seconds before he pulled it back. "My name is Thomas Drake. Call me Tommy."

"I'd like to see Sam Richardson."

"Actually, it's Dracziewicz but I simplified the pronunciation."

"I want to see Sam."

After a few seconds of staring, the man turned and gestured for him to continue down the hall. After three closed doors, Drake stopped him and pointed. "Right here, Mr. Pankowski."

Billy stared at the pebbled glass door and waited for the man to open it to allow him to enter.

It was a narrow office that stretched at least thirty feet to a large floor length window. Two desks, one on either side of the room, faced each other, leaving a narrow aisle that funneled to the window. Both desks had open laptop computers atop green blotters and wire "in/out" baskets at the front corners.

And both desks were empty.

Billy spun to Drake who pushed the door shut. "What's going on? Where is he?"

Drake pointed to the chair that was beside one of the desks. "Have a seat. Mr. Richardson is in conference right now. Perhaps I can help you."

"I'll wait to see Sam."

"Sit."

That single word slammed him into the chair and he fumbled for the briefcase, keeping it against his chest. When Drake moved closer, Billy saw the outline of a handgun in the coat pocket. Drake smiled with a brief nod as he caressed the pocket. "Yes. I can take care of myself, and any problems that arise. We're very security conscious around here." He paused, his hand still caressing the gun, as he let those words settle. "I want to know exactly what is going on here."

"I told you. I want to talk to Sam."

"I understand you told Cyndy that you and Mr. Richardson went to grade school together."

"That's right."

"That's impossible since I went to grade school with Mr. Richardson."

"You?"

"Drake the Cupcake, he used to call me."

Billy slid the briefcase down to his lap. "That can't be. How old are you?"

"I'm twenty-eight," Drake said. "How old are you?"

"I— I'm—"

He leaned slightly toward him. "You did not go to grade school with Mr. Richardson." When Billy started to protest, Drake raised an index finger like a cudgel. "His father perhaps."

"Father?"

"Sam Richardson senior. He would be about your age."

"I'm fifty."

He dropped his head in a slow nod as he stepped back. "That's about right."

"What about the Sam Richardson who works here?"

"His son."

"Oh." His right hand started to tremble and he pressed it against the case on his lap.

"Do you need to use the rest room, Mr. Pankowski?"

"What? No. If he's Sam's son, I guess I've made a mistake."

"I guess you have."

"Well, let me talk to the younger Richardson then."

"Why?"

"I'd like to talk to him about his father."

Drake moved closer, shifting again to make sure the outline of the gun was visible. "That is not going to happen until you tell me what you want."

"Why can't I see him? Are you some kind of bodyguard?"

"Yes, he is." The deep voice came from behind the desk and Billy turned to see a tall slender man with a shaved head standing in a side doorway.

"Sam Richardson?" There was a slight resemblance. Billy remembered that Richardson had always kept his hair short in school. He thought it made him look like an intimidating gang member.

"Tommy screens all my visitors."

Drake straightened and moved between the desks, staying between Billy and Richardson.

"It's all right," Richardson said, holding out a hand to move Drake away. "I'll speak to Mr. Pankowski."

Billy started to rise but Drake slammed him back into the chair with a fierce look. "Are you sure?" he asked Richardson while still staring at Billy.

"Yes, Cupcake." He planted his fists on his hips. "I'm sure. Now be a good little boy and stand aside." He looked at Billy. "Come into the conference room, Mr. Pankowski."

Billy watched Drake's face crumble like melting chocolate

as he leaned against the desk. In just a matter of seconds, he was no longer the tough intimidating bodyguard who'd brought Billy into this room. He looked near to tears.

Billy clutched his briefcase as he struggled from the chair.

"Leave the briefcase," Drake said, a hand extended like he was hoping for a donation.

Billy pulled the case tighter to his chest and looked past him toward Richardson.

Richardson gave a disinterested shrug. "Let little Cupcake have the case, Mr. Pankowski. We don't want him to throw a tantrum."

"But—"

"You heard him," Drake said, his palm jabbing to within inches of Billy's face. His face reddened like a pouting child's.

Billy decided he didn't need the case. Since Sam Richardson Sr. wasn't here, his plans were changing. He had to find out where Sam was to plan his next move.

He set the case on the floor, leaning it against the side of the chair. It was locked and Drake would need the combination to open it, so he wasn't worried that he would find the gun.

He squeezed past Drake. Richardson ushered Billy into a smaller room furnished with relaxing leather chairs. Muted lighting dusted the paneled walls giving them a golden sheen. He closed the door behind him. "Drake can be a bit of an idiot sometimes," he said. "But he's good at following orders. Nothing from the outside is allowed into this office." He moved behind a small table and sat. "I understand you wanted to talk to my father."

"That's right." He remained standing. "Can you tell me where I can find him?"

"Saint Mary's Cemetery."

"I don't understand."

"He's dead."

"Oh." For a moment he didn't react, just let information settle into his consciousness. Sam, his childhood nemesis, the man who had ruined his life, was dead. Billy had been denied his revenge. When he realized that Richardson was waiting for some kind of response, he said, "I'm sorry. I didn't know."

"Obviously."

"What happened?"

"He died."

"When?"

"A year ago."

"I'm sorry. How did it happen?"

"He died."

Billy took a breath. Richardson's sarcastic tone told him he wasn't going to get any details. "Why do you need an armed bodyguard in your office?"

A smile flickered at his lips. "The financial world is sometimes a dangerous place."

Billy studied the man's slightly twisted face. The longer he stared, the more he looked like Sam Richardson. Maybe he was also a lot like Sam Richardson. "Or maybe you have a lot of enemies." He sidled to one of the chairs and sat.

Richardson kept his hands flat on the table. "Are you one of my enemies?"

"I've got nothing against you. We never met. But I'm one of your father's enemies. No. I take that back. Enemy is not the right word."

"What is the right word?"

"I don't know. Victims?" He let his right arm dangle over the chair seeking his briefcase. When he realized it was still in the outer office, he brought his hand to his chest. He decided not to make this visit an entire waste of time. "There are a few things you should know about your father."

"I'm always interested in hearing about my father. Especially from one of his— victims."

"I came here because I wanted to give your father a chance to apologize." He let the words settle to the floor.

Richardson fingered his tie and tilted his head to study him from a new angle. "For what?"

"Because he ruined my life."

"How?"

Suddenly faced with that direct question, Billy erupted like a long dormant volcano spewing anger and resentment. He told the man how Sam was the popular boy in grade school who the teachers loved. Sam used that to secure his dominance. Whenever anybody complained that Sam was bullying them, the teachers always sided with the shrewd abuser.

Because of Sam's bullying, Billy was never able to establish lasting friendships. He lived his life as an outsider. Through high school and college, he was too shy for any girlfriends. He quit college before his senior year because he knew he'd never make it as a doctor, the profession his father had nudged him toward. He could barely talk to people. How could he establish a bedside manner?

He accepted being a factory worker, though he hoped to advance to make his father proud.

"You could never be a supervisor," his boss at the distribution center told him when he applied for a promotion. "You're too much of a pushover. I'm sorry, but I can't see you telling people what to do. The first time somebody whines, you'll fold like a deck of cards."

He was right. Billy was a patsy.

But he had come here to change that.

Finished with his rant, puffing like an exhausted marathon runner, Billy sagged back in the chair his elbows splayed across the arms. "I feel you should know what kind of man your father was." Unable to punish his nemesis, he decided to settle for punishing the son with the truth.

Richardson, who had remained silent, almost disinterested, during the entire speech, said, "I know what kind of man my father was. I'm still dealing with his legacy. In fact, your name is on the list."

"What?"

"That's the only reason I let you in here. My father gave me the names of all the kids he used to pick on in school. He was worried that they might carry a grudge." He stopped and considered his words. "Let's be honest with each other. My father bullied weaker kids in school." He paused. "Don't look so shocked. You were one of them, so you know. He told me the kind of pranks he used to play as a child, the way he used to beat up the smaller kids, how he used to call them names."

Billy found himself squirming in the chair as he listened to Richardson listing his father's crimes, all of which he had witnessed.

"He was a bully as a child," Richardson said. "And he never changed. He was a bully as a father. When I cried, he said it would make me a stronger person." He stopped and raised his shoulders as if taking a deep breath. "And he was right. It made me tougher. It gave me the incentive to advance through this company. I have underlings beneath me who've been here longer than me, but they answer my every demand. We're a finely tuned machine." He paused and studied Billy who cringed under his glare. "My father was right. It made me stronger. But after the accident he started to weaken."

"What accident?"

"A hit and run that left him with a broken leg that never healed properly."

Billy almost said he was sorry, but instead, pressed his lips together.

"That's when he gave me the list of names. Five classmates that he felt were the weakest. He figured most of the kids he bullied would mature and get over it. He actually thought it would make them stronger. But there were a few he worried about. He wanted me to track them down and keep an eye on them."

"Why?"

"My father was convinced the hit and run wasn't an accident. It was attempted murder."

Billy arched his eyebrows, hoping to look shocked, but it didn't really surprise him.

Richardson said, "He didn't want to give anybody a second chance."

"So, what did you do?"

His eyes flicked down for a moment. "I hired a detective agency. It took a while, but they finally gave me a report. Two of the people were dead. One lived in France. You and another guy still live in the city. But none drove a Toyota Highlander." He paused. "What kind of car do you drive?"

"I have a Ford," he lied automatically, realizing what the man was implying. He didn't want him to know he had a Toyota SUV down in the parkade. "What did you do about the names on the list after you found them?"

"I was going to have someone deal with them." The way he said that made Billy think of Drake and his gun. "Warn them to leave my father alone. But my father died before I did anything."

"So, you just dropped it?"

"Oh, I've given it a lot of thought. As his son, I should seek to avenge his death. But I'm in no hurry."

"Well, clearly, you're worried."

"Excuse me?"

"The tight security around here." He waved his right arm back toward the door. "Someone has to go through an armed guard to see you. You're still worried about those people on the list, aren't you? They might come after the son for the sins of the father."

Richardson said nothing, but his tired look answered the question.

"I guess I could understand your caution," Billy said. He

had considered revenge. He was sure others did too.

"Yes. Very cautious." Richardson opened a drawer in the table. "There was always a concern that someone might come here looking for revenge."

"Not me," he lied. "I just came here looking for an apology."

"After all these years?"

"I'm convinced your father's abuse scarred me for life." The sound of the opening door cut off any more words, and he turned to see Drake nod toward his boss from the doorway. He gave a thumbs up hand signal.

Richardson removed a handgun from the desk. "What kind of car do you drive?"

"What?" He stared at the gun. "I told you."

"So that Toyota SUV in the parkade is not yours?"

"No. Never. T—that wasn't—" That was his sister's car. His own was down for repairs. "Was it a Toyota that hit your father?"

"Is it yours?"

Billy tried to stand but couldn't get out of the chair. An invisible weight held him down as he leaned to one side in the chair. His sister also went to Merryside Elementary, one year ahead of him. "I didn't drive," he lied again. "I took a cab."

Richardson shot a glance to Drake.

"There's a gun in his brief case, Mr. Richardson."

Richardson's eyes came back to Billy. "And what exactly were you planning to do with that gun, Mr. Pankowski?"

He swung his head back and forth from Richardson, still

holding a gun, to Drake who stood behind him, one gloved hand now holding his derringer. "Hey. That case was locked. You had no right."

"We have every right," Richardson said. "I knew who you were. No way I was going to let you bring anything into this office. And no cheap briefcase lock is going to keep my little Cupcake out. Right?" He winked at Drake. "He's useful sometimes. That's why he still works here."

"No, P—Please," Billy wailed as Drake trained the weapon on him.

Still holding his own gun, Richardson stood grinning behind his desk.

Drake swiveled his arm, aimed and shot Richardson. Blood popped from the center of his forehead as he staggered back into his chair, his head trembling, his arms flopping to the sides, and his gun thumping to the carpet.

Still unable to move, Billy stared at Drake who dropped the derringer and took out his own gun. Billy opened his mouth to speak as Drake fired, cutting off his words and his life.

Drake moved quickly, placing the derringer in Billy's hand before dashing to the outer office and grabbing the phone. "I need the police," he shouted when someone answered. "The bastard shot my boss. I'm sorry. I had to do it. Hurry." He turned and saw Cyndy, the secretary, standing in the doorway. "The bully is dead," he whispered.

She gave him a thumbs up.

Brit's Rules
Al Hagan

Britney still thought about Cliff a lot.

She thought about all of the dead boys, but Cliff had been her first. Maybe.

She had been 15 and he was a 19-year old sophomore at Southern Methodist University, close to her University Park home in Dallas. They had met at a mutual friend's house. He'd been stricken by the blonde-haired, blue-eyed beauty and had pursued her despite her young age. She had been conflicted; interested but hesitant.

Her family had money, a lot of it, both old and new. The old money had come mainly from real estate and banking. The new was pouring in from commercial rent and other investments and her father's occupation as a neurosurgeon. Cliff's blue-collar father performed manual labor in the oil and gas industry. Oilfield trash, her parents would have called him, had they ever known about him. Completely unacceptable as a boyfriend, even if she had been old enough to date, which her Mother had set at age 16.

The difference in status didn't matter to her, except when it did. Sometimes she wanted nothing more than to be in his arms. Other times, she laughed disdainfully at the thought of meeting his parents in their mobile home. She'd never even been inside a mobile home.

That last night, he'd kissed her slowly, passionately, deeply, and she'd felt things inside her body that she'd never felt before. And she'd stepped back, said "No," then turned and walked away.

Even now, she wasn't entirely sure what she'd meant by that one word. No, I am not going to go any further tonight, but come back tomorrow? No, we're moving too quickly with this relationship? No, I am rejecting you and never want to see you again?

Maybe he took it that last way. An emergency crew had pried his body out of his truck later that night, with a DUI level of intoxication. It was ruled an accident, but could very well have been a suicide. Britney was pretty sure it was. *After all, what did a man have to live for after kissing me?* crossed her mind, but she laughed at herself for being pretentious afterwards.

And it thrilled her. It gave her a taste of power. Would boys kill themselves if she stopped kissing them? That was the power of life and death, the power of a goddess.

*****

The next significant milestone on this path happened a year and a half later. Britney did a hit and run in her cute little red BMW. She'd had a couple of margaritas in a bar on the beach in Galveston. At 17, she shouldn't have been drinking for another four years, but a young bartender somehow neglected to check the IDs of three beautiful girls in tiny bikinis who sat at the bar and flirted with him.

The wreck wasn't anything major. She just scraped down the side of a parked car on one of Galveston's narrow streets and kept going. She confessed to her Mother, who was at her desk, deep in the midst of some fundraiser or other. Her Mother sighed, called the insurance agent, and claimed someone had hit the car while it was in a mall parking lot.

"The normal rules just don't apply to us," she told her daughter, shooing her out of the room.

Britney thought about that phrase a lot, and it gave her a whole new perspective on the world. It put into words something she'd known, and experienced to some extent, but now it was up front so much more.

And it was true. She got things based on her looks, on her smile, on her flirting. Boys bought her gifts. Cops let her off with warnings. Teachers cut her some slack.

She owned the world.

*****

Tanner taught her to shoot, and other, more intimate things. The shooting was acceptable, as it was sporting clays, skeet, and trap, and done with a $5,000 shotgun and not a $600 one. The shotgun was heavy, but Britney's gymnastics classes had strengthened her. She liked the power, the ability to apply a few ounces of pressure to a trigger and to turn a clay pigeon into dust.

She'd been dating Tanner for a few months, and was almost ready to move on when she began to suspect that he was seeing someone else. The more she looked for signs of infidelity, the more she found.

No one breaks up with me! she raged.

187

She went out for a run several nights later, just to clear her head. But the more she thought about it, the madder she got. She veered off of her normal path and headed towards his house to confront him.

He actually lived in an apartment in back of the main house that they called the game room. The bottom floor of the game room had a pool table, a ping pong table, and a wet bar. The upper floor had a couple of guest bedrooms, one of which Tanner had taken over.

When Britney turned into his driveway, she slammed to a stop, recognizing the car that was parked there. It belonged to one of her classmates. Her blood seemed to boil.

If it was one of my friends, that would be one thing. But her?!

She marched up the driveway, past the pool and spa, and through the unlocked game room door. All of the lights were off and the only noise was a faint sound of music coming from above. Moving quietly, she went upstairs and looked into the bedroom. There were two figures under the sheets, apparently asleep.

Brit thought her head would explode with fury. She spun on her heel and marched into the other bedroom, where Tanner kept his shotgun, but she stopped just short of touching it. After a couple of deep breaths, she went back downstairs to the wet bar and found a pair of kitchen gloves that the maid used to scrub the sink.

She fumbled a bit, loading the shotgun with the gloves on, but it was only two shells that slid into two barrels. There were no springs to fight against or actions to noisily rack. And the trap shells would be more than adequate at close range.

Brit stepped back into the doorway and neither figure stirred, so she moved up to the foot of the bed. She stood there for a few seconds, breathing hard, looking at the pair, letting the fury build back up inside. Then she shouldered the shotgun, aimed at Tanner's chest, and squeezed the trigger.

The Browning shotgun bucked in her arms and tried to slide up off of her shoulder. Her previous shooting had been at targets that were level or above her, which made the gun punch into her. Aiming down made it recoil differently and it took her a moment to get it back in her shoulder.

The girl had sat up in bed, wide-eyed, and had her mouth open, drawing in breath for a scream. Brit cut that off with another shotgun blast. She tossed the firearm onto the bed, almost in Tanner's lap, before turning and running.

The normal rules just don't apply to us, she thought.

The police questioned her, routinely, but got nothing. As a last resort, the homicide detective asked if she would be willing to take a lie detector test.

"My daughter politely declines to take a Polygraph examination," her Father had stepped in. "And you can address any further questions to my attorney."

Detective Lowenthal ground his teeth as they walked out the door.

"I kind of like her for this," he later told another detective in the squad room. "Problem is, we got nothing on her. She was the guy's girlfriend, so any fingerprints or DNA we find in the house are useless. Not unless her hair is stuck in the blood, and it's not. There's no video that's usable that shows her running anywhere. No witnesses. Worse, no motive for anyone else to do this."

"We'll keep trying to run down a motive on the female victim's side," Detective Taylor replied. "Her last boyfriend is clear, but maybe there's someone that wanted her and couldn't get her."

The only other piece of evidence was the gloves, and Britney had shredded them with scissors, cutting them up into little strips. The day after the murders, she had driven down Interstate 30 and dumped them out the window, bit by bit, over a ten-mile stretch of highway.

Like her classmates, she was dressed in black and crying at the funerals a few days later.

*****

The summer after she graduated, it was her drug dealer.

She bought a little weed from him, and sometimes some flake, actual cocaine, not that low-class crack. She was careful, getting a burner phone and only using it to contact him. She didn't need a drug conviction to screw up her college admission.

She's also learned that it's easy to swap out the barrel of a 1911-model pistol using only one's hands, and that replacement barrels only cost a couple hundred dollars. And weren't serial numbered. Her newfound interest in shooting turned into plenty of money spent on gear, ammunition, and classes to teach her how to use it.

The drug dealer met her in a secluded little suburban park with a long road that would give early warning of any approaching headlights. That wasn't unusual, but what was different this night was how Brit planned for it to end.

They made the deal standing by the side of their cars, and then she hesitated, running through her mental checklist to make sure that she had everything in order. He mistook the pause for something else. Maybe she wanted to say something to him and was just shy.

"So you know we could party," he suggested. "I could keep you hooked up. Whatever you want."

She looked at him for a couple of seconds with a smile slowly spreading across her face. *Oh. My. God. As if. At least see an orthodontist,* she thought.

He took her smile as an encouraging sign and broadened his own. He opened his mouth to say something else but never got the chance. Brit had reached behind her back and came out with a pistol, extended it towards him, and fired twice, all in one smooth, well-practiced movement.

The two .45 caliber hollowpoint bullets slammed into his chest like baseball bats swinging for the fences and his legs folded under him. He couldn't get any air in his lungs, even gulping in great breaths. Brit loomed up over him.

"How does that feel, you bastard?" she said through gritted teeth. "How does it feel to cheat me out of my money? My cousin was visiting from Houston and she laughed at this trash!" She waved the plastic bag of marijuana. "She said we were paying twice as much as we should. And for poor quality! You made me look like a fool."

He tried to speak but he didn't have enough air. Things were hazy, jumbled and confused. Then he saw the muzzle come up and point at him one last time before everything went completely black.

She bent to dig her money out of his pocket. Not because she needed it, but in case her fingerprints were on it. The empty shell casings the pistol had ejected were nothing. She had wiped the ammunition clean and used gloves to load the magazine. All of her clothing, the burner phone, and the pistol barrel would be disposed of carefully.

It was really, really difficult to drive the speed limit, but she couldn't be caught with a murder weapon and weed.

Detective Lowenthal found a video that showed a red BMW in the area, but only roughly, not the immediate area. Of course, the video did not show the tag number. He also learned that the drug dealer had a pretty elite clientele: he serviced the rich kids, charging them higher rates for the safety of not going into a bad part of town and dealing with shady characters. It was thin, too thin to even run her cell phone records and find out where she had been that night, but he thought about her.

*****

She went to college at UCLA that fall and Lowenthal breathed a sigh of relief on the one hand. On the other, she had gotten under his skin. He kept her social media pages bookmarked, checking in periodically. He was happy when he saw that she was on a ski vacation in Colorado instead of coming back to Dallas on Christmas break.

But he couldn't let it go. He lasted another two months before he called a homicide detective in Los Angeles that he had met at a conference. After some small talk, he came to the point.

"Sean, I have a rich Dallas girl that I think is good for three murders. Well, two, anyway. The third is more iffy, but I like her for it. A lot of things fit, but not enough for warrants. She's now a student at UCLA."

"Really? So you shipped your problem out to us?"

"I wasn't unhappy to see her go, I'll admit that."

"I was just joking. Tell me about her."

"Her name is Britney Hall--"

"Britney Welles Hall?" Sean interrupted.

"Oh, Jesus. What did she do?"

"I'll get the detective working that case on the line, but the basic story is that a professor was having an affair with one of his students, apparently your Britney. He died of a drug overdose. His wife claims he hadn't done drugs since he was a student himself, ten or twelve years ago."

"His wife would probably have also claimed that he wasn't banging an 18-year old student, either," Lowenthal muttered.

"Yeah, that's a fact. The tox screen says he had alcohol, Valium, and there was some indication of GHB in his system. It's not a good idea to mix two depressants with something that may make you stop breathing. So we're open here; accident, suicide, or murder."

"What did Britney have to say?"

"She admitted to the affair, but she had to, because other people knew about it. She seems to have an alibi for the night in question. Apparently she spent it with her new boyfriend.

He claims they partied until they both passed out Saturday night. He says she was still out when he woke up Sunday at the crack of noon."

"And any GHB in his system is long gone. If I had to guess – and, hey, I'm not telling you how to do your job here – but if I had to guess, Britney dosed the new boyfriend up with GHB to make him pass out, went by the professor's place and had drinks with him until she could dose him with GHB, and then stuffed Valium or whatever down his throat. Now, the three here in Dallas were all shot, but two of those were with the victim's shotgun, so I can see her using whatever weapons she has on hand. She's smart, and she's evil. We have to stop her somehow."

*****

It was over a year before someone managed to piss Brit off enough for her to kill them. Oh, there had been minor slights that she had punished. She had zapped one girl's phone with a stun gun and ruined it. She had squirted pepper spray into the air conditioning vents of another girl's car. There was a guy that insulted her, so she poured Coca-Cola onto the keyboard of his laptop. But all that was all minor league for Brit.

What wasn't minor was getting the notes. Britney was out with friends one night, having a great time. It was getting late and they all had class the next day, so some of the girls were leaving.

"Oh, I want to stay," Britney pouted. "Margo, can I get your notes from Dr. Buck's class tomorrow?"

"Sure," Margo had said, but she didn't deliver. She didn't answer Britney's calls or texts. Frustrated and running out of time, Britney got the notes from someone else, but they weren't that good. The exam had been tough, and Britney was furious to find that she had gotten a C. It was going to take a lot of hard work to pull her average in that class up so it didn't spike her GPA.

That was major. That was screwing with everything, impacting her future. This called for blood.

Brit planned carefully. She always did, now, after that first rage killing. That time she'd been lucky. The gloves had been a great idea, but that had been on the fly. No one could rely on luck, so she made her own.

She chose a hoodie and sweatpants that belonged to her boyfriend. If it came down to an investigation, they would find DNA from him and her both, and the clothing would be back in his possession by that time. That would induce reasonable doubt, even a preponderance of guilt on him, and she'd throw him under the bus. *Well, detective, I did tell him about Margo screwing me over on the notes, but I was just complaining. I had no idea he'd go out and do anything to her!* Cue up the horrified and shocked face at that point.

She had a pair of latex surgical gloves that were a kind of beige fleshtone color, not too far off of a natural skin tone. It had been easy to lift a pair from the bio lab.

For the weapon, she happened upon some rebar mesh offcuts at a small construction site where the sidewalk was being repaired. She picked out one that was just under an inch in diameter and about eighteen inches long, making it a nice blunt instrument. And she knew just when and where to use it. She knew when Margo would go on a run, and there was a secluded area for the ambush site on the route.

Brit was waiting off to the side, the hood up and drawn tight, and had even added a baseball cap so she could keep her face hidden under the bill from any security cameras. When Margo went by, running alone, she picked up the rebar and sprinted to catch up. Margo had earbuds in and was oblivious to the footsteps coming closer. Brit clouted her across the back of the skull, sending her off balance, crashing down to the pavement on her knees and elbows.

Skidding to a stop, Brit leaned down and struck the surprised girl on the back of the head three or four times, the rage roaring through her entire being. But she retained enough presence of mind to switch her strikes to other parts of the girl's head. She didn't want to keep hitting the same spot and create a lot of blood splatter. She didn't need obvious spots of blood on her clothing and face as she left the scene.

Another quick half dozen blows to Margo's shoulders and neck, then she turned and ran. She kept the rebar in hand for a minute, going over her checklist, making sure she had the gloves on and wouldn't leave any fingerprints, before tossing it aside. It would provide no clues.

She had two miles to run in order to get back to her boyfriend's apartment, an easy run, not even enough to get warmed up. The gloves went into a dumpster along the route, after she had wiped them thoroughly on the hoodie. The shoes would be gone tomorrow, into a Goodwill drop-off box, after a bath in bleach.

Inside, her boyfriend greeted her without taking his eyes off of the video game he was playing.

"Hey, beautiful," he said. "Where have you been?"

"I went downstairs and cleaned out my car. I was only gone fifteen minutes at most. And I found a hat that I bought for you and then forgot about." She took the ball cap off of her head and put it on his, scrunching it down so it got a good dose of his DNA on it. She stepped back and pulled the hoodie and sweatpants off. All she had on underneath were panties and a sports bra.

"I thought I'd take a quick shower. Want to join me? Or is your game more exciting?"

*****

Lowenthal had Sean's number programmed in so he knew who it was calling.

"Guess what? We just had a girl severely beaten while running in a park," Sean wasted no time with small talk. "Your little girlfriend might have struck again."

"Please tell me you have something solid on her." Lowenthal held his breath.

"Unfortunately, I can't say that. They're in the same class together, and apparently Britney was trying to get some study notes from her. She sent three texts but none of them are anything hostile. They're all pretty courteous, as a matter of fact. Like this one says 'Hey, can I get those notes from you?' Real innocent."

"Damn."

"The girl's injuries may be fatal, or she may survive with brain damage. It's too early to tell at this point, but our department is stepping in because of the severity of the wounds. She was hit in the head multiple times with a piece of rebar."

"Does Britney have an alibi?"

"Yeah, she was at her boyfriend's apartment, about two miles from the park."

"That's nothing for Britney. She's a runner. She's done marathons," Lowenthal interrupted.

"Yeah, but she was only gone fifteen minutes according to the boyfriend. There's no way she ran a four mile round trip and ambushed a girl in fifteen minutes."

"What about her phone?"

"At the apartment the whole time."

"I guess the girl, the victim, can't even talk."

"No chance. And none of the blows were to her face, so it looks like she was hit from behind and went down face-first and stayed that way."

Lowenthal sighed, feeling bleak. "She's going to get away with this one, too, isn't she?"

*****

They didn't even know about the accident. The kind-of accident. The one that started as an accident. Whatever. She was never questioned; that was the important part.

Britney had been at a club in West Hollywood and had left with a cute guy. He didn't live that far away, a little ways up in the hills, and his parents were away on a trip. They sat on the deck beside the pool while he fired up the hot tub.

"Of course, a swimsuit is optional," he mentioned.

She had just met the guy and wasn't quite that ready to jump into bed with him. "I don't know. Do your parents have a security system here? Are there cameras recording us now?" she asked. It was an innocent question at the time.

"No, no, I turned all that off. I don't need them to see my business," he assured her. "Speaking of getting down to business…." He stood in front of her chair and leaned in towards her for a kiss.

"Slow down, cowboy," she said, putting a hand on his chest and pushing him back. She'd done that before, plenty of times. It had always been taken in good humor. She wasn't saying no; it was more of a yes. There was still the potential to get the girl eventually.

This was the one time it wasn't taken well. His face had flushed red in anger and he'd swung a slap at her. Britney was fast and had taken martial arts, and she blocked most of the blow with a forearm. But he was pressing an attack, not just throwing a slap. He moved in on her, trapped in the chair, grabbing her breast with his other hand.

She shoved him hard with both hands, pushing him back a little, enough room to draw her legs up to her chest and then thrust them into his abdomen. He staggered back, the alcohol in his system affecting his stability. The first two steps backwards were on the deck. The third step came down on nothing but water, and he fell into the pool.

It should have been funny. It would have been, if the hot tub hadn't been protruding into the pool behind him. The back of his skull slammed into the rock rim of the hot tub with a disturbing thump, and the angle of his fall spun him around so that he landed face down in the water.

Brit sat forward in the chair, hands on knees, considering the situation.

His face was in the water. He was going to drown, if the crack on the skull hadn't already killed him. She didn't have a problem with that. Of the ten seconds she sat there, nine were used in calculating what she needed to do to get out of there without leaving a trace.

Not much, as it turned out. She had just walked in the door, almost, and all she had touched was a glass and the seatbelt latch. He had been a real gentleman and had opened and closed the car and house doors for her. The cameras were off. At least, she hoped so. That was her biggest worry, that he had botched that somehow.

She stood, pushed the chair back under the table with a foot, washed the glass and put it back in the cabinet, then she'd calmly walked out, using a paper towel as a makeshift glove. The passenger side of the car got a little wipe, and she was gone. Her car was still at the club, only about a mile away. It was further than she wanted to walk in the shoes she was wearing, but doable.

The phone. She almost kicked herself. Maybe the drinks were blurring her mind. There was nothing to be done about it now, other than turn it off. Maybe the club and the house both hit off of the same cell tower. Or maybe she was screwed.

She was jumpy for the next few weeks, but nothing ever came of it. She hoped they would regard it as an accident. He was drunk. He fell in the pool. End of story. Didn't the cops have enough to do? They wouldn't canvass every club and look through all of the video footage to find out he'd been drinking, would they? They knew that already. She just didn't want them to find any video that showed her leaving with him.

Maybe she needed to get out of California. Maybe she should complete her undergraduate degree back in Texas.

*****

Britney came back home to Dallas in the summer, except for three weeks in Europe with her family. And she stayed, pleading homesickness, and laid low for the next two years while she completed her degree. The boy in the pool had scared her. She hadn't planned it and things were sloppy.

It had been easy for Lowenthal to pop a magnetic GPS tracker onto the underside of her car, in the small hope he could catch her doing something incriminating. With her back in the area, he became nosy, checking with the homicide detectives in the surrounding communities, looking for anything that she might possibly be linked to. He really wanted to get her into an interview room, have her lie on camera, and put her in prison for the rest of her life.

But deep down, he didn't think that would happen. He had no doubt whatsoever that she was a serial killer, but she wasn't one of those who was driven to kill, with an obsession that escalates into more and more frequent murders. She wasn't going out every month and killing someone. It was more like one a year, on average. Four murders in four years, plus at least one attempt. Maybe even more murders that no one had yet managed to associate with her. She'd been smart enough to commit all of these without leaving enough evidence to incriminate herself, so maybe she had done some perfect murders.

It was truly depressing.

He had his own little shrine to her; copies of all of the files with a notebook on top of the boxes, explaining all of his suspicions and clues and conclusions about her murders. Maybe someone could use it after he was dead and gone.

Maybe they would think he'd become obsessed with her, fallen in love from afar with the beautiful young lady. Following her. Watching her. Stalking her. Wishing he could be with her.

But he knew better, and that was what mattered. He hadn't fallen in love with her. He was stalking her, like the doctors stalked a disease like cancer. They didn't love the cancer. They stalked it to defeat it.

But the doctors weren't going to defeat cancer quickly enough to save him. The tenderness and the pain in his abdomen and the blood in his stool had driven him to the doctor. The outlook was grim: stage four colon cancer and only a matter of months to live. There was nothing they could realistically do at this point to stop or even slow the disease.

He had sat on his couch, alone, and cried for a little while. Just let the waterworks go. After that, he cracked open a beer, the first of many, and started a mental list of what he needed to do. Calls had to be made, when he could speak of his own imminent death without his voice quavering. There were things to give away to people. May as well do it now and not wait for the reading of the will.

And maybe there was one more thing he could do. He had dedicated his career to public service, first in the Army and then on the police force. There might be one more thing he could do to help society.

About the same time Lowenthal was learning he was going to die soon, Britney was celebrating her graduation from college and interviewing for a job.

Her number one pick had involved a marathon interview process. There had been the first interview on campus, followed by an invitation to visit the company offices. There, she found that she was one of a small group of graduating students who were all given a tour of the facilities, but then broke off for individual interviews.

She realized at some point that she was in competition with another girl for the same position. She had mixed feelings. On the one hand, she felt she had it all over on the girl: *Who would want to work with her? She's not cute or charming or anything.* Of course, there was the other hand: *Is she going to get a sympathy pass because she is plain and awkward, figuring that I'll have no problem getting a job somewhere else?*

A few days later, she put down the phone with exaggerated care instead of throwing it against the wall like she wanted. She was breathing heavily and there was a white-hot rage building inside of her. "Better qualifications"? A "better fit for the company"? That little bitch had taken the position away from her. But she knew the girl's name and where she'd gone to college. She picked her phone back up, starting to run a search to get her address, then stopped abruptly. That would be stupid, to search on her phone. She had to leave no traces, no clues. This required careful planning.

With social media, it wasn't hard to figure out that the girl was still working her part-time job as a waitress until she started her new job in another two weeks. And it wasn't hard to call in, impersonate her, and ask what her schedule was.

Brit cruised apartment parking lots until she found a car with "4 Sale" and the phone number painted in white tennis-shoe blanco on the rear window. She called the number on a burner phone and when she met the guy to make the deal she was wearing sunglasses, no makeup, a brunette wig, short shorts, and a top that exposed a considerable amount of cleavage. Between the cash and the cleavage, the guy never looked at her face. He did offer to show her a good time, which she declined.

She bought a baseball bat for cash at a store 40 miles away, wearing a cowboy hat and keeping her face down, hiding from the security cameras. She wore a tank top for this trip, with large temporary tattoos on both arms. It was kind of fun, secret agent-type stuff.

The day she had scheduled, she told her friends she had a touch of the summer flu or something and was going to stay in. On her email, she scheduled a series of rules that would send automated responses to incoming emails, based on what was in the subject line. That way, all she had to do was to send emails from her burner phone and an anonymous email account to her real email account. The real account would reply with the canned messages and make it appear that she was responding to emails.

Wearing the wig, she slipped out of her apartment after dark and made the short run to the car she had bought. From there she drove that to a parking lot a mile from her target, and made that run. While she was waiting, she emailed herself from the burner phone and got a reply. Then the girl came out to her car and turned her back on Brit to get in. It was a few steps and a swing of the bat to get her down on her hands and knees, then a wicked overhead swing down on the back of her skull. Brit put all of her arm and back muscles into it, even bending her knees some to get a little extra push on contact.

The girl dropped flat on the pavement and seemed to deflate, all of the tension going out of her muscles. Brit just let the bat fall beside her. She had wiped it down with bleach and was wearing gloves. It should be clean.

She ran back to the junker, the driver's area covered in plastic painter's drop cloth. It started, for which she was thankful, and made it to the side street she'd previously picked out, a couple of miles from her apartment. She stripped the drop cloth out and stuffed it into a backpack, leaving the keys on the dash. There was no paperwork that tied the car to her. Someone could steal it and keep it as far as she was concerned.

The walk back to her apartment was uneventful. She emailed herself several times to trigger the automated replies and made it back inside unseen. As soon as she walked through the door, the backpack, wig, gloves, phone, and every bit of her clothing went into garbage bags. Tomorrow she would be on the road, dropping the bags into dumpsters many miles away.

The hardest part was going to be simply to wait and see if the company would call her, since their star candidate was now out of play. She gritted her teeth when that thought crossed her mind – star candidate – but the rage that started to rise inside her was mitigated by the memory of the baseball bat slamming into the girl's skull. The bat was aluminum and it made a nice tink sound when it hit.

Brit smiled.

*****

Lowenthal looked through all of the murders in his spare time, even the ones that didn't involve him, but he missed any connection on this one. He couldn't tie anything about Britney to the young woman clubbed to death in the parking lot.

Until he saw Britney announce her new job on social media.

He'd heard the company name before. The dead girl was going to start a position there. He thought this could be the big break and he hammered at it, working endlessly. And futilely. His initial excitement turned to dust.

"I know it was her."

"What, are you psychic, now?" Lieutenant Saunders countered. "You got nothing. The only physical evidence is a baseball bat that was cleaner than when it came out of the factory. Where did your girl get it? You don't know. Who witnessed the murder? Nobody. All you have is that somebody *might* have seen a dark-haired, *not* a blonde, girl running. Bring me one witness. Bring me one person who says this Britney of yours had too much to drink and bragged about it. Then you have something. I can't go to the D.A. and ask for warrants on a random citizen, which is what this is."

Lowenthal stared off into the distance, seeing nothing. He sighed and nodded. She had done it again.

*****

It was Saturday night around ten p.m. in a trendy little part of

Dallas. Britney liked to go there for drinks and dinner and dancing with her friends. Right now, she was out in front of a restaurant with eight or ten other people in a rough circle. Some of them were calling it a night, forced to go home after dinner because they were new parents with a babysitter waiting for them. The rest were planning which nightclub would be their destination for tonight.

Lowenthal sat in his car for a minute longer, thinking hard. Britney Welles Hall, 22 years old, five murders and one attempt, an attempt that left a 19-year old girl brain damaged for life. That was a fate worse than death, so call it six, plus how many other murders that they didn't know about? And how many more would come in the future?

He took a deep breath and made his decision.

He walked up to the group and conversation dropped off for a second, until it was picked up by Britney.

"Why, it's Detective Lowenthal," she announced. "Aren't you supposed to speak to my attorney rather than coming directly to me? I have nothing to say to you."

She was wearing a little black cocktail dress that was cut low, with a long gold chain necklace that disappeared down her cleavage, inviting one's eyes to follow it. His eyes did, just like every other man's, and he cursed himself for being weak just when he needed to be strong. He forced himself to look her in the eye.

"That's fine," he replied mildly. "You don't have to say anything. As a matter of fact, it would probably be better that way." He had his pistol out in a second and started firing, pumping .40 caliber bullets into Britney's abdomen as fast as he could pull the trigger. She went to her knees, then fell back with five or six shots in her, a shocked look on her face. He took a step forward and added four more just to make certain she was dead.

He ignored all of the screaming and noise and confusion while he turned and slowly trudged back to his car. He threw the Glock and his badge case on the dashboard and sat there, sideways in the seat with the door open, waiting to be arrested. He had done his last service to society. The cancer would kill him long before he would go to trial.

Agatha's Simple Plan

Caroline Tuohey

Agatha had always hated her name. Her mother – a fan of the crime novels of Ms Christie – in a moment of adoration after spending the last two weeks of the pregnancy ploughing her way through ten of the mystery novels, had paid homage by way of name. Had Agatha's father gone to the library and borrowed a selection of romance stories (as he'd been requested to by his wife) for that last two weeks of resting and waiting, he, the unsuspecting husband and soon to be newly proud father, may well have averted a tragedy. But fathers-to-be are generally not thinking their newborn will grow up to be a nasty piece of work. And they usually aren't thinking too deeply about names. They just go with the flow.

So little Agatha was swaddled and driven home to be doted on by her loving parents.

She was largely oblivious to how different her name was until she started school. But by then she'd already begun to hate her mother. She dealt with the playground teasing by retreating into a silent cocoon where she, like Ms Christie, concocted all sorts of terrible endings for those around her. And when she returned home each afternoon, was loved and cared for by her parents (this wouldn't have happened had her mother been privy to the dastardly deeds Miss Agatha had considered for *her*, just a few hours earlier). This combination of hatred and love somehow got her through.

But work – well work was another story entirely. If she wasn't being called Andrea – why would your mother choose Agatha instead of Andrea? – she was usually being asked to solve the latest crime that featured in the news.

Data analysis was something she was very good at, which often made the process quite tedious, because usually, she *did* solve the crimes. It generally didn't take her long to sift through the newspaper reports and trawl the internet, tail the occasional suspect after work, and gather the essentials needed to figure out who was guilty and who wasn't. Why this didn't alert her to the fact she would have been a valuable addition to any law enforcement unit in any major city is a mystery in itself, but the years of name-teasing had skewed her thinking.

So, it was only a matter of time before Agatha took her first steps down the other fork on Life's highway and realized she probably could live out her own Agatha Christie story. And, without the meddlesome Miss Marple or the methodical Monsieur Poirot, she could well get to the final chapter and still escape accountability. She figured it was worth a try. After all, why should the other Agatha be the only one with all the good ideas?

So, she started. It seemed reasonable, given the appalling choice of name she'd been saddled with, to choose her mother. Tick. Victim sorted. She smiled.

Now, the method. Ideally, nothing that involved blood – not so much for the squeamish aspect, but rather, the advanced technology now available meant Forensics could see it on everything, which generally meant a conviction. So no blood. Or at least, not blood that left the body with any great volume or projection. Poisoning would be better. Her mother took a concoction of tablets – she'd seen them when she'd last visited. Packets and bottles all lined up and carefully alphabetized on the kitchen counter top. Agatha had meant to ask her why she needed so much medication – it seemed that her mother was still quite fit and healthy, so what on earth were all those tablets for? Obviously now, she'd need to know. She rang her mother and, after the usual pleasantries, had enquired about joining them for an early dinner that evening (Agatha darling, we'd love to see you – I'll cook your favorite. You bring the wine.) Tick. Research victim's medication with view to poisoning mother with her own prescriptions, sorted. With that successfully engineered, she left for work.

As she drove past Marshall's Autos, she reminded herself to remind herself that her car was in need of a much required service. Tires, lights, brakes, the passenger side door where it had jammed shut…. But tomorrow was always another day.

She arrived at her parents' house shortly before six o'clock, and after wrestling the old wrought iron gates open (why her parents never got them re-hinged and aligned correctly was beyond her), parked the car in the driveway and headed inside. She made for the fridge with wine – she'd purposefully bought white, so it needed chilling – she recalled the tablet collection was nestled on the kitchen worktop, in neat rows next to the fridge.

"Mum, what on earth are all these tablets for?" she asked. She carefully avoided touching the bottles but leant forward to read some of the labels.

"Oh, this and that," replied her mother. "You know what it's like these days. We have a tablet for everything."

"Are they all prescription?" she asked, carefully filming the bottles with her phone, her mother quite oblivious to her actions.

"What? Prescription? No. Well yes, some are and the rest off the shelf, recommended by the doctor. They want you dosed up to avoid problems. Preventative medicine I believe is what they call it."

Agatha straightened up and winced – those blasted gates had done something to her shoulder. "Have you got a Panadol in all this? I've hurt my shoulder. You really need to get those gates sorted. How on earth does Daddy manage them? They need to be dragged. Get them re-aligned."

Agatha's mother reached into the mix of bottles and produced the Panadol. "Here you are. And there's a method to the gates. You just need to know what it is."

If truth be known, Agatha couldn't stand the wretched things. But they'd come with the house when her parents had bought it, apparently 'a credit to the blacksmith's art.'

Agatha took the tablets and stared out the window at her father, who was now dragging the gates shut. She frowned. That wasn't in the plan. She needed to be able to leave quietly. Having to reopen the gates would make more noise that neighbours might remember at a later date. She watched as the rusted gates heaved their way along the cement driveway, her father some sort of modern hunchback of Notre Dame, dutifully shuffling along in their wake.

"I'll just go and have a word with Dad," she muttered and

headed back out to the front.

"Dad, what are you doing?"

"Just closing the gates love."

"But I'm leaving soon."

"I need to keep the neighbour's dogs out. They dig up your mother's flowers."

Agatha sighed. This was not in the plan. Dogs. Gates. Fathers. No wonder Miss Marple sorted it all so easily. The plans were always compromised. The unexpected couldn't be planned for.

"Well, perhaps you could at least oil the hinges or something – so they're easier to open. I've jarred my shoulder from dragging them."

"Yes, good idea. You might help me with the top hinges – save me getting the ladder. It seems I've shrunk! Can't reach up that far anymore."

Agatha watched her father head up to the shed. Hopefully the gates would be sorted and then she could eat and run – she had all the pills to research.

A panting behind her diverted her thoughts. She turned. A large dog had arrived at the gates and started barking. Great, more noise. Right, well this was something she *could* remove from the plan.

She strode to her car as her father appeared waving the oil can.

"Here it is."

"Just a minute Dad, I'm getting the mace to sort that dog. It might think twice before coming back."

"Right, well I'll make a start on the lower hinges."

Agatha sighed again. When did life become so tedious? She opened the driver's door and leant across to the glove box – somewhere in there was a can of mace – yes, there it was. She winced again as her shoulder, and now lower back, resisted as she shifted her weight. As she fell forward from the pain, re-jarring her already tender shoulder, she realized she'd now need something far stronger than a Panadol for the throbbing from both shoulder and back. Sprawled across the car seats, she looked through the back window at her father. Damn him and his gates, she thought. Why couldn't he have just left them open? She winced as she attempted to sit up. Maybe she needed a new plan. She dragged herself back out of the car, slammed the door with a force quite contrary to one suffering a shoulder injury (the power of anger displacement), and headed back inside for an icepack and a whiskey. The gates could now wait.

It was when she was one step from the kitchen door, that she heard the rusty grating again. It was followed almost instantly by what she would, a second later, conclude was her father's last breath being knocked through the wrought iron gates as her car, having deftly rolled down the steep driveway, pinned him with force and accuracy against the now-shut gates.

In doing so, her car (a nice solid European model with a sound safety rating and an eye-catching manufacturer's marque) knocked his head solidly onto the mock Tudor rosette of the gate and extinguished life as he knew it. As she surveyed this unfortunate scene, Agatha realized the nagging pain in her back was when she'd fallen onto the gear stick and accidently knocked it into neutral (or so she would later tell the police). She smiled. How silly to have forgotten about the park brake too – her father was always going on at her about its need to be properly adjusted (or so she would tell the police later still).

While she pondered on whether the icepack she intended for her shoulder, might be of assistance to her father (Agatha, who are you kidding, there's blood everywhere, I think he's dead, best just go and call an ambulance and get it over with), her mother glanced out the kitchen window. Her scream, considerably louder than that of her husband's final breath, was the last sound she omitted before she fainted, tragically hitting her head on the newly renovated stainless-steel and Beechwood butcher's block on the way down. This extinguished life as *she* knew it.

It was only when Agatha ushered the last police officer out of the house, all the while reassuring him that, no, she didn't need to have someone keep her company that night, that she realized her plan – both plans actually – may have worked. She carefully deleted the tablet footage from her phone, walked to the medications by the fridge and took another Panadol – her shoulder was still hurting.

Starstruck

Steve Carr

Sure, it ain't easy being a gumshoe. On some nights it can be a really lousy job. This was one of those nights.

1937 had faded into 1938 uneventfully, or so it seemed, and although it doesn't often rain in L.A., the sudden downpour tonight had washed the trash and debris from the gutters and sent it into the drains to be washed out to sea in heaps. Traffic on the downtown streets was at a standstill, and the drivers showed their displeasure with the situation by laying on the car horns, filling the early night hours with discordant noise. The valets at the nightclubs and upscale restaurants on Sunset Strip did their best, but with little success, in mopping up the puddles as best they could. They had a head start of a couple hours before the wealthy and well-known, the socially elite, along with the gangsters, their molls, and nefarious dames were due to start arriving. The manager at *Grauman's Chinese Theater* stood at the front doors and wrung his hands, waiting for the rain to stop, hoping he wouldn't have to unroll the red carpet and see it get soaked. He had no intention of angering the money men, stars and starlets who would make it headline news if they got their expensive shoes wet while going into the theater for the biggest movie premier to hit town in over a month.

I had time to kill before *Café Trocadero*, the *Mocambo* or *Ciro's* began to swing, and while rain pelted the large plate glass windows of Schwab's drugstore I sat at its counter and slowly sipped on a cherry coke. The others sitting at the counter were dolls that most likely had left their midwest hometowns by bus and traveled cross country in hopes of seeing their names in lights. They'd sell their good names and souls to fulfill their dreams of being discovered by some movie scout. Probably some producer wearing spats, smoking a Cuban cigar, and diamond studs on his shirt. Their pouty lips that were rouged with fire engine red lipstick suggested they were perpetually preparing for a first kiss that would lead to getting a screen test. They batted their mascara'd eyelashes like signal lamps sending out SOS messages. I had been in Hollywood for 12 years. First on the beat as a cop, then another 5 as a Police Department detective. When I'd finally had enough, I crossed over to being Private Investigator. I'd seen thousands of dolls just like them come and go, not once seeing any of them make it to the big screen. Nothing about me said power or money. I wore a brown fedora, a beige trench coat, and scuffed Oxfords, so they avoided me like the plague.

I was almost to the bottom of the glass when Johnny Speckles, known as Headlights, pushed the peroxide-blonde doll next to me from her perch and plopped down on the stool as if he had just gotten tired of carrying around his immense weight. He stared at me through the thick lenses of his wire rimmed eyeglasses that made his eyes appear five times their actual size. When he looked at you, it was like being caught in the headlights of an oncoming truck. An unlit stogie hung from the left corner of his lower lip. Water dripped from the rim of his black fedora.

He opened the conversation. "Word on the street is that you been lookin' for me."

Somehow I couldn't take my eyes off his stogie as it danced up and down on his lip.

"Your stink is all over the Hayes murder," I said. "The cops would be interested in hearing what I know about you and your gangster pals."

He shifted on the stool as if rearranging his excess fat. "I had nothin' to do with that flatfoot's murder," he said. "The racket he had going was encroaching on my territory, true, but I was only waiting for the right time to step in, not to bump him off. He was a dirty copper and that's what got him knocked off."

"By who?" I asked.

"You know how this town operates," he replied. "If I knew that, an' someone found I'd spilled it, I'd most likely end up in the morgue on the slab right next to him." He slid from the stool and stood up with a large grunt as if lifting his own weight took effort. He shifted the cigar to the other side of his mouth. "Go ahead and tell the cops what you know. They'd be interested to know all about your doings with that Hayes clown and I could tell 'em plenty."

"Alright, then who should I be talking to?"

"Talk to the dame he was nuts about."

"The singer? Claire LaLong?"

"Yep, that's the one. She'll be performing at Mocambo's tonight. Go see her and keep your nose out of my business. I'd hate to have to break it."

"I'll keep that in mind," I said.

I watched as he walked out of the drugstore and through the window saw him get into a large Chevrolet limousine that I knew was owned by Teddy The Boot.

*****

The cabbie who took me from *Schwab's* to my office six blocks away cussed throughout the entire journey.

What should have taken ten minutes ended up taking twenty-five. I gave him a five cent tip and told him he would have gotten more but I didn't appreciate the cursing.

"Well, fuck you, buddy!" Then for good measure he threw the nickel at me as I got out of his cab. I kinda felt bad for the poor schmuck. Driving a taxi isn't an easy job either.

As I watched him pull away from the curb I turned and stepped into a puddle, soaking my sock through the hole in the sole of my right shoe. I sloshed my way to the doors and entered the dimly lit foyer. The aromas of curry and cardamon that wafted in from the Indian restaurant next door hung in the air. It was a low-rent building that housed small offices leased to ambulance chasers, unscrupulous accountants and seedy theatrical agents. It also rented out cheap studio apartments to down-and-outers. It was the perfect place for someone such as myself, with few clients and little cash.

I took the elevator to the fourth floor and as soon as I stepped out I ran into L.A. mayor Yardley Hemmings. He was dressed to the nines in a tuxedo with tails and a top hat. He looked like the debonair screen idol he could have been if he'd had any acting talent. His movie career ended almost as quickly as it began, so he turned to politics. This was his first term as mayor, and it was obvious he had no real talent for politics either. His connection to Bugsy Seigel and the local mob mostly went unnoticed, but he was in with them thicker than fleas on a dog. Although he was married he had a reputation as a skirt chaser. It was well-known he had a gambling addiction and he spent more time in Las Vegas at the black jack tables and playing the slots than he did in city hall. The mob would exploit Hemmings and his weaknesses eventually.

"Where have you been?" he snapped at me. "I've been waiting here for over an hour."

I pulled my office keys from coat pocket and inserted one into the door. "I didn't know you were coming," I said. "I was having a soda with one of your friends."

"What friend?" His voice was hushed. As if we'd likely be overheard in the empty hallway.

I opened the door, flipped on the lights and walked into my office. "Headlights," I answered over my shoulder. "He denies having anything to do with Jimmy Hayes' murder."

Nearly stepping on the heels of my shoes, the mayor followed me in and slammed the door behind him. "You can't believe what he says. He spent time in Alacatraz for God's sake."

I took off my coat, hung it on the coat stand, then turned and faced him. "For a convict who has spent time on the rock he has a very noticeable gambler's tell," I said.

Hemmings' left eye twitched, which I'd heard was his tell at the gambling tables. "What tell is that?"

"He grinned when he threatened to expose me," I answered with a chuckle. I walked behind my desk, sat in the chair, and took off my shoes and wet socks. "He said he'd let it out about my connection to what Hayes was doing, which made me wonder how he knew about it." I leaned back and put my feet up on the desk. "You're the only person who knew Hayes was giving me a cut from his shakedowns on the Strip."

"What are you suggesting?"

"You have a big mouth when you're around your pals in Vegas," I answered. I wrung my socks, letting the water fall into the pot of the dying fichus plant beside my desk.

His cheeks reddened. "Why would I say anything?"

I laughed out loud. "You really are a bad actor." I leaned towards him. "I'd hate to implicate you in all of this, but I'll sing like a canary to the police if I have to." I pushed my fedora back on my head and locked eyes with him. "Why are you here?"

"I need your promise, now that Hayes is dead, you won't mention to anyone the money he gave me."

"In Hollywood a promise is as worthless as used toilet paper," I said. "As I told you, I'll keep you out of it unless I'm backed against the wall. And Teddy the Boot should stay out of my way if he doesn't want to wind up back in Folsom Prison. It's not a big leap between what Hayes was doing and what Teddy the Boot does. Headlights confirmed that. "

He nervously adjusted his bow tie. "I have less influence with the mob than you might imagine."

"When possible, I try not to imagine," I said. "In Hollywood imagination is only for those working in the movie business."

"In politics imagination can get you booted out of office," he said, then turned and left my office.

I sat at the desk for a while, regretting that I became involved as a link between Hayes and the mayor; a link where dirty money was passed from one set of hands to another. Jimmy Hayes had once been my best friend. I pondered the question, who went bad first, me or him?

I rose from the chair and went to the closet and took out my dinner suit and wingtip shoes.

*****

The traffic clogging the streets consisted mainly taxis and limousines filled with the famous and infamous. They were on their way to clubs and dives prevalent along the strip that stretched from Hollywood to Beverly Hills. Anyone standing on the sidewalk could have thrown a rock at a passing vehicle and easily hit someone on the noggin, a matinee idol sporting a pencil mustache, or perhaps a vamp with a diamond encrusted cigarette holder held between her gloved fingers. Or maybe a screen siren in a mink stole, or a studio big shot. Mobsters and the like rode in chauffeur driven Rolls Royces. The rain continued to fall, producing a symphony of whooshing windshield wipers and squealing tires.

In the back seat of the Yellow Cab I could feel against my rib cage the weight of my snub-nosed .38 I carried in a shoulder holster hidden under my dinner jacket. Hayes had been carrying one just like it when he was shot in the back at close range. I had no intention of letting anyone get that close behind me to allow that to happen to me. The vehicles waiting to unload their well-heeled passengers beneath the striped awnings of the *Mocambo Club* was a block long. From the end of the waiting autos I handed the cabbie his fare and a modest tip and climbed out of the taxi. Immediately, I knew I had made a mistake. Teddy the Boot and two of his henchmen were waiting for me. Taking me by the arms they dragged me into an alleyway.

I didn't say a word before Teddy slapped me. "I don't like dicks who want to tell Teddy the Boot what he should or shouldn't do, see?" he snarled.

That slimy mayor wasted no time getting back to this gangster, I thought.

Teddy was five-foot-four in Cuban heels, but he still had to stand on tiptoes so his bloodshot eyes could glare into mine. He was dressed in a tuxedo which gave me some comfort since I doubted he wanted to enter the club with my blood splattered on it. His breath smelled of licorice, a sign that his love of absinthe hadn't diminished.

"Teddy the Boot had nothing to do with that copper's murder," he said. "Okay, so I didn't like it that the dead copper was shaking down marks in my territory, but I let it go. I can be a forgiving person, see? Anyone who says Teddy the Boot had anything to do with his murder is asking for trouble."

"Sure, Teddy, I see," I mumbled. "But the police ain't going to let this drop. I'm doing this on my own because Hayes was a pal of mine, but eventually I'm going to have to bring them into this."

"The cops are already breathin' down our necks about this murder. They're just itchin' for a reason to blame it on me, see?"

"Yeah, I see."

"Go ahead and find the killer. Teddy the Boot won't stand in your way, see?" He stepped back and brushed the lapels of his jacket, as if wiping away my germs. "But next time come see Teddy the Boot directly if you got questions, see?"

"Sure Teddy, sure," I answered.

He turned to his two goons and snapped his fingers. "Make sure he heard what Teddy the Boot just told him." He walked out of the alley and turned the corner, heading towards the entrance of the club.

His companions came at me with their fists up, prepared to pound Teddy the Boot's message into my thick skull. Apparently someone forgot to tell them I was a trained boxer. After a brief scuffle, I left them lying on the alleyway's pavement, while I dabbed at a scratch on my right check with my handkerchief. I left the alley, straightened my bow tie, and joined the line of the lesser-knowns waiting at the door of the *Mocambo*.

*****

Backed by a full band, Claire LaLong stood at the microphone crooning a love ballad. Her silver sequined ankle-length gown was slit Geisha style to the middle of her thighs and the neckline plunged almost down to her waist. As she swayed in time to the band, what was left of her costume glistened in the glow of the spotlight. Her platinum blonde hair was in homage to the just-late Jean Harlow, and her elbow-length black gloves were encircled by diamond bracelets. When she finished her number the maître d handed her my business card and pointed at me. She stepped down from the stage and walked over to the bar where I was sitting. She moved as if her body joints were assembled with ball bearings, every limb and hips in synchronized motion.

Originally from Ohio, it didn't take long after I'd arrived in Hollywood to learn how to spot a dame that was dangerous. Claire LaLong was a five alarm fire on high heels. I took a fast gulp of my cherry coke and swallowed hard.

"This better be worth my time." She laid my card down on the bar.

"I don't mean to bother you Miss LaLong," I said, trying to sound a bit more confident than I felt. The look in this dame's eyes could turn water to ice. "You and Jimmy Hayes were an item, right?"

Her look suddenly softened. "Yeah, but it was more than that with him. We were engaged to be married."

Hayes told me almost everything, but he'd had kept this secret to the grave. It took me a moment to recover from the shock. "What can you tell me about his murder?"

"You should ask Yardley Hemmings about that," she said, her eyes suddenly scanning the crowded club like a pair of prison searchlights.

"The mayor of L.A?"

"Yeah. The mayor told Jimmy he would kill him if he continued to see me. Yardley Hemmings is obsessed with me. He's been pursuing me even though he knew about Jimmy and me. For Jimmy's safety I tried to break off our engagement, but he said not to worry, that he had some information that would ruin the mayor's career if the mayor tried anything." She brushed a stray strand of hair from her face. "The mayor's

226

here every night that I sing, watching me like a hawk."

"Why didn't you say any of this to the police?" I asked.

"I have my career to think of." She looked down at her gloved fingers. "I begin filming my first movie with Metro in a few weeks and any scandal would ruin everything." She suddenly stiffened, her gaze fixed on something at a distance. I followed her gaze. Standing on the other side of the dance floor was Mayor Hemmings.

She grasped my arm. "You can't be seen talking to me. He'll kill you too." She suddenly turned, quickly walked away, and disappeared beyond the curtains that separated the stage from the dressing rooms.

I looked back to where the mayor had been standing. He was gone.

*****

My small apartment was a few blocks from my office. It overlooked a narrow street lined with bars and pool joints that had neon signs above their doors which flashed and blinked all night. I made enough to pay the rent, but only barely. I've always had a problem keeping up with my bills, even when I had the steady income from being on the police force. This is where my connection to what Jimmy was doing comes in. I'd seen the money he was handing over to Hemmings, who was extorting the money from him. At first I asked for a few dollars as a loan to pay for food and clothes, telling Jimmy I'd repay him as soon as I got a good, paying case. Then I asked for a little more money to get a cavity filled. Then I asked for some other reason. Jimmy never said no, so I kept asking. It was a snowball effect. Before I knew it I was involved to the tune of over two grand, money that had originally been squeezed from bakers, laundry mat and dress shop owners, and other poor schmucks who were just trying to make their way in the world.

I walked into the bedroom, changed into pajamas and a robe, and was about to shut off the lights and go to bed when there was a knock on the door. I looked through the peephole and there stood the mayor. I hardly knew the guy, other than by reputation, and only saw him prior to this night when I was giving him his dough. Maybe all cops are born with the ability to smell the kind of trouble that a rat like Yardley Hemmings brought with them, or maybe it comes with experience, but the stench was strong enough that I picked up my gun before I opened the door.

I opened the door, aiming the gun at him. "What do you want?"

"I saw you at the club talking to Claire LaLong," he said. "Did you know she was engaged to Jimmy Hayes?"

"I found that out tonight. So, what of it?"

He looked up and down the hallway. "Can I come in?" he asked.

I stepped aside and waved him in. He immediately went to the window and looked down at the rain soaked street.

"You expecting someone?" I asked as I closed the door and put my gun on a hall stand where I kept my mail.

"I thought I was being followed." he poked at the curtain a little more, turned away from the window and looked straight at me. "I'm hopelessly in love with Claire. Always have been."

"So she told me, but she phrased it differently," I said.

Then there was a light tap on the door.

"It's getting to be like the train station around here," I said as I turned to the door and peered through the peep hole. It was Claire LaLong. I opened the door and immediately regretted it. She raised a gun in her right hand and aimed it at my head. She was the trouble that Yardley brought with him.

"Step back," she said icily.

I took several steps back as she walked into my apartment and closed the door behind her. She slowly shifted the aim of her gun back and forth from me to Yardley. "Imagine my luck finding the two of you together. The last time I had this kind of luck was when Jimmy wanted to take a hike up to the Hollywood sign. It was where he first proposed to me. Killing him there meant there was no chance of it being seen by anyone. It put an end to his slapping me around and threatening to ruin my film career even before it began. He said he would take me down with him if I didn't do what he said. I tried to break it off with him, but men get attached to me like butter on bread.

"Claire, I...." Yardley started.

She pulled the trigger, shooting him square in the middle of his forehead. He fell to the floor like a sack of wet spaghetti. She then aimed the gun back at me.

"Jimmy told me what he was doing and who else was involved," she said. "I've been around enough to know that eventually the mob would get to the three of you. That's what the police are going to believe happened to you when this is all over and done with."

"It doesn't have to be like this," I said.

"Shut up," she snapped. "I'm going to be a big movie star,

the biggest. The director of the movie I'm doing predicts I'll get an Oscar for this role. He says I'll be that good. I don't know you like I knew your pal Jimmy, or like that garbage lying on your floor, but what you were taking from folks you don't even know makes you just as worthless."

"Look, I made a mistake. I'm actually a nice guy."

"What's that saying about nice guys?" she asked with a malevolent smile.

She then aimed her gun at my head and pulled the trigger.

A Good Night's Sleep
Bobby Mathews

Corley Brown wasn't fidgeting. He wasn't feigning sleep. He wasn't doing any of the million little tells a murderer's body uses to betray him. He seemed perfectly calm, sitting there and waiting for someone to come and take his statement. His hands rested on the tabletop, steel handcuffs glinting in the low light of a flickering bulb. His wide shoulders were square, and his hair was thin and dry and brown, long over the top to cover a spot of male pattern baldness. His eyes were clear and bright, and he was smiling.

It's the smile I can't forget.

It wasn't a smirk. It wasn't sarcastic or mean. It wasn't hurtful. Corley Brown had the smile of a happy man, and I couldn't understand it. Happy men don't kill their wives. They don't come home from their job at the insurance office and use a framing hammer on their wife and children. They don't leave the bodies in the living room and go upstairs to their bedrooms to nap while their neighbors call the police.

But that's exactly what Corley Brown had done.

I took the thin case file into the room with me, a few pages of notes, initial forensic details of how the Brown family had been beaten to death and left where they lay. The cops who found the bodies—veterans both, guys with more than a decade on the job—had to run the other direction and thrown up. All while Corley Brown slept on, unaware.

Brown didn't stand up when I entered the room. He couldn't. The small gray table where he sat featured a large O ring bolted into the center. The chain of Brown's handcuffs ran through it.

"You ready to talk about it?" I asked as I tossed the buff-colored file embossed with the Las Vegas Metro Police emblem onto the table.

"What do you want me to say? You know what happened just as well as I do."

I dragged a chair out, turned it around and straddled it so I could fold my arms over the back. In silence I opened the file and looked at it, not really doing anything, just letting my eyes skip across the pictures of the three victims. There was Rannie, Corley's wife, and Bradley, who would have been ten in a couple of weeks, and Abigail, who was four. None of them would be getting any older.

I took a white card out of my shirt pocket and read Miranda to him. The uniforms at the scene had already done that, gotten the arrest on video, but I had learned a long time ago that you had to be careful so that there were no questions later.

"I know what happened," I said. "What I want to know is *why*."

Brown shrugged his shoulders and yawned. I could see molars in bad need of a dentist.

"I don't really give a damn what you want," he said. "The

why don't matter, does it? *Why* just fucks everything up for you. I did it. I'll cop to it. Now let's quit fucking around. Put me back in my cell and let me get some rest."

I shook my head.

"It doesn't work that way. I ask the questions. You answer them."

Corley stared at me, and gave another little shrug.

"Whatever, man," he said.

"Why did you kill your wife?"

"Are you married?"

"Sure," I said.

"Then you ought to understand."

I laughed. I couldn't help myself. I've been married for thirteen years. Some of those years were good, and some were bad. Sometimes I wanted to hug Lacey, and sometimes I wanted to strangle her. So in some respects I guess I knew exactly what he meant.

"Was there something specific that set you off today?"

When Corley said no, I believed him. Whatever happened in that gray little bungalow on Third Avenue, it had been building for a long time. I kept my eyes on his, watched how steady they were. It was unsettling. He looked at peace, the sonofabitch.

"Tell me what it was about," I said.

He laughed.

"You're like a dog after a goddamn bone," he said.

I tapped the gold shield hanging from the lapel of my JC Penney suit. "It's my business."

A Good Night's Sleep

Corley Brown's eyes skimmed the room. He wasn't uneasy. He was just looking at his surroundings. Interview One isn't much of a room. If you've ever seen a cop show on TV, you've seen one just like it.

"I never thought I'd end up here," he said. "I thought I could wait it out, you know?"

I didn't say anything, and after a long moment, Corley Brown sighed. He looked me up and down for a moment.

"You got kids? Of course you do. You got the look. Solid citizen all around, right? I could probably tell your life story. Army, right? Used the GI Bill to go to college. Got out after twenty, caught onto the cops right away."

Almost. I'd been in the Navy. Took the exam for the fire department and the cops. Cops came through first. I didn't tell Brown any of that, though. I didn't have to. He was just warming up.

"I sell insurance. Tough game, you know? Auto, home, whole life. Lotta stress. You gotta make sales to keep the money coming in. Pressure all the time."

Since silence was my best interrogation technique, I kept at it. I cocked my head to show I was listening.

"Rannie just—it was a lot of things. We got the country club membership, last year's Lexus. Mortgage isn't upside down, but it's close. Always fighting about money. Kids need clothes. Tennis rackets for the club. But we can't just go down to Wal-Mart and pick up a twenty-dollar stick. Got rackets? Great. Gotta have lessons. It bears down on a man.

"This time it was landscaping. We just had the yard done three years ago, but now she wanted a—what the hell did she call it?—a goddamn water feature."

Now I did interrupt. "A what?"

"A fucking fountain. She wanted to put up a fountain in the front yard, re-do the driveway into a circle with crushed oyster shells, that sort of thing. You know how much money that shit costs?"

I thought about it for a minute. The casinos and hotels all had water features, but they also had money to burn. Even if the Browns were rich, that kind of thing was just throwing money down the drain. So to speak.

"You killed your wife over a fountain?"

Corley Brown looked puzzled, puffed his lips out and blew a lock of his dry brown hair away from his forehead.

"No," he said. "I killed her because she tried to stop me from killing the kids."

My hands lost all sensation. I heard the pen clatter to the scuffed linoleum floor. I couldn't think of anything to say, so I just sat there for a moment. I tried to get to my feet, but my legs bent at unnatural angles. Finally I lunged for the door and made it into the hallway before I puked. I scrambled away from the hot vomit, my numb feet kicking at the floor. I couldn't feel anything. My bladder felt like it would let go at any moment. I put my back against the wall and covered my head with the dead sticks of my arms.

The tears came then, and I let them. Those children—those babies—I couldn't get them out of my head. A shadow blocked out the overhead light for a moment, and I peeked out from between the protective shell of my arms. Eric Church, my captain, had his hands on his hips. He was looking down at me like he'd never seen me before.

"Get back in there," he said. My captain isn't known for his soft, fuzzy side. "I'll get someone to clean this mess up."

Church put out his hand, and I reached across the thousand-mile gap between us to take it. He hauled me to my feet and slapped me on the back. In close, he whispered in my ear.

"It's the worst goddamn thing I ever heard. You've got to finish it, though. You know that, don't you?"

I did know it. It's part of what makes a cop who he is. You gotta be able to take the shit that comes with the job. It's part of being a stand-up guy, part of that thin blue line that protects society from itself. If your brother officers sense weakness in you, that they can't count on you when the shit goes down, it could spell curtains for your career. If they can't trust you—or even think they can't—then you're out. *Persona non grata.*

Church pumped my hand once, hard, and we gave each other a firm little nod. He bent and handed me the brown manila evidence folder that lay on the floor where I'd dropped it. I felt like the quarterback being asked to go back in and win the game with a minute left and no timeouts remaining. There was sweat on my neck and face, and my bladder was full to bursting.

I ignored everything else and crossed the hall back to Interview One. When I opened the door. Corley Brown looked sympathetic, the asshole.

"Everything OK?" He asked. His tone was neutral, slightly concerned. No mocking sarcasm. I couldn't figure out what the hell was wrong with him.

"Fine," I said. "Right as rain." I took my seat again. I was trying to pick up where we'd left off, but I couldn't seem to find the thread of our conversation. I shuffled his file around a little and cleared my throat.

"Your wife was trying to stop you from killing your children," I said.

He nodded, his green eyes bright with earnestness.

"Of course," he said, "she was a good mother. You know how mama bears are, don't want you to mess with their cubs. I guess it's genetic." Brown paused for a moment and stared through the window to the world outside. That window was two panes thick with chicken wire sandwiched in the middle. You could see a little bit of Fire Station No. 6 across Stella Lake Street, but not much else. He wasn't going anywhere, and I still don't know what he was looking for.

"What had the kids done?" I asked.

Brown didn't answer me. He'd wound down like an old watch. He finally rattled his cuffs and said, "Can you take these off?"

I shook my head.

"Not right now. We still have some things to discuss."

Corley Brown yawned again, big enough to make me cover my own mouth.

"I'm so tired," he said. "Tired like this, it gets down in your bones like cancer, and no matter how much sleep you get, I guess it's never enough."

I grunted like someone punched me in the gut. But I didn't have anything to say, so I just listened to Brown talk.

"Bradley was a talker, like me. Talk, talk, talk all the time. He couldn't keep his mouth shut. Got in trouble for it at school and at church. And when Abigail came along, I just—some folks weren't ever meant to be parents, you know what I mean?"

I couldn't bring myself to say anything. I didn't trust my voice.

"Anyway, I put up with it as long as I could. I guess today was the day that everything snapped. I took that hammer and, well, I did what I did. I got to Bradley, and then Rannie tried to stop me. I hit her one good time. I didn't want to kill her, but, well, she got in the way."

I could see it all in my mind's eye. Corley Brown getting home from work, tired like usual. Inside the house, shrugging off his coat and tie, maybe rolling his sleeves up. All he wanted was rest, but then the twin tornadoes of his two kids blow in and make him even more exhausted. All that talk and all of that noise, the constant commotion. Maybe it didn't drive him crazy, but it drove him somewhere close and let him walk the rest of the way there.

"So that's it?" I asked. "You were just tired ... of being a parent? You kill your whole family because you're, what, too lazy to take care of them?"

Corley Brown's eyes blazed at me, spittle in the corners of his mouth.

"Do you know how long it's been since I've had a decent night's sleep? Kid cries in the middle of the night and somebody has to go to 'em, wipe their nose, get 'em water, right? Well, the other parent doesn't just lay in bed and sleep, man. Every time one of 'em woke up, I was either right there with 'em or layin' in the bed and listening while Rannie was up. All I wanted was some sleep."

And then he was done. I waited for several minutes to see what else Brown might say, but there was nothing.

"Are you sorry you did it?" I ask. I didn't need to know for the confession. I was genuinely curious.

When Corley Brown smiled at me, I believed he was the happiest man in the world. Certainly he was the happiest man I've ever seen.

"That nap," he said. "Before your beat cops got there? That was the best I've slept in ten years. I don't regret a damned thing."

There was more, but none of it mattered. I had his confession—easiest one of my career—and I was gonna do everything in my power to make sure Corley Brown spent the rest of his life locked up somewhere. The captain congratulated me when I finished my report. I didn't even have the energy to say thanks, just tipped him a mock salute and headed for the garage.

The unmarked unit is a perk of the job, a late-model Dodge Charger with buggy whip antennas and no hubcaps. It looks exactly like what it is—a cop car. But the seats are leather and comfortably low-sprung, and the AC ran cold enough to circumvent the desert heat on even the worst days.. I made the twenty-minute commute to Summerlin in silence, just like I do every day. I thumbed the button on the garage door opener attached to my visor and pulled in still thinking about Corley Brown and his hammer. Every blow freeing him from obligation, every hit a strike against the chains of responsibility that held him moored to the real world, this stark reality.

Finally, I hit the garage opener again and listened as the big door rattled closed. I shut the car off and got out, wandered over to my little workbench. I keep my tools in a big steel cart that stands about four feet high. The second drawer down holds a variety of wrenches and hammers. I took out the framing hammer, a big old one that my Dad bought for me when we worked construction together near Lake Meade the summer after I graduated high school. The steel head weighed about thirty-two ounces, all by itself. After a summer of using it, the muscles in my forearms looked like cables.

I held the hammer in my hand and swung it a couple of times, just to remember how it felt. I could still see Corley Brown and his family in the back of my mind.

The door to the house opened up behind me, and Lacey stuck her head into the garage.

"Hey," she said. "When are you coming in? I could use some help with the kids."

"Right now," I said.

Then I put the hammer back in the drawer and went inside.

Soiled Dove
Michael Bracken

In the early morning fog rolling in off the lake, I found Ashley Manford's year-old Lexus in the country club's parking lot, an overnight-guest pass propped up behind the windshield. I left my SUV next to it and walked to the far end of the marina where houseboats, vacated for the season, were lined up like floating suburban tract homes. Lights on inside the *Finnegans Wake,* a forty-eight-foot Navigator, caught my attention, so I stepped from the dock onto its foredeck and tapped on the sliding glass door. When I received no response, I slid the door open and stuck my head inside. "Ashley?"

Again I received no response, so I entered the cabin and made my way aft. Dirty dishware from the previous evening's meal occupied the dinette to my right, and a blue backpack, open to reveal *The Norton Anthology of English Literature* and other college textbooks, lay on the sofa to my left. A single saucepan remained on the stovetop and another occupied the sink. On a small counter in the head lay an empty pill bottle that had once contained sleeping pills prescribed to Ashley, a sterling silver purity ring engraved with "true love waits," and a home pregnancy test stick, the positive result all too evident.

As I checked the two lower-deck staterooms, each just large

enough to contain a double bed, a bass boat sped through the marina toward the open water of the lake, rocking the *Finnegans Wake*. I paused a moment to let the boat settle and then descended to a third stateroom below deck.

The young woman splayed across the bed within had been dead for several hours, so I retrieved my cell phone and dialed 9-1-1.

*****

The fog had burned off before Lt. Danvers and I stood on the dock watching the EMTs wheel Ashley Manford's body away. Without turning, he asked, "How'd you tumble to this?"

"She hadn't taken her father's calls in more than a week," I said. "He hired me to find her."

"Why you?"

"He filed a missing person's with your department and with campus police, but had the impression no one took him seriously."

"We get a lot of calls from helicopter parents after their little darlings get their first taste of freedom. We can't chase after every delicate flower that wants to spread its pollen."

"Somebody should have checked on this one."

*****

At police headquarters, I made a full report about my discovery of Ashley Manford's body but didn't reveal that I'd photographed the empty pill bottle and the rest of the scene. As I walked out, I called my client—Peyton Manford, pastor of the Garland Revival Baptist Church—to let him know I'd found his daughter.

"Did you tell Ashley to call?" He noticed my hesitation.

"What's wrong?"

I told him how I'd found her. "I gave the police your name as next of kin. They should be contacting you soon."

This time he hesitated.

"I'm sorry," I said. "Maybe if I'd found her sooner…."

*****

I had encountered several bodies during my years as a patrol officer, but Ashley Manford's was the first I had encountered since becoming a private investigator, and I was uncomfortably numb when I finally returned to my downtown apartment. After opening a beer, I settled onto my couch to watch college football, hoping to drive the image of the dead co-ed from my mind.

ESPN was broadcasting the local university's home game. Though I watched many games, I was a fair-weather fan and had not supported the team through the years it spent wandering in the desert. The possibility that the Revival Rhinos might ever find the Promised Land seemed unlikely until a new coach gave the team direction. Each year since his arrival three seasons earlier, the team had improved and now, halfway through the season and playing in their new stadium, they were 6-0. With the Heaven Eleven playing offense, no other team's defense stood a chance, and sportscasters were throwing around the idea that the Rhinos might have an immaculate season.

*****

While I watched football, Pastor Manford came down from Garland to identify his daughter's body. He spent the rest of the weekend in a cheap motel on the outskirts of town, unable to find anything better because football fans filled the best hotels. Monday morning, the medical examiner completed his work and released Ashley's body. After collecting her Lexus from the impound lot and making arrangements to have his daughter sent home, Pastor Manford visited my office. He found me behind my desk, nose deep in another client's case file.

I'd seen his photograph on his church's website—standing in his office before a wall filled with certificates and awards, including his Bachelor of Arts Diploma from Texas A&M, his Master of Divinity Diploma from Seminary, and his United States Army Honorable Discharge Certificate—but I'd been hired over the phone, and so I didn't immediately recognize him when I looked up. In his early forties, Manford was clean-shaven and had graying hair trimmed fashionably short. He wore a long-sleeve button-down black shirt with the sleeves rolled halfway up his forearms, dark Wrangler jeans, and black cowboy boots.

I closed the file and motioned toward one of the empty chairs on his side of the desk. Though I'd completed the job for which I'd been hired, I didn't think it appropriate to hand him an invoice while he was still grieving. Instead, I said what most everyone says under the circumstance. "I'm sorry for your loss."

He didn't acknowledge my condolences. Instead, he said, "They told me she was pregnant."

I'd suspected as much, but said nothing.

"I want to know who the father is," he said. "I want to know who soiled my daughter."

"He hasn't come forward?"

"I doubt he ever will," Manford said. "Only a coward would leave my daughter alone to deal with her situation."

"And you? What did you do?"

"What could I have done?" he asked. "She didn't tell me what she was going through."

Ashley's mother had died when she was young, and no father, no matter how well meaning, could fill a mother's role.

"So," Manford said as he pulled a prewritten check from his shirt pocket and tossed it on my desk. "You find the boy who put her in a family way. We need to have a come-to-Jesus meeting."

I didn't look at the check until after he'd left, and I found the amount more than enough to cover what he owed for my first assignment and get me started on the next. Out of client loyalty, I pushed aside the case file I'd been reading.

*****

The *Finnegans Wake* was registered to Kelly Flynn, and it didn't take much effort to learn she was an English professor at the university. When I knocked on her office door Tuesday afternoon, I heard her voice call from within. "Come in, Terry. I have your paper."

I pushed the door open.

She looked up, surprised. "You're not who I was expecting," she said from behind her desk. She wasn't what I was expecting, either. She was near my age, with auburn hair cut in a bob, fair skin dusted with freckles across her nose, and emerald eyes that sparkled with reflected light as she examined me in return. "What can I do for you?'

I showed her my I.D. and placed one of my business cards

on her desk. My name—Studebaker Johnson—along with my cellphone number and private investigator's license number were printed on the face of the card. I told her I wanted to ask a few questions about one of her students.

"I'm sorry, I can't—"

"Ashley Manford," I said. "Her father hired me."

A young man stepped into the office behind me before the professor could respond.

"Office hours end at five," she told me. "I could talk to you after."

I took a chance and said, "Preston's for dinner?"

She hesitated a moment, her gaze darting to the student standing beside me before answering. "Five-thirty."

"I'll be waiting."

I left Professor Flynn and crossed campus to the university health center.

*****

I'd earlier examined my photograph of Ashley's pill bottle, knew the prescription had been filled at the university pharmacy, and suspected the prescriber was on the health services staff. I bulled my way in to see Dr. Hahn and found an overworked man nearing the end of his medical career who had no tolerance for bullshit. I showed him the photo of Ashley's empty pill bottle, and told him who I was and what I wanted.

"Anxiety," Dr. Hahn said after he checked Ashley's medical records. "She was having trouble sleeping, said she was having nightmares."

"About?"

He glanced at her file. "Doesn't say."

"Did you ask?"

"Do you have any idea how many whiney, hypochondriac kids I see in a day? I'm not here to make friends with them."

"Did you know she was pregnant?"

"I wouldn't have prescribed those pills if I did."

I was about to ask another question when he silenced me.

"You think I had something to do with her death? Let me disabuse you of that notion. If that girl wanted to kill herself, she'd have found a way without the pills." He stood. "We done?"

*****

I made my way to the dorm where Ashley lived while attending the university. Just as she had when I visited a few weeks earlier, the barrel-shaped guard would not let me past the lobby. Officer Randall said, "Women only."

I shoved my I.D. in front of her, but she didn't even glance at it.

"I remember you," she said as I pulled my I.D. back. "And the answer's still no."

"You know the girl died."

"I saw the news."

"I need to talk to her friends."

"I told you before. She didn't have any."

"You didn't tell me why."

"Goody two-shoes," she said. "Lorded it over the other

girls, but I had the feeling she had a darker side."

"Why's that?"

"She's a PK," Officer Randall said before correcting herself. "She was a PK, and I never met a preacher's kid who was anywhere near as squeaky clean as they pretend to be."

"You saying Ashley was doing things she shouldn't have?"

"I wouldn't put it past her."

"But you never witnessed her doing anything inappropriate?"

Officer Randall shook her head. "I don't get out from behind the desk much, and most of these kids are too smart to do anything in front of me, afraid I'll report their silly infractions. I catch even a hint of alcohol on their breath, they'll be up before the disciplinary committee, put on probation, reported to their parents, and God knows what else."

"That seems harsh."

"Those are the rules," Officer Randall said, "and it's my job to enforce them."

"What's happened to her things?"

"Campus police cleaned out her room as soon as they heard about her death."

*****

The rest of the afternoon proved as fruitless as my attempt to get past the security guard at Ashley's dorm. At twenty past five I took a booth at Preston's and sat where I could watch the door. I rose when Professor Flynn entered a few minutes later, and she walked directly to my table.

"Professor Flynn—"

"Kelly," she corrected.

"Kelly, then," I said, returning her smile with one of my own. "Thanks for meeting with me."

I let her settle into the other side of the booth before I sat. We exchanged pleasantries about the weather until the waitress interrupted to ask if we were ready to order. We were.

After the waitress walked away, the conversation shifted.

Kelly said, "I know you have questions about the young woman who died on my houseboat and you're probably itching to get them answered."

"Ashley was a student of yours."

"Yes," she said. "She was in my Intro to Brit Lit class last semester. She was quite a good student, too. Always did her assigned reading before class, turned her homework in on time, and scored high on all the tests."

"And outside of class?"

"She latched onto me, visiting often during office hours, even when she was no longer one of my students. I had the feeling she was searching for a mother figure."

"And that was you?"

She shrugged. "She wasn't the first and likely won't be the last. Many of these young men and women are away from home for the first time in their lives and they're completely lost."

"So how did Ashley wind up in your houseboat?"

"Something was bothering her. She wouldn't tell me what it was, but she said she didn't feel comfortable staying in her dorm and she couldn't go home to her father." She sat back a little, relaxing. "I gave her the keys to the *Finnegans Wake* and told her she could stay as long as she liked. When she hadn't been to her classes in a week, I went to see her. She told me she was pregnant. I tried to talk to her about her options, but she wouldn't listen."

"Did she tell you who the father was?"

"She didn't know. She claimed she'd never had sex."

"Do you believe in immaculate conception?"

"No." She stared directly into my eyes. "But I believe—believed—Ashley."

Our dinner arrived. I suspected I wouldn't learn any more about Ashley, so I asked Kelly if she enjoyed teaching.

"Things are fine inside the classroom," she said, "but we're expected to toe the party line at all times—no drinking, no smoking, no dancing where students might see us—and we aren't allowed to publically criticize anything the university does."

"I'll bet there's a lot to criticize."

She didn't take the bait. Instead, she said, "What about you? Do you enjoy what you do?"

"Not when I stumble into cases like this," I told her.

Later, over dessert and coffee, our conversation grew personal.

"Are you married, Mr. Johnson?"

"Divorced." I'd not anticipated the question, but I followed up with, "You?"

"Three years now, but we knew it was over long before

that." She toyed with her empty ring finger. "He left when the new football coach took over and cleaned house."

I didn't remember any coaches named Flynn and said so.

"Dumbowsky," she said. "I never took his name, so I didn't have to take mine back when we divorced."

*****

Despite the dorm security guard's effort to cast aspersions on Ashley Manford's character, the girl certainly appeared squeaky clean. During the next few days I talked to some of the young women who lived in the same dorm as my client's daughter. I learned that Ashley did not smoke, did not drink, did not use drugs, and everyone believed she was a virgin who had taken the chastity vow in high school and fully meant to honor it until her wedding night.

I had her class schedule from when her father first hired me, so I again visited her professor—who still wouldn't talk to me—and tried to talk to some of her classmates. Those willing to talk confirmed what I'd learned from her dorm mates, though her male classmates were less kind in their assessment of Ashley, telling me she acted as if she were too good for them.

*****

I didn't recognize the number when my cellphone rang Thursday afternoon, but I answered anyway.

"Do you like football, Mr. Johnson?"

I recognized Professor Flynn's voice, so I said, "As much as any man."

"I have tickets to Saturday's game and I'm wondering if you'd care to join me."

"Shall we meet there?"

"No," she said. "You can pick me up."

She provided her address.

*****

Friday, I finally learned something about Ashley that no one else had mentioned. A pimple-faced young woman approached me outside of the science building. "You the guy asking questions about Ashley Manford?"

I told her I was.

She looked around. "She was a Rhino Girl, escorted football players to events, showed prospects around campus, told them how great a place this is. That's the cush job."

"How did you know her?"

"Bible study," she said. "A group of us meet every Wednesday. She once told us about being inducted as a Rhino Girl, but she never mentioned it again. It's like a secret sorority or something."

"And you think—"

"Ashley changed after that," the girl said. "She was always holier-than-thou, but not long after she became a Rhino Girl, she seemed more high-strung. Something was wrong and she wouldn't say what it was. Then she disappeared. Now she's dead."

I didn't learn anything more from the young woman. When she refused to give me her name, I slipped her my card and told her to contact me if she had any other information she wanted to share.

*****

Kelly wore a loose-fitting university sweatshirt and form-fitting jeans when I arrived at her McMansion. She made me wait on the porch while she grabbed her purse and a jacket. During the drive to the stadium we discussed the team's chances that day before she asked, "Are you having any luck finding the young man who impregnated Ashley?"

"Almost everyone I've met said she walked on water. She didn't drink, smoke, or do any recreational drugs. She took the chastity vow in high school and everyone who knew her is convinced she never broke that vow. Even you told me she'd never had sex."

"So how did she get pregnant?"

I had no answer, so I said nothing until I joined the long line of cars trying to enter the stadium parking lot. Then I said, "Did you know she was a Rhino Girl?"

The professor looked up sharply. "A Rhino girl? Those girls are nothing but bait. They pick the prettiest girls and parade them in front of football prospects, make those young men think—"

She stopped herself and I had to prompt her to continue.

"My ex-husband told me stories about what those girls were expected to do. Those who didn't comply didn't remain Rhino Girls for long."

At Revival Baptist University, just as at many universities, the football program is made of Teflon. Football players ace tests for which they don't study, receive grades they don't earn, and pass classes they don't attend, all because they earn millions for the university. At Revival, the new coach was hailed as the second coming when the team started winning, and well-healed donors had built the team a new stadium and a new practice facility. The team was playing its first season in the new facilities, and they were winning.

*****

Monday morning, the coordinator of the Rhino Girls refused to talk to me, even refused to acknowledge that Ashley had been a member.

"It's a simple question," I said. "Was Ashley Manford a Rhino Girl or not?"

"If you don't leave on your own, Mr. Johnson," the tightly wound woman said. "I'll have campus police escort you out."

We stared at one another for a moment. Then I turned away and let myself out of her office.

After that, I focused my attention on the football team, and I spread word that I was interested in talking to any player who knew Ashley. The team was a closed community, so another two weeks passed before my efforts panned out. By then I'd been seen around town in the professor's company, our relationship moving almost too fast for me to keep up.

One afternoon, a walk-on punter I recognized from the football program I'd picked up at the game I'd attended with Kelly, caught my attention.

"I can't be seen with you," Carson Greer said, so that night I found myself sitting in my SUV behind an abandoned H-E-B slated for demolition. Precisely at eleven p.m., he tapped on the window and I rolled it down.

"Don't get out. This won't take long." Carson told me how he knew Ashley and how he and two other players had accompanied her while showing two prospects around campus. "The guys knew she wouldn't put out, and that she didn't drink, so one of them slipped roofies into her Dr Pepper."

He played a video on his phone, turning the phone so I could see the screen.

After Ashley passed out, the four other players took turns with her, showing no more concern than if she had been a blow-up doll.

"And you?" I demanded. "Did you?"

He shook his head. "I could never."

"But you did nothing to stop them."

"You don't know what it's like," he said. "I'm just a walk-on, and I've seen what they do to guys who don't fit in. I just want to play ball, Mr. Johnson. That's all I want to do, but I knew this wasn't right."

After his teammates finished with Ashley, Carson said, he cleaned her up, dressed her, and left her sitting outside her dorm.

I could identify all four of the players in the video, but I had him confirm their names. They were all part of the Heaven Eleven, the eleven offensive line starters who were leading the Revival Rhinos toward their best season ever.

"Has anyone else seen this?"

Carson shook his head. "After Ashley died, I didn't know what to do. Now I've shown you, maybe you can do something about it, but not with this."

Before I could stop him, he deleted the video.

*****

After I reviewed my notes the next morning, I realized that Ashley had visited health services a week after the assault. She apparently didn't remember what happened to her, but it nonetheless traumatized her.

I stopped asking about Ashley and tried to learn more about other Rhino Girls and their relationships with football players. I soon learned that several had been victims of non-consensual contact. Because the girls were in violation of school rules at the time of their assaults—drinking and being out after curfew the two most common violations cited—they were afraid to report the incidents. They feared being suspended, expelled, or reported to their parents. Some even thought they brought the assaults on themselves. The few who tried to report the assaults to campus police were discouraged from filing formal reports. One who dared to file a complaint with the city's police department was later expelled when she admitted to consuming alcohol at the time of the event. None of the football players were ever disciplined.

Campus police took to following me, but never approaching me directly. One afternoon when I was visiting Kelly in her office, one of the officers poked his nose in. He glared at me as he asked, "You okay, Professor Flynn?"

"I'm fine, Charlie," she told him.

"This man isn't bothering you, is he?"

"Not at all."

"He's been bothering a lot of people," the officer said. "You let me know if he bothers you."

"I will, Charlie," she said. "I'll let you know."

After the officer left, she turned to me. "What was that all about?"

"I'm on to something," I said. "I think the athletic department—or maybe just the football program—is covering up something far worse than what I was hired to find."

"Things have changed under the new coach," Kelly said. "The players weren't saints when my ex-husband coached, but there have been rumors that the new couch is bringing in players with questionable morals."

*****

I took Kelly to dinner that night. Afterward, she invited me inside for the first time. "Would you like something to drink, Stu? I have Balcones."

I couldn't think of any reason to decline the offer, so I said, "Sure."

A few drinks led to a few kisses, and as we kissed Kelly took my hand and guided it to her breast.

After a moment I withdrew my hand and said, "I think I should go."

She caught my wrist. "So soon?"

"We've been drinking," I said. "Let's not let the alcohol make decisions for us."

She stared into my eyes. "I made my decision before I opened the bottle," she said. "Don't let me think I made the wrong one."

She took my hand and led me into her bedroom, where the covers were already turned back.

She unbuttoned my shirt and stared at the ugly pucker in my shoulder, the result of a shoot-out with a drug dealer that left him in Huntsville wearing an ostomy bag and me with early retirement. Kelly touched it and looked up at me. The scar fascinated every woman who'd ever seen it, so I knew what she was going to ask. I said, "No, it doesn't hurt. Not after all this time."

We didn't speak again until after, when we lay together in her bed.

*****

Two days later, I was roused from sleep by a telephone call from an unfamiliar police officer named Harvey Edwards who suggested I meet him in the emergency room of the local hospital. He wouldn't tell me why until I arrived.

He held up one of my business cards, one that had been crumpled and then flattened. "We brought a woman in a little while ago. She's unconscious, doesn't have any form of I.D., but she did have this in her hand. I need to know if you recognize her."

I told him I'd handed my card to nearly every woman on the Revival Baptist University campus, so I didn't expect to make a positive identification. That changed when he opened the door.

Professor Kelly Flynn lay on the bed.

I rushed to her side. "What happened?"

"We don't know," Edwards said from behind me. "Someone called 9-1-1 and told us where to find her. How do you know her?"

I told him I'd been dating the professor, that she owned the houseboat where Ashley Manford's body had been found, and that he should phone Lt. Danvers.

I remained at Kelly's side the rest of the day, and when she finally came around late that evening, she seemed surprised to see me.

"What happened?" I asked.

She told me two large men in dark clothing and stocking masks had grabbed her in her garage as she was returning home from the university. They put a bag over her face, pushed her into the back seat of a car, and drove her to the abandoned H-E-B where I'd met with the walk-on punter. Then they'd beaten her unconscious.

"Why?"

"They don't have any leverage with you," she said, "except through me. They want you to stop asking questions about Ashley."

*****

I knew I was unlikely to learn any more about Ashley's assault, and I hadn't been hired to investigate the activities of the entire football team, so I decided to wrap things up. I drove to Pastor Manford's church in Garland and met him in his office. I opened a copy of the football program I had picked up a few weeks earlier and placed it on the desk in front of the pastor. I had circled photos of LaDavid Washington, Roy Rickers, Juan Montoya, and Ed Huley. "I've narrowed it down to these four young men."

"You can't be any more certain than this?"

I told him what the players had done to his daughter.

The pastor's eyes narrowed as I spoke. Through clenched his teeth he asked, "How do you know?"

I told him about the video, and I told him the video no

longer existed.

"So there's no proof?"

"The only witness, the young man who took the video, is unlikely to testify against his teammates."

Pastor Manford stared directly into my eyes and said, "Those boys might not have put the pills in my daughter's hand, but they killed her just same."

*****

Kelly didn't feel safe returning to her home when she was released from the hospital on Friday, so I took her to the *Finnegans Wake,* and we spent the night together. As I was preparing breakfast and listening to the news the next morning, I learned about the murders of four Revival Baptist University football players, all members of the Heaven Eleven and each shot to death in his own bed.

The Revival Rhinos forfeited that day's playoff game, instead hosting a candlelight vigil in the new stadium. The community was rightfully outraged, and remained so until investigators examined the dead players' cellphones and discovered video evidence of numerous assaults on female members of the university community. The severity of the assaults ranged from coerced toplessness to rape to the violent beating of Professor Flynn, and each member of the Heaven Eleven was ultimately implicated in one or more crimes, as were many others.

As the investigation expanded beyond the murdered players to the rest of the team, the coaches, and the support staff, several young women identified in the videos and many who had previously attempted to report similar assaults, sued the university. With Title IX and other lawsuits flying, the entire football coaching staff, the athletic director, and the university president were terminated. Several players were charged with crimes and many others lost their athletic scholarships. NCAA opened an investigation. The strength coach and a defensive lineman were convicted of the assault of Professor Kelly Flynn, who retired after receiving a healthy cash settlement from the university. Carson Greer transferred to another university but did not return to football. Through it all, Ashley Manford's suicide was not connected to any of the other events, and the murders of the players who assaulted her remain unsolved.

None of this will bring back Pastor Manford's soiled dove, but he paid his bill promptly, and I haven't spoken to him since that day in his office when I'd pointed out the four young men who assaulted his daughter.

A Winter's Day

June Lorraine Roberts

It's a sharp-winter, sandy day. A day when the wind blows sand in your eyes making them brim over. One piece of grit feels like a hunk of pumice, grinding against my cornea. I press my fingers to my eye, the tears warm against my skin.

It's the kind of day your stupid cousin spends at the beach anyway. Flapping around in the waves like an idiot. I sit farther back along the sand in the sea grass and scrub. Huddled in my hoodie, arms wrapped tight against my body

My head is turned away from the water, but I keep one eye on her. It may be Florida, but today it's only 61 degrees. She laughs at me shivering in the sand.

The same kind of laugh she bellowed when I found her in bed with my boyfriend, 15-years ago. That braying laugh even now like a cheese grater on my shins.

It's a sharp-winter, sandy day and the afternoon grows late. I can't seem to budge whatever is grinding inside my eye. A couple walking their dog turn their collars up against the strong breeze. They shake their heads at the woman in the water but don't look my way.

The wind catches their voices as they yell caution to my cousin. She flips them the finger and pulls from the bottle.

Tequila is her drink of choice in Florida. Fuel for her antics and today, protection from the cold.

It used to be vodka, her hand waving the bottle at me while laughing in bed with my boyfriend so long ago. Memories of other times run across my mindscape as the ruckus from the water continues. The lies told my family that they believed.

The shoplifting she blamed on me. The joints she said were mine. The pregnancy test-kit found in the bathroom garbage. Cousin was a busy girl back then.

It's a sharp-winter, sandy day as laughter from the water changes from a bray to a bark. I look up and see a pelican's brown body lifting from the water beside her, flying away with its prey.

Moving to SW Florida years ago had been a relief, and not just from the Vermont cold. But she lives here now, all false hugs and shrill compliments like nothing happened. Like she never happened to me.

More sand in my hair now and the salt sticky against my face. Cousin calls to me from the water, the gusts whipping her voice away. We are alone on the beach. I wave at her as the swell moves her sideways in concert with the spray.

It's a sharp-winter, sandy day and the sun lowers in the sky. I can't see cousin for a moment, then she stands up. The waves have moved her farther out and the water is up to her armpits. Even from my blanket I can see the confusion and fear on her face. Her actions are jerky, as she slides on the Gulf's sandy bottom.

I pull up my blanket and head to the facilities around the other end of Lovers Key. Got to get that grit out of my eye before it causes real damage.

It's a sharp-winter, sandy day and the cry of the seagulls are all that can be heard. One of them seems strangely stricken.

The Usual Unusual Suspects

John Gerard Fagan is a writer from Glasgow in Scotland who writes in both English and Scots. He has published over 50 short stories and essays, including in *Black Static, The Sunlight Press*, and *Write Ahead/The Future Looms*.

Nick Boldock is a writer from Hull, East Yorkshire. His short stories have appeared in a number of print anthologies such as *Radgepacket, The Fathom Collection, The Epocalypse – Emails at the End*, with short stories in *Pulp Metal Magazine, Thrillers Killers 'n' Chillers*, and *A Twist of NOIR* – as well as the darker recesses of the mind.

He is also a dedicated and avid Vinyl Man behind http://www.hullmusicarchive.co.uk/author/nboldock/ *Superstition* is his nod to the classic short story format. He does not have a cat.

Weldon Burge is a full-time editor, freelance writer, and publisher. His fiction has appeared in many publications, including various horror and suspense magazines and anthologies. He is a frequent writer for Suspense Magazine, often writing author interviews. In 2012, Weldon and his wife founded *Smart Rhino Publications*, an indie publishing company that focuses primarily on horror and suspense/thriller books. You can find his author page at www.weldonburge.com.

Chris Phillips is the former editor of a motor industry magazine. Now retired, he has published two novels available on Kindle—*The Compassion of Trees* and *East Wind*—along with two compilations of blogs available on Wordpress.

St George's Day Massacre is from a collection of short stories—*Playing With Fire*—due to be published later this year.

Dan Meyers sadly passed away in 2018 after becoming the victim of a massive stroke, from which he never recovered. We first made contact in a writer's forum in 2015, where he asked questions, then asked if I would become his beta reader. The pieces were not quick in coming – he owned and worked a farm in the US, but wrote during the winter periods when he had a fraction more spare time to do so. The two that were completed were originally destined for a proper anthology of his work, to be titled **Tales from the Travelling Carnival**. We hope to print them individually in the Crimeucopia series.

Jeff Dosser is an ex-police officer and current software developer living in the wilds of central Oklahoma.

In addition to winning Oklahoma Writer's Federation awards in best new horror for 2019 & 2020, I've also had short stories published in magazines such as *The Literary Hatchet*, *JJ Outre Review*, *Tales to Terrify*, *Shotgun Honey*, and *Mystery Weekly*.

Eve Fisher has been fortunate to have had almost 30 stories published with *Alfred Hitchcock Mystery Magazine*, as well as additional publications in other mystery, science-fiction and fantasy magazines.

Emilian Wojnowski comes from another planet, which is why he feels bad on Earth. A philologist and translator by education, a hobbit by nature and appearance. He is constantly looking for peace, lost time, and books. Emilian has never drunk alcohol but fears the future all the time. His name can be found in such literary places as *Intrinsick*, *Curiosities*, *Amon Hen*, *Ghost Orchid Press*, and Graham Masterton's official website.

Fabiyas M V is a writer from Orumanayur village in Kerala, India. He is the author of *Monsoon Turbulence* (Poetry Nook, US) *Shelter within the Peanut Shells* (Red Cherry Books, India) *Kanoli Kaleidoscope* (PunksWritePoemsPress,US), *Eternal Fragments* (erbacce press,UK), *Stringless Lives* (Budding Light Press, Australia), and *Moonlight And Solitude* (Raspberry Books, India). His fiction and poetry have appeared in several anthologies, magazines and journals. Western Australian University, British Council, University of Hawaii, Rosemont College, Douglas College, Forward Poetry, Off the Coast, Silver Blade, Pear Tree Press, Poetry Nook, Zoetic Press, Typehouse, Structo, Encircle Publications, Pendle War Poetry and Creative Writing Ink are some of his publishers. He has won many international accolades including Merseyside at

War Poetry Award from Liverpool University; Lest We Forget Poetry Prize from Auckland War Memorial Museum; and Animal Poetry Prize 2012 from RSPCA (Royal Society for Prevention of Cruelties against Animals, UK). He was the finalist for Global Poetry Prize 2015 by the United Poets Laureate International (UPLI) in Vienna. His poems have been broadcast on All India Radio. Poetry Nook, US, has nominated him for the 2019 Pushcart Prize. He has been working as a teacher in English at Gov. Higher Secondary School, Maranchery in Kerala.

Lamont A. Turner has appeared in numerous online and print venues, including *The Half That You See, Horror For Hire, Death And Butterflies* and *Scary Snippets* anthologies as well as, *Theme Of Absence, Tales From The Moonlit Path, Frontier Tales, Terror House, Lovecraftania, Abandoned Towers, Jitter, Serial, The Realm Beyond,* and *Dark Dossier* magazines.

Ed Ahern resumed writing after forty odd years in foreign intelligence and international sales. He's had over three hundred stories and poems published so far, and six books. Ed works the other side of writing at Bewildering Stories, where he sits on the review board and manages a posse of six review editors.
https://twitter.com/bottomstripper
https://www.facebook.com/EdAhern73/?ref=bookmarks htt
ps://www.instagram.com/edwardahern1860/

Robert Peyto's most recent stories have been published in the anthologies: *EconoClash Review, COLP: Big, Hardboiled, Suspense Unimagined, Transcendent, Serial Magazine, Classics Remixed, Thuggish Itch, Flash Bang Mysteries, The Black Beacon Book of Mystery*, and *COLP: Treasure*.

Al Hagan is a retired IT project manager. His career also included a four-year tour of duty with the Marine Corps and a number of years in the intelligence community, working in Washington, D.C. and in foreign countries.

Caroline Tuohey is a writer and poet whose main interest is picture books. She has six published picture books in print. She has also been published in children's literature magazines in Australia and Ireland as well as in anthologies and poetry sites online. Her other interest is bush poetry – which she writes and performs. Then, from time to time, she writes short stories for adults. She enjoys holding story time sessions at libraries, schools and preschools and conducts workshops for both school students and adults.

Steve Carr, from Richmond, Virginia, has had over 470 short stories published internationally in print and online magazines, literary journals, reviews and anthologies since June, 2016. He has had seven collections of his short stories, *Sand, Rain, Heat, The Tales of Talker Knock* and *50 Short Stories: The Very Best of Steve Carr,* and *LGBTQ: 33 Stories,* and *The Theory of Existence: 50 Short Stories,* published. His paranormal/horror novel Redbird was released in November,

2019. His plays have been produced in several states in the U.S. He has been nominated for a Pushcart Prize twice. He is the founder of Sweetycat Press. His Twitter is @carrsteven960. His website is https://www.stevecarr960.com. He is on Facebook: https://www.facebook.com/steven.carr.35977

Bobby Mathews is a writer based in suburban Birmingham, Alabama, and his fiction has appeared in *Close to the Bone, All Due Respect, Bristol Noir, The Dark City, The Sandy River Review, Southern Discoveries, Flash Fiction Magazine*, and *Shotgun Honey*. More of his work is forthcoming in *YELLOW MAMA*, *Gleam of the Blade*, and *The Dillydoun Review*. His crime novel, *Magic City Blues*, is set to publish in February 2022 through Close to the Bone.

Michael Bracken's short fiction has appeared in *Alfred Hitchcock's Mystery Magazine, Ellery Queen's Mystery Magazine, The Best American Mystery Stories*, and in many other anthologies and periodicals.

June Lorraine Roberts is a Flash Fiction writer of crime fiction, whose stories have been featured by Punk Noir Magazine, Akashic Books and The Flash Fiction Press.

As the creator of MurderInCommon.com, a website about crime fiction books and authors, she features debut and mid-list writers worldwide. Murder in Common is a FeedSpot Top 100 Crime Fiction Blog.

June Lorraine is a graduate of the London School of Journalism, a member of Sisters in Crime, and the Short Fiction Mystery Society. She has served as a Derringer Judge, Bouchercon panelist, and has read her work at Noir at the Bar—Toronto. As time permits, she beta reads for crime fiction authors.

She is married to a very patient man, who prays fervently at night before closing his eyes.

https://murderincommon.com/

https://twitter.com/JuneLorraineR

https://www.instagram.com/junelorraineroberts/